CADUCEUS

A Beth Harper Supernatural Thriller
Book Two

BY

S. E. ENGLAND

ISBN 979-8-5255-5294-4

1st Edition
www.sarahenglandauthor.co.uk

DARK FICTION BY
SARAH E. ENGLAND

ABOUT THE AUTHOR:

Sarah England is a UK author. At the fore of Sarah's body of work is the bestselling occult horror trilogy *Father of Lies, Tanners Dell,* and *Magda,* followed by *The Owlmen.* Stand-alone supernatural thrillers include *The Soprano* and *Hidden Company,* followed by occult horrors *Monkspike* and *Baba Lenka.*

Masquerade is the first in a new series of Beth Harper supernatural thrillers, with *Caduceus* the second. These books are based on the experiences of a spiritual medium and healer, who works on police cases and demonic infestations. Although the story, characters and location are all fictitious, the spirit guides, exorcisms, clairvoyance and ability to remote view are real. References in relation to quantum physics, sacred texts, and also the shadow councils are at the back. This is dark to light, and we hope you enjoy the read.

If you would like to be informed about future releases, there is a newsletter sign-up on Sarah's website. Book Three will be underway shortly, so please feel free to get in touch – it would be great to hear from you!

www.sarahenglandauthor.co.uk

DEDICATION

This book is dedicated to the following people.

To Ada, with more love and gratitude than could ever be expressed in words, thank you.

And to my mum, Valerie Patricia, a retired English teacher. I started with her cast-off Victoria Holt novels at the age of seven, and haven't stopped reading since. Thank you also for 'marking' my short stories nearly two decades ago, before I dared submit them to magazines. At the age of forty I had to re-learn grammar and syntax. Thank you, Mum, for your practical support, and for the inherited love of literature.

PROLOGUE

CREWBY, NORTH WEST ENGLAND MARCH, 2013

THE CEILING was a dazzling glare, painful in its brilliance. Beth quickly closed her eyes again. Was this the after-life? Her body felt…weightless… floating away on a dream…

"Lily? Lily? Can you hear me, sweetheart? We need to move you now."

She squinted into the blinding light. Two faces were peering down.

Who's Lily?

"She's still well out of it."

"I know, but we need the bed."

"I just gave her pethidine."

"Well, Mr Freeman said to move her, so… I'll call the ward to check they're ready. Just do her obs again, will you?"

Where's this? A hospital?

The bed rattled and jiggled as it was pumped higher. A tight band squeezed Beth's upper arm, followed by a hiss of deflation. Something sharp nipped the tip of her finger.

"Blood pressure's a bit low."

She tried to reply but her lips were caked together, her throat too dry. A babble of muffled voices echoed in the background as if this was a local swimming pool, and her head felt swollen, sickness swilling in her stomach.

"I'm just going to take these sticky pads off now, Lily."

Strong hands shovelled under her shoulders and began to loosen the ties at the back of her gown, but as she was prised from the mattress she noticed a man peering in through a gap in the curtains. Her chest had been exposed and she cried out. A group of people were shuffling around the perimeter, too close, staring in. She tried to grab for the sheet but couldn't quite reach it.

"Yeah," said the nurse, turning round to talk to someone else. "Cubicle four needs a catheter."

Eyes were on her as she lay half exposed…someone still peeking in… She scrabbled to cover herself but could not. "I…I…Excuse me!"

The nurse turned back to finish removing the cardiac monitor pads. "Ooh, hang on a minute, we're giving Joe Blogs and his wife a front row view here." With one swish of the curtains she shut them out.

"Now, listen. Can you hear me, Lily? We're taking you up to the ward in a few minutes - we're just waiting for the porter. Here's the buzzer in case you need anything, okay?"

The racket beyond the curtains was escalating. She tried to nod but pain thudded into her head. Swallowing repeatedly, she motioned for water.

"What? Oh, water? No, you're not supposed to in

case we need to operate. You've got a drip up, love."

Beth tried to clear her throat, the words coming out in a croak, "It's noisy. Where am I?"

"Is it? It's a lot quieter than normal, actually. You're in A and E."

"A and E?"

"Don't you remember?"

"No."

The nurse raised her voice, kindly, but as loudly as if Beth had lost her hearing. "You've had an accident, a car crash, Lily. We're going to keep you in overnight."

"No."

"Yes. And don't worry we've got your belongings. You can have them back tomorrow."

"No, no. Please–"

"Calm down, pet. You can't go home in this state, can you?"

You don't understand...

"Once you're on the ward, they'll contact your husband or your family. Try to relax. I'll be back in a tick."

The blue blur of the nurse's uniform vanished in a flap of material, a barrier which did nothing to abate the cacophony of voices reverberating around the walls. It was getting ever louder and now she realised why. A crowd of spectral faces began to float through the flowery print. With outstretched hands they loomed in close-range like inquisitive old women clamouring to peer into a pram.

You can see me...She can see...I have to explain...Can you tell George...can you find Mary...They cut me open...I wasn't dead...I never got to say good-bye...

3

She could not and would not stay in a hospital - every single unit, bay, ward and corridor contained hordes of spirits stuck in a cobweb of fear and confusion. But this one was by far the worst. Many of the spirits were skeletal, some with sunken heads or weeping cavities where their stomachs should be, others in a state of partial decay. A gnarled finger pulsing with open sores poked through the watery air, and she heard a voice shout, "No!" Her own?

Oh God, where's Billy? Where's Gran?

She tried to lift her head from the pillow, to fumble for the buzzer, but the sledgehammer of pethidine knocked her slam backwards again. The surrounding curtains swam as fragments of cloth swirling in oil, and voices carried on waves of disinfectant. Time merged with the dull thump of her heart, as in between moments of lucidity, camera shots of brilliant whiteness flashed like electric shocks.

What the hell have they given me?

"Billy? Gran?"

Prayers would not take form, familiar words fizzling out long before they reached her lips.

"Billy?"

She drifted into a haze, and then woke with another jolt, this time to the sound of a man's shout. Had he called her name?

He was standing at the bottom of the bed. A porter? The nurse had said they were waiting for one. She tried to focus, to train her eye, as his image wobbled like a television picture not tuned in. Maybe it was the drugs they'd given her?

He was wearing a funereal suit and a top hat, his

face and hands pasty-white and made of spaghetti. Spaghetti? As soon as her attention settled on him he began to unravel like a spool of wool. And his eyes…She swallowed hard…His eyes were tar-black pools.

"Billy!"

The curtains whooshed back. "All right, Lily. We're taking you up to the ward now, love."

The fluorescent lights reflected in the dark glass of the window showed it was evening. And the thought came to her again - why were they calling her Lily?

"Sorry we took a while. You can blame Darren here. Porters take special lessons in the art of disappearance."

A laugh rang out as the bed swung around. The nurse liked him. A spark had flown between them.

"Who's Billy, anyway? Is he your husband? Only we couldn't find a next of kin for you."

"He is more…no…not…"

Her voice trailed into nothing as the bed clattered down a corridor in a cool breeze, followed by the metallic clunk of a lift door opening. Chatting over her head, the nurse and porter pushed the bed inside, the suspended cubicle bounced slightly on entry, and then plummeted. They were going down? Down not up?

"We've got to go through a tunnel to get to the women's ward on the other side, Lily. Nothing to worry about. She's been shouting out a lot. I think she's worried. Aren't you, love? Worried?"

"Um, tunnel?"

The man standing behind laughed. "Thank your lucky stars it's not two in the morning. We could tell you some hair-raising stories, couldn't we, Terry?"

"You're not kidding. And don't start trying to spook

me, either. I'm on nights again next week. Honestly, he's terrible for ghost stories."

Beth closed her eyes.

What would be nothing but a creepy shiver for them would be a theatre of horrific images for her. As the lift plunged her stomach balled into a knot. Where was Billy? And Gran? In a woozy state of dislocated consciousness, she concentrated on visualising a pearlescent bubble of protection around herself, in readiness for the barrage that was surely coming the second the lift door opened.

Briefly she glanced up. As if he'd been waiting for her to notice him, peering down from the elevator ceiling was the inquisitive face of a jaundiced boy, a spectre with hollow eyes and a smile that cracked open without mirth.

The lift now docked into the basement, and they emerged into a dimly lit tunnel lined with racks of laundry and stacked boxes.

"Did I ever tell you about that time we brought a body to the mortuary at three in the–"

Beth tuned out.

God, you know my heart!

It was not the mortuary they needed to worry about. It was the ice-cold floor beneath the Victorian tiles. This hadn't been a normal hospital...She tried to shut out the visions of cadaverous bodies skulking in the shadows, of a ghostly figure lying on a gurney, prodding in confusion at blood-sodden bandages, of grimy hands beginning to push through the layers of time, nails ingrained with dirt...

The bed was hurtling along towards another set of

lifts at the far end.

I wasn't dead…she can see…the foxes…the pain…you have to help…she can see…

Repeated powerful white flashes jarred her out of a coma-like stupor, and she struggled again to protect her aura. Was this still the tunnel? Would they ever get out?

"Gran? Where are you?"

"Calm down, Lily. You're all right. We're not scaring you with our spooky talk, are we? It's not real, you know?"

Any one of these spectral creatures could walk right into her. As a powerful spiritual medium she would appear to them like a lighthouse beaming into a dark ocean, and as such they sped towards her. Dozens of them now rose in a ground swell, floating out of the walls, zooming in from every angle.

"Gran!"

The soft touch of a hand on the top of her hair was all she needed. The lift pinged open, the bed was pushed inside, and she sighed with relief. Billy and Gran Grace were here. No doubt the opiates had dulled her senses, although losing her power of self-protection was a shock. What the hell had they given her? That was not nice. Not nice at all. In fact none of this, she thought, when a few seconds later they clattered into what was obviously a much older part of the hospital, felt remotely normal.

***

PART ONE

'Know what is in front of your face, and what is hidden from you will be disclosed to you. For there is nothing hidden that will not be revealed. And there is nothing buried that will not be raised.'

Jesus Christ. The Gospel of Thomas. The Nag Hammadi.

CHAPTER ONE

CREWBY
ONE MONTH PRIOR

This was one of those places you had to make the best of, Beth thought. Crewby. But to those who'd always lived here, it was home and they wouldn't be anywhere else. Landmarked by a power station, it was a small, sea-facing town on the north-west coast of England. Historically a fishing port, it had now morphed into a predominantly non-descript, wind-battered sprawl of housing estates and business parks. Moorland hills rose sharply from sea level, the harbour and market place flanked by warehouses.

The terrace rented by Beth Harper and Jeannie Lockwood was on the end of a row of Victorian back-to-backs. It wasn't difficult, Beth thought, looking down from the bedroom window, to picture post-war housewives of yesteryear pegging out washing in these back yards. Images of them flashed before her - women in stout brown boots, flowery aprons and hair rollers, cigarettes balancing on lower lips while the whip-raw winds flipped sheets high over the line.

"Like the old days," said Billy, her spirit guide.

She smiled, recalling her own family in Liverpool, and how Nan and Gran Grace had lived in a similar fashion. It seemed a lifetime ago, a different age, yet she had been there and lived in that reality, so it really wasn't. Time - it was the strangest thing.

The house today was a silent shell, gloomy and hollow. Rented to whoever the letting agency could find for a place with yellowing wallpaper and dark brown woodwork, not to mention a stand-alone rusty cooker, sagging single beds and threadbare carpets, it stood with an air of pained endurance. And the imprints of past occupants remained.

On the day they'd been given the keys, last October, the first thing Beth had done was to place her hands on the kitchen wall. A bickering angry couple flashed before her...the presence of a teenage boy brooding with resentment, slamming the door so violently the frame shuddered...A woman with her hands over her face as she sat and wept at the kitchen table...

Beth had pulled away. This had not been a happy home and the misery lingered. Trapped anger was to wake her repeatedly in the early hours: the sound of pummelling on the dividing walls or fists banging on the front door. And the cold rose in plumes of mist in a stairwell peeling with damp.

"Will it do us, do you think?" Jeannie had asked anxiously.

She'd nodded. "Do we have a choice?"

"At least it's a roof. Somewhere to be."

Beth agreed. "I'd draw the line if there was anything

sinister here, but you're right, we need to be somewhere."

Moving-in had actually been a good day and it hadn't taken long to clean the place up. They'd scrubbed the kitchen and bathroom on their hands and knees, and pulled up nylon carpets in the bedrooms, only to roll them back again after noticing stains on the boards. A couple of vats of cheap, white emulsion now coated what had been nicotine-stained walls; and after the first wage packets they'd bought duvets, throws, rugs and ready-made curtains from the market. Nothing short of a costly professional make-over was ever going to transform it into a thing of beauty, but as winter set in and sleety winds howled off the North Atlantic, they acknowledged they'd been blessed. The house had been built to last and the thick stone walls provided a strong buffer. No, there really was nothing to complain about, far from it.

The town's market turned out to be excellent, well stocked with local produce and cottage industry goods - everything from beeswax candles to home-made cushion covers and hand-painted birthday cards. Seagulls squealed over the day's catch and the stalls selling crabs, mussels and whelks; and The Lighthouse Inn was nearly always full in the evenings, laughter lubricated with ale spilling out onto the harbour. It wasn't a bad place to work and Beth was more than happy to be its part time chef.

Jeannie had also found employment - as a cleaner at a nursing home on the outskirts of town - and both thanked God every day for their good luck. Sleeping in the car on an old fairground site, and queuing up in the job centre each day was now a distant nightmare. Again, it seemed such a long time ago. Really, she thought, it was quite surreal, almost as if those worrying, bone-weary days they thought would never end, had never existed at all.

There was, however, a seam of discontent running through Crewby. Things had changed over the course of recent decades, and tensions bubbled under a surface of congeniality. So stealthily as to have gone unnoticed, at first a trickle, an ever-increasing influx of the world's most desperate people - the penniless, the disenfranchised and the war-torn – had streamed in. Having left native countries with utopian promises of safety, housing, money and food, they were instead to find themselves in one of the coldest, dampest backstreets of Britain. Initially accepted, the increasing numbers had, however, gradually begun to erode goodwill and engender resentment. Language and cultural barriers made integration difficult and gangs had formed on both sides.

And it was this which now turned over in her mind. Standing at the window on that February afternoon, peering through the slats in the blind, Beth frowned. Why cross entire continents? Who engineered it that way? Because it didn't just happen. No one found their way from an African refugee camp to a rundown terrace in Crewby unless it was orchestrated.

At the very moment the question formed, a shadow flickered across the wall. Blacker than black was the colour of that shadow, the feeling psychopathically cold…before it vanished as quickly as it had appeared.

Beth shook her head. Odd! And was about to let the

blind shutter into place, thinking it must be time to get ready for work, when a flash of silver caught her eye and she twitched the slats open again. There. A filament of light sparked atop the houses on Mailing Street. It was the row closest to what was the kind of bog standard retail area found in every town in Britain. Ugly and soulless, the car park was almost empty, as were the outlets for carpets and sofas, white goods and computers.

Where they lived on Portland Street the houses were just as old and in various states of disrepair, but Mailing Street had a very different atmosphere. Shaded by warehouses and garages, the occupants hid behind grimy nets, rubbish blew around like tumbleweed, and a low level stench of bad drains permeated the whole.

As she stared, it happened again - a star-like glint of silver over one house, or was it two? She squinted to see.

"There's always a reason," said Billy.

She glanced sideways. Billy had appeared today in fleeting form, a bright outline like sunshine behind a storm cloud.

"You mean why I'm in Crewby?"

No answer. He'd gone. And she let the blind rattle shut.

Well, of course – everything had fallen into place far too easily, hadn't it?

***

CHAPTER TWO

As it turned out, only two days elapsed before the subject of Mailing Street resurfaced. It was a particularly cold February evening with flurries of snow in the air, and Beth was already regretting having walked to work, because now there was the walk back again. One mile wasn't far, but when tired and battling against a prevailing sea wind, it felt like forever. On impulse therefore, she cut away from the promenade and took the longer route past the warehouses, ducking out of the blast to emerge on Mailing Street.

Genals connected the rows of terraces, and the plan was to use those and arrive home from the opposite direction. However, hurrying and keen to get out of the cold, it wasn't until she had actually turned the corner that she realised something was badly wrong.

All the houses on Mailing Street stood in total darkness, with the exception of the second one in, which was lit up like an all-night supermarket store. Two police cars were parked outside along with an ambulance. The pavement was empty and shiny with rain, both neighbouring houses gloomily silent behind drawn curtains, not so much as a television light flickering from within.

As she stood watching, an officer opened the front door and she stepped back. There was something unnaturally dark about the entire street, but most particularly the houses around the one fully lit. Methodically and without speaking, the authorities began to seal off the scene, before a body on a stretcher was lifted into the back of the ambulance and it glided away.

By the time she stepped out of the neighbouring gateway, the entire scene had ended as abruptly as that of a theatre show, its audience of one left staring at an empty stage.

There was no option but to walk past. Cautiously she levelled with the house, its darkened glass panes reflecting amber streetlights and swaying branches; and paused. A tiny movement had caught her eye and she glanced up at next door's bedroom window. Someone had seen her. Not a good idea to hang around…Yet she found herself completely unable to drag her gaze away from the house, and instead of passing by, drew closer. Mesmerised she walked up to the large bay window, until nose to glass, she found herself staring through the mirror of her own image into a myriad of fragmented shifting shapes within.

It happened fast. No warning. One moment she was peering in, the next a shutter fell with such guillotine precision across her vision that she almost fell. Holding onto the window sill, she closed her eyes while one image after another flashed into her mind. First, a woman with smooth dark skin, her hair tucked into a scarf, was pleading with someone, a man. His fists were raised but she wasn't frightened. An argument was spinning out of control quickly though, and now the woman's eyes widened in shock. Suddenly she was slammed face down onto the table, a hand on the back of her neck. There was confusion, a heavy grainy atmosphere…a spurt of blood hit the wall…but it was the man who was sliding down on his haunches, dropping something to the floor…

When Beth came to, it was with a hot, sickly sweat. She stood clutching the sill. No doubt incidents of domestic violence like this were commonplace, although it didn't make them any less tragic. Nevertheless, that's what it was. And she told herself this was the case, as possibly every man and woman in the country would. And she carried on telling herself that's what it was, none of her business - an argument that got out of hand - even as the axe of blackness, total blackness, descended on the street behind her, and the sound of inhuman screams, the howls and cries of base animal fear, ricocheted around the bowl of her head.

Conscious of Billy's presence around her, she hurried through the genal. Unlit, with brick walls on either side, the alleyway was no place to linger, and the prospect of being mugged crossed her mind. This area was known for gangs, and hooded boys scooting about with silent stealth could and did appear out of nowhere.

With the only sound her own rapid footsteps, she exited the first genal, then after glancing over her shoulder, sped down the next one to Portland Street. The feeling that someone was following, and closing the gap, was growing by the second. Was that her own heavy breathing, or that of another? The end was now in sight - an amber streetlight, the outline of a car – and the fast walk became a sprint, until finally she burst out into the middle of the road and swung around.

But the genal was empty, a hush of silvery sleet. No stealthy hooded gang members. No sinister looking man in a trilby and raincoat. Half expecting to see a spectral imprint or for something to materialise out of the litter strewn shadows, she held her breath. No, there really was absolutely no one and nothing there.

A quick nod of relief and she walked smartly home. Most of the terraces here were warmly lit, and in contrast to Mailing Street, which had few cars, here they were parked end to end.

"That was weird," she whispered to Billy, putting the key in the front door. "Like the frickin' twilight zone."

"Jeannie, it's me! You still up?"

It looked like she hadn't yet gone to bed. The kitchen light was still on and the television was blaring. Jeannie's shifts started early at seven, which meant getting up at six and being out of the door by half past, so she wasn't often up this late.

"In here!"

"The television's on loud. This isn't like you, has something…?"

The local news had Jeannie transfixed. Pixie-like in appearance, she was sitting on what was a dilapidated faux-leather sofa, now draped with throws, knees pulled tight to her chest as she bit her nails. Despite all the home-cooking and left-over desserts Beth brought home from the pub, Jeannie had remained a wisp of a girl with haunted eyes and a nervous conviction she was constantly followed. Maybe, the thought occurred to Beth, that feeling had been contagious?

"What's going on? What have I missed?"

"There's been a violent incident and a man's driven off across the moors. No one's to approach him. It was on that road nearest the retail park, Mailing Street. I bloody walk along there every day."

Shrugging off her coat, Beth flopped onto the chair closest to the electric fire and closed her eyes for a second. He had driven away? The scene replayed in her head, of the man sliding down the blood spattered wall. But something didn't fit...he hadn't looked angry or murderous...rather his expression had been one of stunned confusion.

Like the woman's.

She shook her head as if to clear it. The man had been shocked to the core, but something else, too. She tried to re-conjure the energies, the essence of the vision. It was grainy, vague, but yes - tears had been streaming down his face.

"Doesn't make sense," she mumbled, half to herself.

"Bit too close to home for me," said Jeannie. "I hope they catch him. I've got to walk to work in the dark in the morning."

"I don't think you need worry," Beth said firmly.

Jeannie glanced up. "How do you make that out?"

"I came that way home and when I saw the coppers I hung back. Anyway, after they'd gone I stopped and, you know, tuned in? It was a man and wife argument. I don't think he meant to do it..." She shook her head. "It was odd. They both seemed shell-shocked."

"Hmmm."

"I don't think there's a serial killer on the loose, anyway."

"Okay, well that's a relief, at least."

"Do you want a roll-up or are you going straight to bed?"

Jeannie nodded still frowning. "Go on then, ta. I could do with a chat to be honest. There's something on my mind."

Beth began the process of filling cigarette papers. Fleeting images of the murder scene were flashing into her mind: a dimly lit kitchen…the blue light of a television set filtering through from another room…a table strewn with the remnants of meal…candlelight… yes it had been a candle-lit dinner…

"You look miles away."

Beth jumped. "Ooh, blimey. Sorry, here you go." She handed her a roll-up. "So what's bothering you? It's funny, we live in the same house but we hardly see each other." She flicked a glance at Billy who was on the stairs playing with the spirit cat.

"Okay, well don't give me that look, but you know when I said someone was following me the other week? Well, this is the thing, they really are. I'm not making this up. And it's not just me. It's us - both of us."

***

CHAPTER THREE

It was difficult to know what to make of Jeannie. Beth took her time rolling her own cigarette, aware of Billy on the stairs. The spirit cat he was playing with was skinny and black with a white spot on his head. She smiled to herself, knowing he'd been called, Spot. Emaciated, the little cat had lived off scraps thrown from the table and whatever mice he caught in the outside walls. That said, this was his home and he wasn't leaving it.

If Jeannie wasn't significant in some way, then Beth would not have been urged to go back for her in Curbeck. But she was also a damaged, traumatised child from a family that had suffered generations of abuse at Scarsdale Hall. So what was real and what was not? Was Jeannie really being followed? Knowing for sure was difficult because Jeannie's nerves were frayed and her fear contagious. Increasingly, Beth was leaning towards suggesting professional help, but officially registering anywhere, especially with regard to mental health, was a problem. The grip of the Mantel family, with their extensive network of power, was not something from which anyone had ever escaped. Even after death. Perhaps especially after death.

Now however, as Jeannie talked, the skin on the

nape of her neck prickled. Had Allegra Mantel had them physically tracked? Four months had passed so it wasn't beyond the bounds of probability. Why, though? What threat did people like herself and Jeannie pose were they to talk about Scarsdale Hall? They would likely be ridiculed or ignored - easy to discredit, easy to smear. Besides, neither of them could prove a darned thing. No, this was paranoia… had to be…Yet, all the time she told herself that was the case, a deeper knowing informed her otherwise. This was no more Jeannie's imagination than the murder on Mailing Street was a run-of-the mill act of domestic violence.

What if she really does need help?

Jeannie stared into the bars of the electric fire. "I can't explain any better, really. The whole place gives me the creeps. I know nursing homes aren't given to being a laugh a minute, but Moorlands is horrible. I swear I see silhouettes creep across the walls. The residents watch them like spooked ponies. It's not just me."

"I didn't realise you didn't like it there."

"It's getting to me a bit. Honestly Beth, these poor wizened creatures in nightdresses and slippers, left in chairs staring into space all day. What do we do to our old people? It's like they were never real, never had families, never fell in love! They don't matter anymore, just discarded."

Beth nodded. Gran Grace's presence was shivering around her shoulders and she knew Gran agreed.

"I really don't want to get old, Beth. I don't want to end my days like that - years and years stuck in a chair all day then tipped into bed."

"Me neither."

"I think May gets to me more than most. She was a historian, you know?"

May? The name, for some reason, registered.

"She always smells of talcum powder, even her hair. Anyway, it's a spooky place is what I'm saying. It's like there are eyes and ears everywhere. And that doctor sneaks up on you." She visibly shivered. "Creepy bastard. I don't know what it is about him, but...ugh!"

The thought occurred to Beth that Jeannie was creeping herself out. Perhaps she'd never be able to throw off the invisible clutches of Scarsdale Hall?

"Who is he? What's his name?"

"He owns the place, wears glasses, shoulders narrower than a girl's. You wouldn't look at him twice, to be honest. Although you would at his car."

"What about the others? The staff?"

"Yeah, Polish mostly. I like them, they just get on with it and they're nice to the oldies. It can't be easy doing what they do and the pay's shite."

"I can imagine. But anyway, you said you're being watched? So do you mean in the nursing home or–?"

Jeannie stubbed out the roll-up and reverted to hugging herself again. "Well, first of all, that doctor. He keeps looking at me. I mean I'm just the frickin' cleaner, right? And let's face it no one looks at me: I'm seven stone wet through, and pale as Casper the ghost. But every time I glance up from mopping the floor he's staring, and the minute I catch him doing it he looks away again."

"What's his name?"

"Freeman. I only know because the old dears keep

saying, 'Thank you, Doctor Freeman. Oh, you are kind, Doctor Freeman.' They clutch at his hands, just trying to touch another person, I suppose, to get a response. But you can tell he doesn't like it – you know, like he's gritting his teeth and holding his breath?"

Beth shook her head. "So apart from him looking at you funny, and bear in mind he might fancy you–"

"Oh for fuck's sake. Don't make me laugh."

"I'm not. You're really pretty. Have you ever been out with anyone, Jeannie?"

She shrugged.

"One of the lads at Curbeck?"

Jeannie looked away.

"Sorry, none of my business. It's just that not everything's suspicious. He could genuinely be attracted to you."

"Beth, listen up, right? The Polish girls are stunning. One's about twenty three with white blonde hair and the longest legs I've ever seen in my life. She looks like a Victoria's Secret model–"

"I heard some of them are men."

"Shut up!"

"No, seriously," Beth said, trying to keep a straight face at Jeannie's expression.

"You've got a weird sense of humour, I'll give you that. Anyway, he does not fancy me. It's more like he's trying to identify me. Like a scientist scrutinising a bug under a microscope."

"Okay, so is there anything else giving you the impression of being followed?"

"Yes, shadows everywhere. I'll be sitting on my own in that basement kitchen when one just towers over me on the wall or sweeps across the floor on a cloudy day - always on the very edge of my vision and nothing I can particularly put my finger on. But it's as if someone walked past the window or they were lurking in the corridor."

Recalling the shadow on the bedroom wall earlier, Beth narrowed her eyes. No, that had been an insight, a vision. "I have the house fully protected. Nothing can get in here."

Billy was nodding.

"No, not here," said Jeannie. "It happens at Moorlands or when I'm walking home. The branches of just one tree start swaying even when there's no wind and all the others are still. And a couple of times I've seen…I can't say…once or twice at the bottom of the stairs in the nursing home or at the end of the genal…a woman…But there's no one there, Beth. Or something catches my eye in a crowd, the shape of someone, but when I glance up they've gone."

Beth nodded. She hadn't noticed any of this until tonight, and that was likely down to what had happened on Mailing Street. No, a far more likely explanation was that Jeannie was stuck in a cycle of fear that she couldn't get out of.

"What about your dreams? Are you still getting the same ones or are they beginning to fade?"

She shook her head. "Same scenes stuck on repeat – either it's running up the steps to the top of the turret or scrabbling to get out of the tunnels. And then there's always that point where I'm high up on the cliff looking back down at Scarsdale Hall, at its black stone walls and the way it sucks the light from everything around it."

"Yes, it's quite a view. And the sparrow hawk...always there..."

Jeannie stared at the floor a while. "And then there's that other one I told you about. That's the worst. All these hooded people in masks looking down at me, swaying and humming. There's a baby screaming and the humming gets louder and louder. I've got a view as if I'm up on the ceiling looking down, and the baby is in the middle of an iron pentagram on the floor. And I think it's me who's looking down at myself. It's me who's stuck on the ceiling and I have to get back into the body but I can't. To be honest, I'm scared to nod off even though I've got to because I'm shattered."

"You remember how to wake yourself up? And you know to pray and protect yourself every single time before you go to sleep, no matter how tired you are?"

"Yeah. But Beth, I never get any further in any of the dreams. They're always the same and I never move on. It's a needle in a groove, gouging deeper and deeper on constant replay."

She took a deep breath. "I think the trick is to tell yourself it was an experience and it is their sickness, not yours - to un-mesh yourself, if you will, from the emotions."

"Well, that's just it. I can't."

Beth nodded. "Look, I've been thinking, and please don't shoot the messenger, but maybe we could think about professional help?"

"What?"

"Someone who specialises in post-traumatic stress disorder–"

Jeannie was already shaking her head. "I thought

you of all people, of all the people in the world, would understand. You said yourself these are not dreams they're memories and past lives, and definitely nothing I would ever want on official documents. People like the Mantels get you locked up for insanity if you say stuff like this, and you don't ever get out again. And when I say we're being followed I am talking about HER! She knows. She can see me, read my mind, and follow my every move like an eye in the sky. And she's doing it to you, too. Want to know how I know?"

Stunned, Beth nodded.

"Because every time I look out of my bedroom window there's a geezer standing on the pavement opposite the house. And I'll tell you summat else: the rest of the street is black as soot when he appears. Not a single light on. And I never told you about the black shapes, did I? But back in Curbeck no one came out after dusk because of them. They're like fat giant slugs slithering round the houses. We all saw them, not just me. We all saw them, do you hear me? And that's what we've got here now! They're everywhere." She stood up. The sinews of her face had tightened and her fists were balled. "She can do this. She sends demons into your mind, and she sends people mad."

"Jeannie, I didn't mean to upset you. I believe you, okay? I just genuinely want to help in every way possible. We have to discern what is real and what is not."

Jeannie was glaring at her but her eyes were full of tears.

"Yeah. Right well, I'd best be off to bed or I'll never wake up in the morning. It's bad enough as it is."

"Me too."

Jeannie turned at the door. "Night, then."

"Jeannie?"

"Hmmm?"

"I didn't mean to upset you. It's just the more help we get the better, because what's happening at Scarsdale isn't just sick it's demonic. I may as well tell you straight - they don't care about people or their children because they're Satanists, and that means blood, torture and pain. Dark magic. Inner circles. That's what we're up against, and no one believes it until they come across it themselves. By which time it's too late. You did incredibly well to break out of it."

"But I've brought the insanity with me?"

"Damage, not insanity."

Jeannie managed a tight smile. "You know about the black slithery creatures, don't you?"

"Yes, I saw them in Curbeck."

"Right. So at least that's not my imagination, then? I'm no more crazy than you are. You talk to your spirit guides all the time. You're looking at something on the stairs every few minutes now and think I don't notice."

"You're scared, though. All the time. Which means you're not free. And fear's the worst. It accumulates more and more until you go under."

"Mmmm."

"The demonic feeds off it. It's called loosh."

"Mmmm."

"Anyway, sorry. But that's why I thought maybe a professional could help – to separate past events from reality–"

To her surprise Jeannie began to nod. "You're right.

I can't sleep and I'm so frickin' tired."

"We could find someone privately and pay cash."

"I don't think we should take any chances. If you saw what happened to my sister and to Viv, after they went into Laurel Lawns–"

"The physical threat is real." Beth agreed. "We have to be careful and we will be, but nor can we live in fear or life isn't worth living. If the dark magicians have your mind they control you. So we take our control back."

Jeannie's smile was weak but it was a smile. "Okay, I'll have a think. Night, then."

"Night."

"Thanks, Beth. Sorry, I didn't mean to shout. I'm just that tired."

"I know, it's okay."

"Night."

"Night."

For a while, Beth sat and stared into the burn of the electric bars wondering about Jeannie's sister, who was probably heavily sedated in Laurel Lawns psychiatric clinic. Was she locked in a constant replay of horror, or had her mind wandered off into tales of mice families living under the daisy fields? Stories that one generation after another had taught their children as a way to escape the terror. Imagine, she thought, if anyone ever exposed the Mantels for who and what they really were?

"Imagine!" Billy said, from his position lying on the sofa.

She glanced up. "I've got a feeling we're not done with the countess, are we?"

He shook his head. "Beth, it's only just started."

***

CHAPTER FOUR

Beth's bedroom overlooked the built-up side of town. She peeped through the blinds, hoping to see the stars, or hear the crash of the tide against the promenade. Instead, there was a glare of lights over the retail park and someone a few doors down was having the mother of all rows.

"You've got a nasty personality!"

"I've got a nasty personality? You're the one with a nasty personality!"

She tuned out.

Another neighbour was on speaker phone, a conversation amplified from their parked car directly outside. And a couple of kids were kicking cans down the road, every other word an expletive. She watched as one balled up a fast food wrapper and lobbed it into someone's front garden. She frowned. At what point had consideration for others turned into, 'fuck them'?

Knotted up inside, she took several deep breaths. There was an air of foreboding these days. Everyone was so angry.

"Look at Mailing Street," said Billy. Standing beside her, this time he was dressed in jeans and t-shirt, his black hair pulled into a pony tail.

"Interesting. Not a single light on."

No sooner had she spoken, than the black slithery creatures Jeannie had just been talking about began to ooze into life. As muscular as pythons, they pulsed along the eaves and coiled around chimneypots. What were they? Gungy oil-slicks, they stood out from the shadows - gleaming holographic monsters reminiscent of the sticky black tar of karma she'd often seen. Was dark magic at work? Maybe there was stagnant negative energy here that made astral projection possible, as it had in Curbeck?

But if she wasn't here to observe, or if Jeannie wasn't, would the black shapes be here at all, she wondered? That was a strange thought, bit of a mind twister.

"I need to talk to a quantum physicist."

Billy spluttered.

She turned to face him. "Are you saying I'm thick?"

"Of course not."

She stared a little longer.

He shrugged.

"Okay, good. Because I'm just trying to work out how I'd explain this to someone who couldn't see it. I'm sick of people telling me I'm nuts. Until they play Ouija and frighten themselves to bloody death, that is. Then they want to know, don't they?"

Billy nodded.

The last case they'd been called to had been in London. Travis, her ex, had casually told one of their customers in the restaurant that she was an exorcist. She recalled the moment, caught him looking at her steadily as he said it, the word, 'exorcist' forming on his tongue as if it was an exquisite morsel. There'd been a burst of laughter, and words like, 'nonsense' and, 'poppycock' had fired out like crackers from a box. But a few days later the woman who'd prompted the episode by mentioning she had a poltergeist, waylaid her outside. She really did need help. As it turned out, the woman's son was an extremely gifted medium. And the look on the boy's face, when Beth switched on the spirit box and the resident ghost spoke his name, and that of his grandad and his best friend at school, had been worth all the ridicule.

"Anyway," she said to Billy, nodding towards Mailing Street. "I wonder what really happened over there tonight. I mean, did the man really murder his wife, because I can't quite make sense of it. He was shocked, wasn't he? Almost as if he'd just found her or been attacked himself? Still, I suppose they'll find him and then the house will be rented out to an unsuspecting family like it never happened."

She shuddered. By and large, what people couldn't see they didn't believe existed, but that didn't mean it wasn't there. They would feel the residual energy and it would give them nightmares. The rooftops were now covered in a pulsating mass of giant leeches. Everyone in those houses would be able to feel that heavy, omnipotent menace as thick as molasses. It was what bound and weighted them down, made it hard to breathe, to think, to lift away in dreams.

Or death...

Sleep didn't come easy for Beth that night, either. The murder replayed continuously, its horror embedding a little deeper each time. Flicking in and out of consciousness, she rolled onto her back, then onto one side, then the other, switching position every few minutes. Greatly agitated, her heart thumped hard against her ribs. These emotions weren't hers. The memory wasn't hers. Murmuring the Lord's Prayer, she eventually woke herself up, before flopping back against the pillows and trying once more to sleep.

No, the scene was coming again: the crack of the woman's neck beneath an inhumanly powerful hand now her own…the head yanked back, a silk scarf falling away from smooth black hair…and the slash of a carotid artery with one backhand slice…

Beth tried again to wake herself up.

But madness was blinding the murderer, the replay crackling and grainy - the only sound now that of static from a television set in the next room, and the steady drip-drip-drip of blood onto the carpet. The metallic fresh stench of it filled the room, dominating his senses as he slid to the floor. He was looking into an apocalyptic wasteland, his soul an abandoned tunnel echoing with the howls of winter. Nothing sat in his heart. Or his mind. All was empty, lacking, a hopeless void. No God…

Where was God?

What had he done?

The feeling was terrible, of non-existence, of being completely cast out. She half woke up, the desolation icy in her veins. "No…no…"

Eventually, Gran Grace's soothing hand lightly brushed the crown of her head, and a soft cool mist washed over her face like the spray from a mountain spring. And soon she was floating, being lifted and pulled somewhere…

Let's go fly a kite… up to the highest height…

The comforting presence of Yukon weighted on the bed, guarding her body, and she sank into relaxation once more. Those feelings had not been hers, the energy not her own. But the man, that poor man! To add to his pain there would be shouts to hang him high and throw away the key. But he hadn't done it.

Then again there was no one else there. So he must have?

"Don't try to work it out," came Gran's voice. "Let it go!"

Where are we going?

Through a cloud of fog she was floating on the astral plane, looking down at a car parked on a mountain pass. Driving sleet merged the grey of dawn with a craggy, bleak ravine, rendering the car - old and battered with a rusting number plate – almost invisible in the gloom. On the driver's seat, a man sat with his hands still gripping the steering wheel, staring unseeingly at an empty road, sleet blowing across the tarmac in spectral gusts.

His energy signature was that of neither rage nor fear. Rather, she noted in the brief moment of time and space afforded, it was the opposite. He radiated love, painfully so, intense waves of it. Dark skinned with smooth chiselled features, he was refined-looking, his far-away expression one of absolute catatonic shock.

He didn't do it…

But he did…

A sudden white camera flash heralded a complete

change of scene, and she struggled to adjust.

Where am I? Where's this?

Inside somewhere. A house? A man was staring up at a skylight, at stars that flickered now and then between fast-moving belts of cloud. Was he in the same groove of thought as herself? Thinking about the same man on the mountain pass?

He was sitting on an old-fashioned, seaside deckchair, his mind on over-drive. It looked as if it was a potting shed - possibly his man cave or just a private place to be when he couldn't sleep or needed to think? There was an impression he was allied to the law in some way, trying to puzzle something out but the pieces not fitting. Tangled in a web of confusion, his aura was clear blue, like his eyes when suddenly he glanced up and clocked her.

Shit...

The remote view had lasted less than a second but she was snatched away by an invisible cord, vanishing as fast as a cut light switch. The face, though, she would know again. Blue eyes as sapphire bright as those were extremely rare, and so were clairvoyant coppers. Or lawyers.

I wonder who he is.

For a while she and Billy traversed Crewby on the lower astral plane, the vastness of the parallel realm as deserted as a ghost town. The atmosphere on Mailing Street, however, was brooding for a storm, crackling with inhuman cries, palpable fear seeping through the ages. Wind whistled down the genals, and now, rising from back yards and waste ground, the long dead began to gravitate towards her in a granular mass. Bloodless and sickly, they wore drab coats and hats, the grinning man at the helm showing stubs of brown, jagged teeth.

Immediately she changed her appearance to a dull silvery orb, and while Billy protected her she began to probe through the veils of time. Layers of imprinted energy fell away, the sinister mobs faded and the houses vanished, until what looked like an old warehouse emerged. There it stood, somewhat incongruously on its own, amid acres of fields coated in fog.

An overpowering smell of blood filled the air, and puzzled she moved towards it. What was this? Why was it being shown to her?

And then she saw what it was and her stomach clenched.

Into view came a yard of cattle standing chained to railings in the drizzle, hock deep in mud and filth. Voices caught on the air as the scene came to life and additional carts arrived for unloading, the animals' bony spines poking through hide - slaps, shouts and whips punctuating the moans and groans of protest.

The cattle shuffled ever closer to the building, beginning now to sense their impending doom, yet unable to break free from the shackles. Terror passed from one animal to the next as they were shunted into corridors so narrow they couldn't turn around. Too late! Some stalled but were whipped. Others fell to their knees and were yanked back up.

"I don't want to see. I can't. I can't…There are some things I can't do. Gran! Billy!"

Beth pulled away.

Fleetingly she landed in the white room, her place of sanctuary, then with a confused lurch and a slam back against the mattress, woke up in bed. Tears were streaming down her face. Her stomach ached along with her heart. There was nothing like the innocence and purity of animals and children. They would not know that kind of evil even existed...She screwed up her eyes until the tears dried, hot and stinging. Oh God, though, the pain, the cruelty, that shocking turnaround of trust.

It came to her then, that although those events were in the past, the terror was still here. It still existed. So that was the sticky black goo crawling all over the streets? Right where the powers-that-be decided to build houses? Those same houses now used for people who were lost, desperate and in need.

Billy was sitting on the end of the bed.

"There are a lot of problems brewing up here, aren't there?"

He nodded.

"And it's going to get worse?"

"Yup."

"And the copper or lawyer?"

He grinned. "Ah! You'll have to wait and see."

"At least those things crawling around don't mean the countess is working dark magic. Karma is karma..."

A frown flickered on his face.

"What? This is a totally separate issue, isn't it? I don't understand."

"Don't rush it, Beth," came Gran Grace's voice from somewhere in the deep, dark space of her head. "Get some sleep, child! Rest, you're going to need it."

***

CHAPTER FIVE

In the hypnagogic state before falling asleep again, Beth slipped into the white room. This time a transitory visit, she did not fully process it until later. But Jeannie was there.

The meeting was brief, although Jeannie seemed startled - as if she'd arrived by accident - looking around her in a daze.

"Hi!" said Beth.

"You're very tall," said Jeannie, just before she bounced out faster than a pinball.

On waking next morning, however, Beth immediately recalled the encounter and tried not to laugh at the comment about her height. So was Jeannie a spirit walker like herself? Who was she? Over the past few months they'd talked a good deal about meditation and chakras, but to her knowledge Jeannie hadn't yet accepted there was such a thing as an astral realm. It did sometimes happen by chance in dreams, though. Many children wandered onto the astral that way, and always there would be a silver being watching over them. Jeannie, though… There was something about her. And it was quite incredible, Beth thought, stepping into the shower, that Jeannie had survived her ordeal at Scarsdale, having clearly been mind-controlled from childhood. Yet she'd had enough awareness to break free at the first opportunity, and been the one to suggest they both change their names as soon as possible. In short, it was likely Jeannie was not only being guided but listening; at least sub-consciously.

And the name change was inspired. It had been while they were still camping out in the car at the old fairground site on the outskirts of Blackpool.

Following a particularly uncomfortable night in the Peugeot, they'd sat sipping coffee from polystyrene cups, watching the dawn tide ebb away over miles of wet, rippled sands.

"You don't know how much they control everything," Jeannie was saying.

"I don't care."

"Doesn't make it not true."

Billy, cramped into a space on the back seat, was nodding.

"Go on then, but I can't see what the countess can do. It's a free country."

"Beth, it really isn't. They're above the law. People vanish into thin air and no one ever questions them. We've got to be smart and we've got to watch our backs. All the time. Stay under the radar is what I'm saying. So anyway, we need to change our names."

"I'm not scared of her, Jeannie. And I don't want to change my name."

"I've decided to be Maria Kitlowski. I met an Olga Kitlowski yesterday in the job centre and liked her name."

"What about references?"

She grinned. "Got it sorted. We all have and it won't cost much. So what do you say?"

"Erm…"

"Beth, listen. My sister's trapped in a psychiatric unit. My mother works at Scarsdale Hall and she's so spaced out she walks right past me in the street. There's no conversation other than what duties she performs, which are the same every single day. Their minds have gone. Both of them…"

Jeannie's voice trailed away as both stared ahead, transfixed by a seam of ocean that was now a narrow band of grey on the horizon, fine gossamer threads of light sparkling here and there like dew on a spider's web.

"We can't be frightened of them. And there's the police–"

"No! Keep away from them. Especially them. There was this couple in Curbeck who rang that lot about their little girl. I don't know the details, but next thing there's a court order for the child to be removed from the family, the father vanished, and the mother was found hanging in the woods. The local paper said they were a problem family, that he was abusive and left her. Anyway, if you don't want to change your name that's fine, but I can't share a house with you if you keep it. I cannot take the risk and I'm not going back."

Beth faced her. "Maybe you're right."

Jeannie raised an eyebrow.

"I've got to say I've never come across anything like this before. It feels…deeper than I realised–"

"So are you going to be Polish, too?"

"What?"

"Your name?"

Beth smiled. "Oh yeah, why not? I'll be your sister. How about Lily Kitlowski? Actually, I'll say Lily Beth Kitlowski then I can still go by the name of Beth. If I don't I'll slip up. I've been Beth since forever."

"I'm happy to have a new identity, to be honest – didn't like the old one. Anyway, we'll have to pay for the paperwork at some point, but that's the thing, this is a really good crowd. None of us have got a bean between us and we don't speak the same language, but we help each other. I think we're going to be okay here, Beth."

Jeannie's words rang in her ears as she stepped out of the shower. That day had been a good day, a pivotal one of change and new beginnings. She'd gone for a walk, settling on a sheltered area at the far end of the bay, as a place to sit quietly and pray while Jeannie sorted the paperwork. And what she asked for had manifested miraculously. Within days they both had interviews for part time jobs, accepted the low rate few others would agree to, and shortly afterwards found the house here on Portland Street.

And now I know why!

She filled the kettle to make tea, staring unseeingly into the concreted yard just as dozens of other people had done before, in this exact same spot. The steely morning sky was spitting hard rain, spattering against the window. A sharp gust buffeted the eaves and whistled through cracks in the window fastenings, gulls screeching in the wind. It would be freezing by the coast. She nodded to herself. Yup, best to go to work via Mailing Street again: it was broad daylight and would be far more sheltered than the promenade. And with less than a gallon in the tank it would save money to walk.

Buttering toast while the tea brewed, she warmed to the idea. And then it came to her – even if there wasn't such a biting sea wind today she would still opt to go that way. She did, in fact, *want* to take that route.

Okay, why do I need to walk past that house again, Billy?

Billy's presence had been hovering, but now he'd vanished without saying where. Shrugging, she finished breakfast, washed up, and then took another cup of tea upstairs. While getting dressed, her thoughts settled amid a silence permeated only by fresh blasts of wind and the cries of seagulls. And it was not, in fact, until she was level with number three, Mailing Street a good hour later that her question was answered.

Boom!

He was sitting on the front wall, which was still sealed off with black and yellow tape. The front door was ajar and two police vans were parked outside. She kept her head down, about to hurry past, when the man looked sharply up. She stopped. Their stares locked. And his eyebrows shot up so high they almost touched his hairline.

Sapphire blue eyes.

Blood rushed hotly into her face. There was absolutely nothing remarkable about this man's physical appearance - late forties, a round, pleasant face, clean shaven, tad on the heavy side - apart from the laser beam eyes.

"Morning," he said.

"Morning." Shoving her hands in her pockets she

took a deep breath, and in the vain hope he wouldn't keep looking at her burning face, nodded towards the house. "I heard about what happened yesterday. It was on the news. Sounds terrible."

His eyes didn't leave hers. "Yes. You local?"

On the edge of her vison she noted a couple of officers in high visibility jackets knocking on doors further down.

"Um, yes. Portland Street. I walked past on my way home from work last night and saw the ambulance."

"Did you notice anything else? We're going door to door, as you can see."

"No, not really." Her skin was on fire. "Although, I…" It was always difficult but the urge to offer help was overwhelming, and despite her best efforts to stop it, it began to bubble over. "I work at the local pub on the harbour and I've not been here long, but…"

He closed his phone.

"I'm a spiritual medium. I had some visions, some insight into what happened here. It was just as I walked past…" She flicked a glance up at the bedroom window of number five, and again had the impression someone was watching from behind the nets: a man in a vest, pale, unshaven, overweight… "I didn't know the couple who lived here. I've never met them but—" She faltered, regretting saying anything.

"Go on."

"I've helped police out before back in Liverpool and also in Ireland. I don't think it's as straightforward as it looks here." She looked down at the pavement. "So anyway, if you need any help—"

"Have you got a card? Erm, I didn't catch your

name?"

Keep away from them. Especially them!

With a sudden stab of alarm she remembered Jeannie's words about the police, and another rush of heat suffused her neck and face. Had she been stupid? Yet Mailing Street could be the entire reason for being here, and this man had been shown to her.

"No, sorry. And Beth. My name's Beth. Anyway, I'd best get to work. It's just…" She cocked her head to listen. Was that the wind roaring off the ocean, or those same inhuman cries heard last night? There was something else this time, too - human laughter – gleeful, maniacal laughter. She glanced over her shoulder. It had sounded so close as to be right behind her. "Anyway, I hope you get it all resolved."

He nodded, and she began to turn away.

"Just a minute!" He pulled a card from his pocket and handed it over. "Joe Sully. CID. Where did you say you worked, Beth?"

***

CHAPTER SIX

The Lighthouse Inn stood at the far end of the harbour, its namesake silhouetted against a grey-white haze on the headland peninsula behind.

Beth wended her way through the market amid a congenial bur of conversation. The cold, fresh sea air was invigorating, and the stall holders were beginning to pack up for an early lunch. Maybe it was the sight of trawlers and nets, or the quay-side shops touting buckets and spades, but suddenly the memory of childhood holidays with Nan and Gran Grace before the car accident, struck with painful clarity. The crash had killed them both outright. Beth had been just ten years old. But those halcyon days lived on - their picnics on the beach, shielded by windbreakers and building sandcastles, sublimely happy.

Spring was coming soon and with it the crowds. The boarding houses would be full, children fishing in the rock pools, the tinkle of the ice-cream van on the harbour…But just as she stepped over the threshold of the inn, stooping beneath the low beam, fresh knowledge hit her head on... *I won't be here to see it.*

The words thudded into her heart.

Why? Why won't I be here to see it? Where am I to go, then?

This was too quick. They'd only just arrived. She reached for a nearby table, dizzy, in freefall as the walls she had built around herself collapsed. The episode lasted only a few seconds but it was long enough. Perhaps a stark reminder not to get too comfortable and make this home? There could be no attachments like there had been in London. No Travis. She must remain an outsider or it would be very difficult to see the wider picture.

"Trust! Don't stress."

She nodded at the sound of Gran's voice, hung up her coat and walked into the kitchen. Whatever was coming would unfold as it should. For now though, it would be a relief to simply prepare good food.

Relax, relax!

The morning's catch had been delivered, and smiling at the sight of it she tied on an apron. Today there would be crab pate with warm toast, battered cod with chips, and steamed mussels in wine. She set to work, content to be alone during these quiet winter months, absorbed in thought.

Joe Sully was significant. He wanted to know what was wrong with that street. Why that particular one? It wasn't the first case they'd had there and he was puzzled, sensed something deeper.

I'm a spiritual medium. I had some visions, some insight...

For some reason the memory of their encounter made her insides tingle a little and pushed those feelings away. No ties. No mistakes. Besides, he was undoubtedly married – that shed had been his own private thinking place. He needed a shed!

She began to whisk batter and switched her focus to Jeannie. No one could carry on feeling as scared and persecuted as that for long. Still, at least she'd agreed to think about seeing a psychologist. Maybe if she found someone for her? Nudged things on a little? Jeannie could still use the alias name, couldn't she?

Cutting into her thoughts, a male voice made her jump. "Are we good to go? Two more orders here for you, love."

"Ooh blimey, I was miles away! Yes, no problem. Thanks."

The landlord was Gareth Banks. Cheery, with a thick-set neck and a ruddy face, he referred to himself as a grafter who worked hard and played hard. All day long Gareth chatted from behind the bar. 'You want to know anything, you know where to come,' was his favourite line, along with, 'No rest for the wicked.'

He leaned now against the doorway. "Bit of a to-do on Mailing Street last night? You heard about it?"

"Yes, I went home that way and saw the cop cars."

"They caught him, mind. North of Lancaster. One of them what-do-you-call-'ems, wasn't he? Caved 'er 'ead in apparently."

"Yes, I heard."

"Funny place, Mailing Street. You don't live on there, do you?"

"No. Portland Street. I only cut through that way last night because it was freezing on the sea front. It's still raw out today, isn't it? Do you get much snow here, with it being on the coast?"

"What? Yes, course we do, on the hills. We've been cut off before now. So did you see anything at the house or were they clearing off by the time you got there?"

"Clearing off. So why did you say it's a funny place?"

He tapped the side of his nose and waggled his head as if it would be fun to try and extract the information from him.

She waited.

"Well, there've been quite a few murders there over the years, did you not know?"

"No."

"It's why none of the locals, those of us in the know anyway, would ever buy or rent a house on that street even if they were giving them away for the price of a dead rabbit. I've got a new place up on the Windermere Estate, myself – a pretty decent four bedroom house for me, the missus and kids. All mod cons. The rooms aren't as big as those in the terraces but…" He shook his head and drew in a sharp breath. "Wouldn't live there if you paid me. My grandma lived on Mailing Street. There was this 'orrible atmosphere. It was always dark even with the lights on, and she had this dog she kept chained up in the back yard. Anyhow, it went mad and hanged itself."

Beth, who'd picked up a knife to start chopping onions, paused, saw it - a red setter climbing onto a high brick wall before throwing himself over the drop. Tears filled her eyes. His old grandma had watched through the kitchen nets, cold as a dead-eyed fish.

"No one could ever put their finger on what it was, but there were more divorces and strange goings-on in that street than anywhere else in town. Or anywhere come to think of it."

She recovered as quickly as possible and began to chop. Incidents like this, and far worse, went on every second of every day. One battle at a time!

"Erm, strange goings on?"

"Well, one woman, back in the seventies this was, knifed her old man in the chest while he was asleep then left his heart out on the front wall for the birds to peck. Afterwards she said a young lad told her to do it, only she didn't have any kids and there was no one else in the house. I think they put her in the loony bin. She might be out now, come to think of it, so we'd best watch out. Whooo….."

She tried to smile at his impression of scaring her with an imaginary ghost.

"There've been quite a few weird tales, actually." He put his hands in his pockets, rocking back and forth, warming to the theme. "But there's a story about that ghostly young lad. They say he was adopted, between the wars I think it was. Anyhow, the couple who took him in, and this is what will shock you - the woman killed her 'usband while he lay in bed and then hanged herself. But here's the thing, her tongue had been cut out. And they say the lad had a satanic bible and when they found the dead couple he was reading from it and laughing. Whole house was decorated with rotting flowers…"

Fucking hell. She carried on chopping onions. Gareth looked so cheery while he was relating all of this. "I'm surprised they keep housing people there, to be honest. Trauma lingers."

"Only immigrants. Got to put them somewhere, haven't you? At least it's a roof over their heads. Beggars can't be–"

She shut out the rest of his sentence by plunging chips into the deep fat fryer, reminding herself she had to keep this job, at least for a little while.

"Won't be long now. Sorry, I am listening."

"Right. Anyhow, I'd best get back to work. No rest for the wicked."

As he pushed the door open, a cacophony of voices bellowed in from the bar, a woman's raucous laughter carrying over the top - the kind of four-sheets-to-the-wind abandon that comes after an entire evening of drinking.

Someone's started early, Beth thought, noticing the woman perched on a bar stool, her head thrown back so far the sinews of her throat stood proud. She sat in a cloud of vape smoke, the black roots of her yellow hair a stark contrast to the bleach; nail varnish chipped as she clutched a glass of clear spirit, no ice. And in that snapshot second, as Beth stared, the woman's spider-mascara eyelashes opened like a fly-catcher, to reveal bloodshot eyes and pool-black irises.

The door swung shut.

Beth forced herself to concentrate on the fryer as one boom after the other now flashed before her: Joe Sully's face, then Jeannie's, followed by the dripping walls of an underground passageway. And just as she was struggling to work out what she was being shown, the presence of someone new floated in. This was someone as yet unknown, a woman of slight stature with eggshell-fine skin, so white as to be almost translucent. She had delicate features and a web of lines at the outer corners of pale blue eyes. The appearance was one of fragility, a porcelain doll that would shatter if squeezed. Sometimes a person's signature came to her as a fragrance, sometimes a taste. This one was taste, of pear drops, a sweet from childhood that was both sugary and sharp. Two tones then, a contrast, a surprise?

All the visions were disjointed with nothing making sense. And again, as with Curbeck, there came an impression of multiple levels and dimensions, stories and lives to be peeled back and disentangled in order to get to the root. One single root.

"We need to talk to Jeannie," said Billy, who was standing at the back door watching the hull of a trawler being repaired in dry dock.

"Is anyone really following her? Us? Or is she imagining it?"

He nodded. "We haven't got a lot of time."

"For real? Physical or on the astral?"

He shook his head. "Both. There are troops on the ground, as it were."

"So Jeannie's not wrong. And she doesn't need help?"

"That's for her to decide."

Beth frowned. He could not tell her what to do or infringe on free will, and besides, if Jeannie was told they really were being followed it could make matters worse.

"I'm confused. I need to tune in. Everything feels adrift. All I know for sure is we need to help with Mailing Street but–"

"He'll chase you up, the man, Sully."

She nodded. "Are we in danger?"

"Gran's gone to Scarsdale Hall to have a look-see. I'll catch you later."

Beth was about to ask more but he'd vanished. Billy had, however, left something to make her smile – one of the bananas on the table had a face drawn on it with a biro, complete with bushy eyebrows and a moustache. And next to it was a small, plastic coffee carton, the kind of chemical powdered cream hardly anyone liked, but used because it was better than nothing. She picked it up and twirled it between her fingers, only now noticing the peel-away lid decorated with a tiny red jester.

The Mantel's presence infiltrated everything. It was everywhere.

***

CHAPTER SEVEN

"We need to talk," said Gran.

Billy had said it and now Gran. Clearly it was time to go within.

The February afternoon had faded early, a storm riding in off the Atlantic. After walking home along the wind-battered promenade, Beth let herself into an empty house and hurried upstairs for a hot bath. Closing her eyes, she lay in the soapy water thinking about her friend and house-mate. There was nothing particular, no one thing to say this or that wasn't quite right, other than the distinct feeling a chasm had appeared between them. Or it was going to. For a moment she was standing on a shore, calling and calling, frantically waving to a figure on a sandbank being swallowed by fog. But they couldn't see her. They couldn't hear…

Weary, she drifted into deep relaxation, allowing guidance to come. It would. Half the trick was unwinding from the minutiae of everyday life, in becoming still and quiet. Scents of lavender, rose and frankincense from the candles merged with the steam as she began the process of contracting then releasing each muscle; and by the time her head hit the pillow twenty minutes later it was easy to slip into trance.

Golden, silver and white light streamed in through the crown chakra, spreading out in a buttery cone of protection until it became a cocoon of radiance. Now her heart chakra opened up as a flower to the sun, filling her whole being with indescribable love. There was nothing that could possibly touch the euphoria, the bliss, and tears welled and streamed down her face as the connection with the divine was made. The radiant cocoon now expanded further and further, until it reached the seals of Solomon placed at each compass point of the grounds, the entire house now protected. Around that she then created a black flame of invisibility, a cloak. Those who tried to remote view or invade either her or Jeannie's auric fields and personal space while they slept, would be repelled.

But who or what was hunting them down? Why had she and Jeannie been drawn here? All of these questions she spoke out loud.

We need to talk...

The Lord's Prayer tripped from her lips as she drifted higher and higher, like a hot air balloon hacked loose, soaring into the ether. She would go to the white room, and from there to the forest to talk to the soul family. They would show her what to do...would be waiting... Suddenly, however, a vision flashed before her and she was unexpectedly yanked sideways onto the astral plane.

Below was a dimly lit bedroom. With only one lamp to lift the gloom, the faces of both Jeannie and an elderly lady were reflected in a darkened window, periodically spattered with sleet. They appeared to be talking in confidence, heads bowed and voices hushed, one wizened hand with prominent veins clutching that of the younger woman's. The wind soughed and whined around the building, sweeping off the moors in gusts that rattled the windows.

Caught off-guard, Beth had only just recognised her friend when Jeannie glanced up - directly at the corner of the room as if at a CCTV.

Beth cloaked her presence at once. Did Jeannie have the sight? Had she seen her or sensed her presence? Deciding to withdraw, Beth sent deep violet waves of loving energy to envelop them both. They needed the healing. Both seemed equally agitated and disturbed. And besides, something was circling and prowling around that nursing home like an unwanted guest.

Gran's voice cut in sharply. "Beth!"

She jerked back into consciousness and in a blinding flash, found herself in the white room. Here, in a lucid dream state, she altered her appearance to that of an impossibly slim, sylph-like creature. Dressed in the style of Queen Guinevere, she examined the room carefully, appreciating the serenity and the security of coming home, before slipping out of a side door and walking to the special place in the forest where the elders would be waiting. The soul family included Gran Grace and Billy, Gran's sisters and father, the tribe healer, the elders, and for the first time ever, the heyoka.

The heyoka was an outsider, a mirror, often comical. Considered a spiritual enlightener by the ancients, he or she would copy or ape a person's behaviour and reflect it back. Often hilarious, sometimes cutting, it depended on the observer as to how this was received - whether the heyoka was welcome or not. Lessons could be painful, humour essential. In their tribe, the heyoka was an elderly woman with a face painted pale, who sat watching with glittering eyes until the chosen member realised it was their turn.

It had taken eighteen years to master memory retention from dream state, but when Beth woke an hour later, to the flicker of just one dying candle, she could remember the lot.

The tribe had sat on boulders by the river for a while, Beth enjoying the fresh, cold mountain water rushing over her bare feet. Sun baked the ground and bioluminescence glinted in the spray as it cascaded over rocks to the aqua lagoon below. Children splashed in the clear water, wild and free, horses grazing nearby. After a while, when the sun began to descend in a fiery ball over the purple mountains, a fire was lit and smokes of ayahuasca and marijuana were passed around. The colours were vibrant, as sharp as a rainbow after a spring shower. Time slowed, and once the pipe had been passed around a few times, what they wanted to show her appeared in the tongues of the flickering flames.

Every moment was a flash of knowing – of what already existed, existed now and was to come - simultaneously exhibited across a quantum reality. And thus, in stark contrast to the quiet forest clearing and star-studded sky, the antipathy of paradise appeared before her.

A slaughterhouse of screaming, bleeding animals.

Horrified, she sprang back. The sickening stench of

terror was palpable. A knot of fear and confusion had been trapped beneath the earth, and remained bound in a mass of sticky black tar that imprisoned the souls of hundreds of murdered animals. They could not escape, constantly reliving their final moments. She tried to focus. There was something keeping them there, a presence they could not bypass for fear of it. What? Who?

She began to probe through the layers of time, the energies sickly and thick...down and down and down....until she found him... Standing in a pit of sawdust, the granular form of a man had emerged. Maniacal laughing that jarred like grinding metal plates rang through the bones of her head...

No soul.

Not human.

But before she could think further, the vision died as fast as a doused flame, quickly replaced by another. And her heart lurched with recognition. This one was much closer to home.

A girl was hurrying along a darkened street. With her hands thrust deep into coat pockets and her head down against the wind, she was picking up pace. She had the energy of one in flight. Unseen by those behind rows of closed curtains, her quick footsteps fell lightly on a pavement shiny and wet. Confetti snow fluttered around the streetlights, settling on the roofs of houses and cars. However, it wasn't the cold that was bothering the girl, but the shadow in her wake. Blacker than those of the terraces she passed, and even the moors beyond, the shadow stretched three or four times her length, encroaching on her own, merging with it, looming over her head as if to devour her.

From time to time she swung around as if to catch the shadow out, only to see it recede like a slick of oil.

Beth caught her breath at the sight of the girl's face, tuning into her fear.

Jeannie, it's all in your mind!

But no sooner had the words left her lips when a van glided alongside the girl and slowed to crawling pace. Charcoal grey with sliding side doors, it was unmarked, the number plate obscured by mud. Beth's heart slammed into her ribs.

The genal's on your right. Now. Immediately.

Jeannie didn't hesitate. The second the van drew level she shot down the genal and vanished. Whoever was in that van would not have had time to even put the handbrake on.

Beth's heart was pounding in synchronicity with Jeannie's as she relayed instructions. Billy was already on the scene protecting her. And Jeannie was fast and fleet of foot. Bolting down the next alleyway she all but flew...Until finally her key was in the door.

With a pang it occurred to Beth that this child had spent her entire life either running or hiding, and still there was no end in sight. But it was only as she was withdrawing from the visions in the flames, and her own breathing began to return to normal, that a glint of something indecipherable caught in the fire.

Gold, it looked like a brooch or a pin.

Gone.

She woke with a bump to the sound of a key slotting into the front door, and for a few seconds lay with her eyes wide open. Snow pitter-pattered against the window, the night icy and black as soot. Where was this? A border of light suddenly framed the door. There was the sound of boots being kicked off in the hall, and a mumbled expletive under the breath. Ah! Jeannie was home safely.

"Thank you, God!"

And seconds later she fell deeply asleep, dreaming of a rippling mountain stream, while vaguely aware of the taste of something familiar - a sweet, pear drops - and the image of something she was supposed to remember but could not.

Dreams flew in and flew out before she was visited, though. Of course, the heyoka had never attended any of the soul meetings she'd been to before. How had she not suspected?

Crap! It's my turn!

The heyoka's tiny, crooked figure, face painted white, eyes glitteringly watchful, appeared to her now. And her wiry hands flew to her face in mockery as she imitated Beth flushing and stuttering in front of Joe Sully.

Initially affronted, Beth watched the performance in the dream and realised she was laughing. There was a feeling the rest of the tribe was laughing somewhere, too.

Yeah, okay. She'd made a tit of herself.

***

CHAPTER EIGHT

By morning the storm had largely abated, leaving in its wake the hush of snowfall. A good inch coated pavements, roofs, and the tops of the moors; and the air was laced with ice.

Jeannie had once again left early for work, her lone footprints a track across the road leading to the genal. Beth didn't need to see her friend's face to know she was bone weary and had only slept for a few hours. Maybe keeping busy to the point of exhaustion staved off the nightmares? What should she do to help her?

Beth washed the dishes and made a start on the housework, and by the time she'd hoovered downstairs an answer had formed. She could find Jeannie a professional psychotherapist. Get the ball rolling!

Sitting down with a coffee, she scrolled through a few websites. Most therapists were affiliated to larger organisations, and by and large were situated in city centres, which for Jeannie would be stressful and difficult. No one in particular jumped out. What might be best for Jeannie, she thought, would be an older lady - someone kindly who worked with those who'd predominantly suffered mental and emotional abuse.

Someone spiritual?

Ah! The name, 'Estelle Vickers' caught her eye. No, she was miles away in Fleet. After another half hour, however, she returned to Estelle, made another coffee and decided to investigate further. Estelle Vickers had originally worked as a mental health nurse, before becoming a hypnotherapist and counsellor specialising in post-traumatic stress disorder. Beth's eyebrows lifted at the inclusion of spirit detachments in the list of professional expertise. Hmmm….had she found the one?

It was so important to get this right. And were the reviews genuine or did people buy them? Maybe friends and family helped out and just made them up? Her mind flicked back to a woman Travis had insisted she see last year. He'd repeatedly told Beth she was mentally unwell because, and how she regretted this now, she'd cried every time he lambasted her for asking where he was going, often for days at a time. Come to think of it, he'd never actually provided that information, which was quite an art in itself. Instead Travis had managed to convince her she was needy and over-emotional. As such, worn down, she'd eventually agreed to see the GP, who referred her to a psychologist. Annoyance screwed her up anew as the memory rose up from its hidden place. Yup, and that had been a mistake she'd known full well the second she walked into the therapist's office. The young woman had been unable to drag her attention away from the computer screen for longer than a few seconds, as with long, two-tone blue nails she tapped, 'yes' or 'no' into an endless checklist.

Beth had replied with whatever came into her head

for the first ten minutes, and then exited on the pretext of needing the loo. Travis had been livid. No amount of explaining to him how she'd felt had sufficed. The younger, infinitely more qualified woman knew best.

Let it go, Beth!

What hadn't the man who said he loved her, not understood when she told him that relating her innermost feelings to a computer was not only unhelpful but insulting? Dehumanising! And to take her side against…

Beth! Let it go!

Gran's voice was faint but she heard it.

Okay, so here was Jeannie, a damaged girl who now had every chance of living a full life. Imagine persuading her to receive professional help only to send her into the computer checklist situation! Not only that, but who wanted their deepest fears immortalising on a database? She bit her lip and closed the phone.

Immediately the memory of Travis's angry face loomed large again. 'You should listen to me. You need help! Serious help…'

Two old ladies locked in a lavatory… they'll be there from Monday to Saturday.…

She looked up to find Gran Grace standing over her with her hands on her hips, just as she had when she was a child. Gran was wearing her favourite turquoise shawl pinned with a topaz brooch.

"Hello, Gran!"

"I told you to let it go. He's a dead weight stopping you from cutting the rope. Can't you see, child? All that mattered to Travis was Travis. He's stuck in his own importance and he managed to get you stuck in it, too.

People like him leech the light off others because they don't have any of their own. They make you feel worse to make themselves feel better and because it's not honest they have to make a story up. We've discussed narcissism countless times."

She nodded. Gran Grace was in full Victorian disciplinarian mode.

"I suppose that therapist incident snagged a bit. I'm okay."

Gran pursed her lips then sighed indulgently. "Good, because there's important work to do and you can't get bogged down. There's going to be an escalation of events now. You must keep watch, and be especially alert walking through the market place. Make a note of any details."

"How–?"

Gran put her fingers to her lips. "You will make contact with this woman, Estelle. And then you will tell Jeannie to go for the appointment." She stared at Beth's phone. "I really must work out how to send a text."

Beth nodded. "Someone is definitely following her, though. So who was it in the van last night?"

"My uncle and I are watching out for you both. Don't be fearful and don't get sucked into the drama, because that too will escalate. Just be hyper-alert."

"Where's Billy?"

The lights dimmed and flared, dimmed and flared.

"Is that you, you bloody idiot?"

Billy appeared on the sofa behind Gran, shrugging.

"Can you stop pissing about? It's not funny."

She couldn't help but smile though, noticing now that every piece of fruit in the bowl had a face drawn on it.

"Okay, well I'll give Estelle a ring. I hope Jeannie's going to be okay with this. Mind you, I suppose I can always cancel—"

"She will," said Gran. "In fact, I have a feeling that after today she'll snatch your hand off."

As it turned out, the escalation happened way sooner than Beth expected. She was wending her way through the market place that afternoon, and although most of the snow had melted, squally winds whipped her hair this way and that. Despite battling with being able to see properly and occasionally slipping, she was miles away as usual, puzzling this time over last night's visions, notably the flash of gold in the flames. What had it been? A pin of some sort…familiar yet elusive… And what had Gran meant when she said Jeannie would snatch her hand off with regard to Estelle Vickers? Was it to do with the old lady in the nursing home or the shadow trailing her on the way home last night? And the van! The van was real…

So distracted was she, that it was therefore a near heart attack moment when a man suddenly jumped out in front of her.

She leapt sideways to avoid a collision and fell sprawling into a stack of wooden trestle tables. With her arms out in front, she narrowly missed a head injury by twisting onto her back at the last second; and in the confusion her shoulder bag flew across the tarmac, the contents scattering. Momentarily stunned, she watched the scene play out in slow motion - a tube of lipstick taking forever to roll into a drain, a hairbrush skating underneath the table opposite.

Several people rushed to her aid.

"You all right, love?"

Someone laughed. "What happened there?"

A woman retrieved her bag. "Here you are, love. I think everything's still there. Your purse is in it anyway, that's the main thing."

She watched the lipstick wash through the grille and plop down the drain, now on its new journey to the sea.

I can't afford another one...

Her knees and elbows began to sing. They'd be grazed, sore...She heard her own voice thanking people, assuring them she was absolutely fine as she struggled to her feet. Shaken, she looked left and then right. The man had burst out of nowhere. True she'd been away with the fairies but the aisles had been completely empty, with the stallholders packing wares into vans. The only thing there'd been time to note was that he'd been dressed in a long black coat and hat.

"Did you trip over your own feet?"

"Er, no. There was a man about to bump into me—"

The crowd of three, maybe four people, all looked up and down the market aisles, which were as empty as they had been a minute ago. A look of confusion passed between them.

"There was no one there, love," said the one who'd laughed, a ruddy-cheeked man of about sixty, jaunty as a garden gnome. "It was quite spectacular actually. I was just over there – couple of yards away. You jumped into the air as if you'd been bitten on the arse, and then you just..." Here he demonstrated with arms spread-eagled, "Leapt into the tables. Are you sure you're okay?"

She nodded, trying to laugh it off along with the

others.

There'd been no one there!

***

CHAPTER NINE

"His name's Crispin," Jeannie was saying. "Doctor Crispin Freeman."

Beth opened her eyes to find Jeannie sitting on the edge of her bed holding a mug of tea.

"Where am I? Am I back home?"

"Yes, you asked me that already."

The bedside lamp was on, curtains closed. A quick glance at the clock showed it was eleven o'clock at night. She must have nodded off.

"Sorry."

"No, it's me who should be sorry. You sent me a text to say wake you up when I got in. I didn't realise you weren't with it yet. I feel a bit daft now."

Beth giggled as she sat up. She had most definitely not sent Jeannie a text. Gran must have finally worked out how to do it.

"What's funny? Anyhow, I brought you some tea." Jeannie handed her the mug. "Sorry, I know it's late but you said it was urgent and we had to talk."

She took a sip. "Did I indeed? Thanks. What day is it? You're doing a lot of double shifts lately. Are you okay?"

"Sunday," said Jeannie, nodding.

Good grief! Three days had passed since the accident in the market, and there hadn't been chance to mention the appointment she'd made with Estelle yet. Jeannie's aura was narrower than usual. A shadow hovered around her, too. But as she watched it faded away.

"You can't still be cleaning this late at night?"

"No. The agency offered me some extra hours – making teas and coffees, manning reception, all sorts of stuff. There's a staff shortage. A lot have gone off sick. I knew most of them because they started at the same time as me. Anyway, word is some don't want to work there anymore because they're saying the place is haunted. To be fair, there have been a lot of deaths but then you'd expect that, wouldn't you? Anyway, I want to save some extra money, so…"

Beth tuned in while Jeannie talked. She was looking at an empty lounge with rows of olive green, high-backed chairs lining the walls. Beneath fluorescent lights, a television set was blaring with a fast, animated commentary, but there was no one there to watch it. Not a soul.

"Thing is, they were all complaining of the same thing - stomach pains and headaches - saying they can't concentrate and they can't sleep. And the old people can't sleep, either. They're out for the count all day, heads lolling over the side of their chairs, but at night they're wide awake, calling out and screaming. May Morris, the lady I was telling you about, said the lights in the corridors are on all night and the television's left on, too. Full volume."

"Can't you turn it off?"

"I've tried but it's impossible. You can't turn it down and you can't turn it off. I feel really sorry for the residents because they can't get out of their chairs to escape the noise. Most of them can hardly walk. And it never stops. You can hear the television people all the time, even upstairs in the bedrooms when it ought to be quiet."

That television....

Beth had the sudden image of a man in a long, black trench coat crawling out of the screen head first. He seemed to be manifesting from the frequency waves, taking form, easing himself out on a low vibration of sickness, helplessness and confusion. A long shadow preceded him, stretching out across the carpet towards the high-backed chairs.

"It's not a healthy environment. Not natural. That television should be switched off, especially at night."

"I told you, it can't be done."

"Unplug it?"

"Nope, a wire goes directly into the wall, and I swear to God no matter what button you press on that set it will not go off."

"I'd get an engineer in."

"I asked because May - she's ninety-three by the way - said it was really bothering her. So I spoke to one of the care assistants and she said she'd ask Doctor Freeman. Anyway, the upshot was he wasn't going to the expense of calling out an engineer just to turn a television off."

"Who's in charge there? Keep talking." An impression formed in her head of a female in her forties, with shiny, raven black hair. There was a nursing uniform of the old style, but this woman was not a nurse, and something on her lapel…something seen before, but where? Also, she had a connection to the doctor on a personal level…

"Daphne French. I think her and Doctor Freeman are more than friends, if you get my drift?"

"Hmmm."

"So anyway, why did you need to speak to me urgently?"

Beth took a sip of tea. "What?"

Oh, the gold flash was the pin, the one seen in the flames? A highly distinctive pin. A snake, more than one, with something on top like the wings of a bird.

Billy was peering through the blinds as something clattered in the yard. And just as the shape of the pin registered and formed in her mind, he turned to face her and nodded. Right, so that pin was significant and it was connected to the nursing home in some way.

"Beth?"

"Sorry. Okay, well I do need to speak to you as it happens. Did a van draw up alongside when you were walking home the other night? Grey with sliding doors and–?"

Jeannie's eyes widened. "Oh my God, yes! And this was the funny thing: the second it drew up, I knew exactly what to do. It was like a voice told me to run like hell. I shot immediately to the right without thinking, and I just kept running until I got to Portland Street. It was only when I'd got the key in the door that I dared glance back, and I really did expect to see the van cruising up, or a bloke behind me. But there wasn't anyone there. I scanned the entrance to the genal.

Nothing. It was only later I remember thinking, you know, one more second of hesitation and someone could have got out of that van–"

"Yes, that definitely wasn't your imagination."

"No, it wasn't. And the fact I sprinted off like that was a miracle."

"Yes."

"I told you we're being followed for real. But the shapes and shadows aren't." She lapsed into thought for a while. "There is a blurred line between what's real and what's not. I suppose I've been watched all my life, so…"

Beth nodded. "You're the one who has to be clear, to be able to discern? If you think it's just your own fear but turns out to be real, then that's dangerous, but if it is imagination then it's going to ruin your life–"

"Sort of, trust God but lock your car?"

Beth smiled. "Exactly, we can't be stupid." She downed the rest of her tea and put down the mug. "Just to highlight the point, something odd happened to me the other day, too. I don't want to alarm you but if I don't tell you and you let your guard down…well you get my drift?"

Briefly she described what had happened at the market and that Gran had warned her it might. "And like you, I don't know if it was real or imagined. I have a feeling it was an astral projection. The dark magicians can do that, it's not unknown."

Jeannie started to bite her nails.

"Think about those black shapes you've seen, with your own eyes. Ritual magic can cause heart attacks, car accidents – all sorts – and the vast majority of people will never know. There's no trace. The victim went mad or just jumped off a bridge or—"

"Beth!"

"Sorry, it's a balance between making you aware this stuff is real and making it worse. It's all about understanding the energies and separating out your own fear."

"You've made me that appointment, haven't you?"

Beth pulled a face. "You know me better than I thought."

"I might look daft and sound daft, but I promise you I'm not. A lot's come back to me since I escaped from Curbeck. I'll tell you something else an' all - May Morris confided in me. Turns out she's got some extremely interesting information about the Mantels."

Beth's eyebrows shot up, and she smiled to herself at the sight of both Billy and Gran Grace poised on the end of the bed, waiting to hear what Jeannie had to say.

"May Morris knows them?"

***

CHAPTER TEN

It wasn't often Gran Grace jumped up and down like an excited child at Christmas. But May Morris had obviously opened up to Jeannie.

"Do you feel this clicking into place?" said Gran.

Beth nodded.

"I thought you weren't going to tell anyone where you're from?"

"That's just the thing," said Jeannie. "I didn't. Why would I? As far as May Morris was concerned I was just Maria Kitlowski, the new cleaner. No, all this came from her. One day she asked me to take her back to her room early because frankly she was sick of the television. So I helped her into bed, brought her a book and gave her a cup of tea. Then she patted the side of her bed and asked me to keep her company for a while. She wasn't like the others. I don't know how to put it really - she had something about her, a light behind her eyes. There was a connection."

Beth nodded.

"Anyway, she wanted to know if I was happy in my work, and I said it was all right. To be honest I didn't want the focus on me for obvious reasons. So I switched the conversation around and asked how long she'd been in the home, and what kind of history she'd taught."

"Had she been there a long time?"

"Less than a year. She'd had a stroke, a mild one, but as she lived alone the hospital staff suggested she consider moving into Moorlands instead of going home. She said she couldn't recall the details or how she came to agree, but wishes she hadn't."

"Probably she felt vulnerable after the stroke and thought it was a good idea at the time? Does she have any relatives?"

"Apparently not. But it turns out she wasn't a lecturer at all. She worked for the government. When she left it was to research history, which was her degree subject and she loved it. Anyway, at first she had several books published, but then suddenly the publisher dropped her and after that she couldn't get anything into print. All doors closed."

"Why?"

"Well, this is where it gets interesting. The book that ended her career was on the aristocracy."

"Oh?"

"Yeah, that's what piqued my interest. I was desperate to ask if she knew about the Mantels."

"I bet."

"So I asked her, as casually as I could, what had happened. Turned out the publisher stopped distribution of the book in question and wouldn't commission the next one she'd proposed, either. No explanation."

"Wow."

"So she dug around for another publisher. No joy.

She was persona non grata. Nor could she get her articles published and all the interviews dried up."

"What did she do?"

"While she was telling me all this, I kid you not, we both thought there was someone lurking outside in the corridor. There wasn't, I checked. So I came back into the room and she told me to lean close so she could whisper. She wanted to tell someone but I was to keep it to myself. Turns out she'd worked in the foreign office, and while she knew the book on the aristocracy wasn't going to please certain factions, she didn't know that the families she'd written about now own most of the media, control the intelligence agencies, and vet every bit of information that goes out to the public."

"The names change. That's why she didn't know."

"Yes, how did you know that? That's what she said. Basically, there's a ruling club that the rest of us aren't in. So it looks like ordinary people make their way to the top of the ladder fair and square, but they don't. They're all part of the same set-up or they soon will be. And at the top of that club is the Mantel family. So by the time the scale of this hit May, she'd already written to ask the countess for an interview regarding her hereditary line through European royalty. She'd started to work on a sequel, you see? And it was after that her career came to an abrupt end."

"The countess had her book checked out."

"It was as if an axe had fallen. The world just cut her out. She did manage to land a deal with an American publisher, but within weeks of the book's release it was swiftly withdrawn."

"Not just a British club, then?"

"In the end she put the work online."

Beth thought back to her time in Curbeck, when she'd researched the Mantel family and found almost nothing on the countess. But there had been some highly comprehensive historical information on the shadow nobility that she'd been immeasurably grateful for. The writer had traced certain bloodline families, those hiding in the shadows, back to the seed of Cain. Had that writer been May Morris? What a coincidence!

Never a coincidence…

Beth flashed a look at Billy and Gran Grace.

"What a shame for her, though. She must have been destitute."

"That's what I said. But she told me she spent her entire life reading and writing – it's all she ever wanted to do - so she just scrimped and got by."

There came a snapshot glimpse of a lady with powder soft, white hair cut into a bob, a pale pink scarf around her neck, tapping away on an old-fashioned typewriter. She was cold, her breath steaming on the air. And a cat was curled up on a two-seater sofa, huddled into a crocheted blanket.

"So what more did she tell you about the countess? And why did she need to whisper? I mean, the work had gone out already and who in that place would be interested?"

"Well, that's what I'm coming to. She told me what you'd already explained about the Club of Rome – interlinking royal houses with the banking dynasties - but that the real power was behind those names; behind the stately homes and behind the corporations."

Beth was already seeing long robes, a black altar, masked

faces, a black and white floor…

"When she started to talk about this bit I had a funny moment, and she grabbed hold of my hand. She's a bit like you in the way she just knows stuff. So apparently, there's something that binds those at the top together, and it's so bad they know that no one outside their inner circle would ever believe it. This would be a circle within a circle and no one knows about it except those who are in it: existence of said inner circle denied. The families are born to it, but successful outsiders who make it to positions of influence for example, are locked in. No secrets ever get out. Not ever. It's on pain of death, and worse than death – if not to them then to those they love."

Beth tried not to look at Billy and Gran Grace.

"And at the helm of the inner shadow circle is Allegra Mantel?"

"She's called the dark mother. I pretended I was daft, that the name meant nothing to me, but I swear I felt someone was watching us while May was telling me this. I don't think I was imagining it but you might think–"

Tell her!

Beth shook her head. "Ah, so she was telling you all that when….? Actually you weren't imagining that one. It was me. Don't worry, I got pulled to check on you, that's all."

"Oh–"

"Only briefly. I was shown who you were with and as soon as I saw it was a private conversation, I left. But you saw me, that's amazing."

Jeannie nodded. "Just an orb of silver but it was

dull, as in you'd miss it if you weren't looking."

"I can see now why they pushed me to go back for you in Curbeck."

"You've lost me, I don't get it."

"May Morris and you connected. You were supposed to. We just don't know why yet."

Jeannie searched her eyes.

"Their worst nightmare is being exposed. That's why they go to such lengths to bind people in. Can you imagine if you committed something so horrific that if it got out you'd be publicly ruined or your family would be killed?"

"And they own everything."

Beth flicked another glance at Billy and Gran.

"Yes, absolutely everything. Nothing is public even though people think it is. Everything is a corporation and everything is owned. All bases covered."

"Don't they have enough fucking money?"

"It isn't about money, Jeannie. That's just another control system."

They stared at each other.

"I keep seeing the shadows on the walls at that nursing home, Beth. Like it's her…catching up with me…"

As Jeannie spoke, the image appeared again of a gold pin with snakes coiling around it – not a pin as such, but a sword plunged downwards with wings spreading out at the top. What was it? What did it mean? How was it relevant?

"It's a Caduceus," Billy said.

She frowned. *A what?*

"…They've found me. And you. I know they have.

It's her, I'm telling you. I've seen her standing at the bottom of one of the genals like she's waiting for me – a nine or ten foot soot-black shadow. A woman in a long black dress. Just standing there watching. And the air freezes. I've seen her at the foot of the stairs in the nursing home, too."

At the same time Jeannie was speaking, Beth was trying to hear Billy.

"What's the matter?" said Jeannie, glancing over her shoulder. "Is something behind me?"

"Kadooseeus? What's a kadooseeus?"

"I don't know," said Billy.

Beth shook her head in frustration. "Gran and Billy are trying to show me something."

"May's scared, Beth. She says it's black magic giving everyone nightmares and sending them mad. Things go missing then turn up again. And May said one night her lamp went out while she was reading. Another time her curtains started to billow like there was a strong breeze in the middle of the night, but the windows were shut. She also told me to watch Freeman, to stay out of his way."

"Fear feeds fear."

"I know."

"Can you try and explain this to May? Tell her what I've passed on to you about protection and–?"

Jeannie was shaking her head. "I do all that stuff you taught me – opening up chakras and clearing negative energy, filling with love and light - but we've both seen those shadows and shapes on the walls, following our every move. They're not going away, Beth. In fact, the more I meditate and connect, the worse it's getting."

"Caduceus!" Gran Grace shouted.

Beth screwed up her eyes as image after image now bombarded her. Jeannie was still speaking and it was hard to concentrate. May Morris ...someone she's seen from her bedroom window...And images of the caduceus symbol on a red door... on a stone archway...underground at the end of a corridor...

"There's something else I should tell you, as well," Jeannie was saying. "It's to do with the house next door, the one May overlooks."

***

CHAPTER ELEVEN

Busy in the pub kitchen next morning, Beth thought over their conversation. Poor Jeannie! None of what May said could have done much to alleviate her fears. She shook her head. Jeannie was going to need a lot of help coping with what was undoubtedly dark magic, in addition to trauma. What a relief she'd agreed to see Estelle Vickers on Wednesday. Hopefully talking it through would help.

She began to mix her popular and now famous batter, when suddenly the sweet tartness of pear drops wafted on the air again, and she paused. That was the third time, wasn't it? A woman....someone's signature...Closing her eyes, she tuned in, trying to make a connection, when the feeling someone was staring at her intensely brought her up sharp.

A man was standing in the doorway. How long had he been there? Just watching?

"Gareth! You made me jump. I was miles away."

Far from being puffed-up and bursting with gossip, however, his shoulders had slumped, his demeanour that of a deflated balloon.

She put down the whisk and wiped her hands.

"What's the matter? What's happened?"

"It's Molly. She's gone missing. No one's seen her for days."

As soon as he spoke, she saw Molly as last viewed through the door into the bar – head thrown back, bloodshot eyes through spider lashes – and instantly knew! Her skin goosed cold and an upsurge of nausea rushed into her throat.

Molly, without doubt, was dead.

She ran to the sink, swiped away the pots and pans, and retched. An overpowering stench of rotting flowers and incense gripped her in wave after wave of colic. It was like the worst travel sickness, closeted in an over-heated car perfumed with synthetic fragrance and someone smoking a pipe. And for several minutes after the vomiting had subsided, she stood with her head hanging over the bowl, clinging to the tap, gasping, eyes streaming. One vision after the other was flashing before her.

Eventually she dabbed at her face with a wodge of kitchen roll and still reeling from what she was being shown, turned around.

Gareth was still there, his expression one of both surprise and revulsion. "Are you not well?" He lunged for the deep fat fryer as it began to smoke. "What about all these covers? Can you finish the battered cod?"

His voice sounded a long way off as she stood swallowing down stomach acid and trying to breathe steadily, to think of an excuse for what just happened, and was still happening. A woman's body had been laid out like a corpse on a table. Or was it a patient awaiting surgery? No, because the operation had already happened: where the stomach and intestines should be, there was a huge, crimson crater. The smell of decaying flowers and incense now began to mingle with candle smoke and sausages...cooking meat... Flames were dancing around a room, leaping across wallpaper...

"Yes, I'm okay." She poured a glass of water and glugged it down.

"Well, if you're sure."

"Don't worry. I get erm...I'm someone who can tune into things others can't, and sometimes I kind of know what's happened–"

"Like a psychic, you mean? Like Mystic Meg?"

Recovering a little, she washed her hands and began to slap the cod with batter. "Not like Mystic Meg, no."

"Well if you're psychic you'll know where Molly is. I've tried ringing and Bob's been round, but there's no answer–"

"No, I don't."

"If you want my opinion, that psychic stuff's a load of bollocks. What you've got is likely a stomach bug, and speaking as your boss that's far more concerning. Could be a public health issue. In fact, now I come to think of it, maybe you should go home and I'll take over?"

Shivering, she nodded gratefully. "Actually, yes. You're right. You wouldn't want your customers to catch anything. Thank you."

"I'm sure Molly will turn up. Probably slept over with someone. She did put it about a bit. Hardly a secret."

"Yep."

Beth was already flinging off her apron, seizing the

chance to flee before he changed his mind. It was as if an invisible hand was compressing the crown of her head with a brick. The pain was intense and getting worse. Not only that but Billy had appeared, and he was hopping up and down, pointing to the door.

Already looking as if he regretted his offer, an air of martyrdom hung over Gareth as he took the apron from her and shouted to the girl on the bar that she'd have to do the work of two. Beth slipped out just as he was mumbling about no rest for the wicked, grabbed her coat and dashed through the bar, intent on getting home as soon as possible. Things were escalating, for sure, just as Gran had said. But at the exact moment she pushed open the door to the market, it swung wide open from the other side and she almost fell out.

A man caught her head on. "Whoa!"

"Ooh, sorry."

"No, I'm sorry. Are you okay?"

She looked up, realising with a thud of embarrassment who he was.

Oh, no!

"Yes, fine. Sorry. Thanks." Acutely aware of having just been copiously sick, she ducked her head and tried to edge past. "Thanks, I'm really fine. Absolutely fine. Completely fine."

Oh no, this is horrible. I want to go home.

His laser blue eyes bore into hers. "Erm, aren't you Beth? The spiritual medium?"

Behind her, a couple of men who'd been chatting, stopped. The silence hummed.

Keeping her voice to a near whisper, she answered. "I don't really …um…you know, tell everyone?"

He flushed very slightly, gently pulling her to one side and out of the way of an incoming couple. "Sorry, my fault, that was tactless. I didn't mean to be." He smiled, revealing even white teeth. "You know that thing where you're in a crowded room and suddenly it all goes quiet except for yourself and you were really loud?"

She relaxed a tad. "Think we've all been there."

"I was actually coming to find you after our chat the other day."

"To be honest, I'm on my way home – not feeling too well."

Joe Sully looked into her face for a second too long, a slight crease of concern around the eyes. "Sorry to hear that. You do look a bit peaky." He handed her another card. "Thing is, I could do with a bit of insight regarding a missing woman. Mailing Street again. No worries if it's not convenient. Would tomorrow be better?"

A shaft of light through the bay window caught one side of his face, cutting across the floorboards to the wall behind. And in that shard of a moment, the clock stilled and a cog logged into place.

Molly. Crap! He means Molly. And Molly lived on Mailing Street, didn't she?

The words she subsequently blurted out were without any forethought. "I just heard about that. Gareth said no one had seen Molly for days. Anyway, as soon as he said it I had a bad reaction. I saw things – well, you'll know already what happened to her. It's made me physically sick as you can imagine. That's why I need to get home. I have to lie down. I feel terrible."

Joe nodded. "I understand. Well, maybe we could catch up later. What time's your shift start tomorrow?"

"Four o'clock."

"I'll meet you at quarter to, if that's all right?"

"Sure."

Later that afternoon, going over the encounter word for word, nuance by nuance, she reclined against the pillows and closed her eyes. Recalling Jeannie's words not to trust the police, had she made a mistake? He may be trustworthy but what about his colleagues? Did he have to report all his contacts to a chief officer?

We'll be working together, though. I can see it…

A headache began to cluster above her right eye.

"Gran? Billy?"

Billy appeared at the bottom of her bed, along with Yukon. "He's going to be important. Steady does it."

"He's probably stunned by what happened to Molly. And the same street so soon after the last one, as well."

"He didn't know she was dead, Beth. She's only just been reported missing."

"What?"

"Anyway, he does now."

Beth's heart missed a beat. She sat bolt upright. "Oh my God! He didn't know and I told him? He'll think I'm a suspect. And here's me with a false name."

***

PART TWO

He grasps the wand which draws from hollow graves,
Or drives the trembling shades to stygian waves:
With magic power seals the watchful eye.
In slumbers soft or causes sleep to fly.

(Statitus, 'The Baid.' Translated by Lewis)

CHAPTER TWELVE

The second Beth closed her eyes, the weight of Yukon dropped onto the bed and a cool mist wafted across her face.

Underfoot the sand was roasting, the air oven hot on a Saharan wind. The colours were vivid, from the whiteness of the beach to the shimmering turquoise ocean. She was in a crowd of men, women and children, voices raised to shouts as they raced towards a fleet of dinghies being pulled ashore. The men in the boats snatched at rolls of cash, cigarettes balancing on their lips while they counted. Now the families climbed aboard, weighting down the boats until they were heavy and low in the water. It seemed to happen quickly, frantically almost. The dinghies were shoved back out to sea, and the men who had brought them walked back up the beach, laughing, smoking, sharing out the money.

Out on the ocean swell, the children soon began to wail, clinging onto women in thin, brightly coloured clothing as the boats disappeared into the haze, the buzz of outdoor motors a faint whir in the vastness of the ocean.

Where am I?

There was a feeling of being among them, as further out to sea the height of the waves increased, each boat pointing up to the crest before plummeting into the dip, climbing, dropping, climbing, dropping…With no end in sight, crowds of souls clung grimly to the sides. The men fell silent, the women stony. Ocean-going ships originally on the horizon now loomed closer: piled high with containers they emerged like dinosaurs, dwarfing the families in the orange dinghies. All signs of land had fallen away. There was nothing now but the quiet swell of the water, the waves higher, the liners nearer…

Briefly, Beth woke with a bang to her chest, before falling back into dream state.

Why am I seeing this?

Back on the high seas, a crimson sun was dropping over the skyline, and afternoon tipped into dusk. Between those in the boats and certain death, there was just an inflatable plastic boat. And the glances between the men and women aboard were now akin to those exchanged between the animals unloaded into the yard beneath Mailing Street. No going back. That realisation. Too late.

For a while she and Billy remained with them, entranced by the gold and silver beings surrounding the families, guarding their journey. There were many spirits around them as the people bowed their heads and prayed, holding onto their children. If only it was possible to tell them they were not alone.

After a while, she found she was no longer out at sea. There was a brief feeling of everything being enclosed and dark, before blinking into the light once more. Where was this? At first it looked like England. No, not an English port – heat was shimmying off a concrete quay stacked with containers, and the smog was so thick that visibility was down to a few yards. Her attention was drawn to mountains of green and black containers marked, 'fine art.'

What of it? Why is that important?

Her questions remained unanswered as the scene panned out like a movie, and it occurred to her this was the Pacific Rim. China or America? Wide roads, palm trees, five or six lanes…billboards…

America? California?

Why?

She rolled over into sleep for a while, committing to memory the sequence of events.

People on the move…false promises…fine art…

For a while she slept, but just before waking she was pulled back onto the astral realm, and with a jolt instantly recognised Scarsdale Hall. Early morning and dawn was breaking over the Yorkshire moors, the blackened wings and turrets of the great house starkly framed against a rose-streaked sky. As before, the lone sparrow hawk circled, squealing, once again announcing her arrival.

The majestic beauty of both architecture and landscape took her breath. It would be impossible not to admire the brutal splendour of it. Yet if the eye were to be slightly off focus, the house changed to that of a large black hole. To non-existence. No matter how palatial, how intricately carved the masonry or beautiful the gardens, Scarsdale Hall drained the life from all in its radius. Everything the dark magicians did was to satisfy an insatiable evil that would always want more. It devoured sacrifices, blood, misery and fear... Should they fail to provide more and more and more, the balance of power would shift and like the portrait in the attic, their façade would crack and crumble. Rapidly. That was the deal. They were blackmailed all the way to hell and they knew it.

No sooner had she acknowledged the location, however, than she was pulled underground, as if sucked into the pit itself. Yet these were not the narrow tunnels beneath the house. Briefly the memory of suffocating panic rose inside, but as her eyes adjusted to the darkness, it became clear this was something else altogether.

Billy's voice cut into her dream state. "Look Beth!"

Row upon row of human beings sat locked in cages. At first she saw only their eyes. Round eyes in deep, hollow sockets.

She began to probe the energies. They were alive. Some were either very small adults or large children, others definitely infants. Stick arms and legs were folded at unnatural angles into emaciated bodies, and like caged, transported animals, there was no way they could get out. Pitch dark, the air reeked of excrement and decay, the silence broken only by scuttling rodents. It looked as though the prisoners had long ago given up crying, pleading or even praying – instead they simply stared, and waited.

The full horror of their plight rose and rose in a claustrophobic nightmare until she thought her heart would give out. Were they to starve to death, cramped, broken and enslaved? And there weren't just a few cages, either. She looked around. There were hundreds, stacked on top of each other, row upon row like cans in a supermarket. In fact, this wasn't so much a tunnel as a vault, the roof an arch. Shelves were fitted along the walls, and on the ground were rail tracks. Trains? They had trains under here? The tunnel or vault stretched into coalmine blackness and occasionally there was a rumble far away... Was this underneath or alongside a railway? It was as if a train had passed. The abiding image, however, was that of the cages: every single one containing a human being, some babies, and some dead and partly decomposed. Bile lurched into her throat at the sight of a hand hanging out of one of them... and the rats...

No!

When she woke it was with an electric volt to the heart. Every pulse was searing and her face was wet, body drenched in sweat.

"Gran? Billy?"

A quick glance at the clock showed eleven minutes past eleven. 11:11.

"Oh God, oh God! That cannot be real."

"You've got to know, Beth. You've got to know how bad it is."

She nodded. "My stomach's burning. My head's thumping."

Falling back onto the pillows she tried to steady her breathing. Everything the captured souls had felt, so, for a few fleeting seconds, had she.

Oh, that was horrible. That was the worst...that was...oh God!

Through the gap in the curtains, stars flickered

between scudding clouds and she watched them sparkle and spin like wheels. All of that had passed in minutes, yet hours had been spent with those families on the high seas, and the last part, in the vault of darkness, had seemed like weeks. She blanked the worst parts out. But where was that and what could she do?

Billy's presence hovered nearby.

"What the fuck are we dealing with? What kind of people do this? No, don't answer that. I mean who carries out the orders and lets this happen? It looks organised. That's a big operation. I mean there were hundreds—"

"Hundreds of thousands."

She took the impact. Let it hit the shock absorbers and finally lodge as true. It took a while.

Eventually she asked. "And this ties in with Scarsdale Hall? I knew we hadn't finished there, I knew it."

Billy was nodding.

"So what's the connection with the people on the boats and the docks in America? Where was the vault? What can I do? I'm not police—"

"You're going to be the one to expose it."

"What? How? I'm nobody. Nothing. People don't even believe me when I say their house is haunted, despite the fact they've seen ornaments fly off the mantelpiece in front of their own eyes."

"You will be the one."

"And it connects to here? To this little seaside town in northern Britain?"

"It does. Don't worry, we've got plenty of time and it will all come together."

Exhaustion and panic swept over her in equal measure. "I'm worried–"

"Yes."

"About all of it. And about Joe Sully. I know I need to work with him but he might have to tell his boss about me. I've got fake ID."

"Bit tricky," said Billy.

"Cheers."

"We need to find who his boss is."

"Okay." Her eyelids were weighting down. "I can't stay awake any longer. Can I sleep or do I need to wait for Jeannie?"

"Gran's with her and May Morris, so yes you can sleep."

Her eyes closed. "That gold pin, the caduceus…"

Billy's voice was faint as she dropped into sleep. "Doctor Freeman…Beth…"

***

CHAPTER THIRTEEN

From far away, a phone was ringing. Beth woke from a vivid and very real conversation. Why was the phone ringing downstairs at…she glanced at the bedside clock… five in the morning? It took a minute to register: there was no downstairs phone. They did not have a landline. She and Jeannie had a mobile each and that was all.

The ringing stopped, leaving an impression of its echo in the chill, early morning air. She lay with eyes wide, heart thudding in her ears, slowly becoming aware of the sound of soft snoring coming from the other room. At least Jeannie was home safely. After a brief trip to the bathroom, on tiptoe across the landing in case she woke her, Beth peeped through the bedroom curtains. Veils of grey shrouded the roof tops as an icy dawn emerged by degrees, the moors beyond dusted with a faint hue of blue-white snow. Her eye was drawn to the road leading out of town, winding into the hills. Lined with large, detached houses set well back, the streetlights petered out about half way up.

She narrowed her eyes. Those last few houses… One would be Moorlands Nursing Home that Jeannie walked to each day. She leaned forwards, trying to work out what had caught her attention. What was she looking at? From this distance the orange glow of the lights seemed fuzzy and it was impossible to pick out details, but those houses really were huge. Whatever purpose they had once served, they now housed the kind of businesses normally found on the outskirts of towns – solicitors' offices, retirement homes, healthcare practices and so on. Why was it relevant? Her thoughts trailed away. She was missing something. Had seen but not seen…She shook her head and scurried back underneath the bedclothes. No matter, it would come. Besides, it was freezing.

What was happening today? What day was it? Oh yes, Joe Sully said he wanted to talk! Why was her stomach bouncing around at the thought? Because of what they might be working on? Because of what was to come? She wriggled her toes, moving back into the warm spot she'd been in a few moments ago. Whatever the case, no more coherent thoughts would come.

And when Jeannie burst in a couple of hours later with two mugs of tea, it was a shock. That had seemed like less than a minute.

"Sorry to wake you, but I need to talk. Anyway, I brought you this."

She struggled to sit upright while Jeannie stood over her, shivering in thin pyjamas.

"Take your time. I've got aaaall day!"

Beth took the tea and handed her a throw. "Thanks. Here, have this. What's the matter? What's happened?"

May Morris!

"I've had a bollocking from Daphne French, the

manageress. Got called into her office yesterday afternoon."

"Why?"

Wrapped in the throw, Jeannie perched on the edge of the bed and took a sip of tea. She had the fragile, wishbone appearance of one who might snap in too high a wind, and there were rings of blue beneath her eyes, the veins mapped close to the surface. With fine brown hair and parchment skin, she seemed quite ethereal, Beth thought. Yet there was a diamond core in there or she would not have survived Scarsdale, let alone escaped. Those left behind in Curbeck were dead-eyed and numb. While Jeannie's spirit sparked and flared like a lantern in a storm. How had she eluded notice?

"I'm not going to lie, she's a right bitch. Mid-forties, black hair that's too harsh for her age, cut into a bob. You can see she was maybe pretty once, but there's a brittleness, a tough shell. Like there's no way she's ever going to see your point of view? I can't explain better than that."

Beth nodded. "I can imagine."

"You know what I mean, don't you? So she's super nice to relatives, and she fawns all over Freeman, but to me she's just a nasty piece of work."

"Different for each. So who is she, really? Yes, I get you."

"She wears a nursing uniform like you'd see from the old days, but she's not a nurse, well not there anyway. I don't know. It's odd. Anyway, so she called me in and sat there behind the desk, glaring like I'm a cockroach that just jumped in her soup."

Beth smiled.

"Didn't ask me to sit down or ask how I was getting on, nothing like that."

"Rude."

"I know. So I was standing there, thinking, 'go on then spit it out, what have I done?' Because, and I'm being honest, right? I'd done nothing wrong and I had absolutely no idea what was coming."

"No."

"Do you know in four months she's never so much as said, 'Hello'? She walks past me in the corridor like I don't exist."

"Wow."

Jeannie took another sip of tea, then another. "Anyway, she said, 'It's been brought to my attention you're spending half your day sitting on the bed of one of the residents. I might remind you that you're not paid to sit gossiping.'"

"What did you say?"

"What was I supposed to say? She hadn't asked me a question."

"True."

"There are some benefits to a background like mine. A mare like her doesn't scare me one bit. I was about four years old when my training started. Me and the others had techniques with the teachers, particularly Miss Elridge. We eyeballed them right back 'til they lost it. If you don't say owt and just stand there, even if you're scared inside, they can't handle it – sends them apoplectic."

Beth nodded, picturing how tiny Jeannie must have been when she first had to learn that lesson. "So did she? Lose it?"

"You're not kidding. Went on and on about how they'd taken me on over and above far worthier candidates, given me a chance because they thought I was a nice girl who needed a break. Had never asked for anything in return other than a fair day's work, and now I was taking advantage. I'm telling you, it was 'we' this and 'we' that. The rant went on forever and it sent me all the way back to that dusty schoolroom on Scarsdale Estate. Then suddenly she snapped, 'Haven't you got anything to say?'

I must have drifted off and I had to think fast, because the only accusation seemed to be that I'd sat on a bed. So I said, 'I've only ever sat with one lady here and that's because she asked me to, and it's her bedroom. She was lonely and wanted to talk. I'd done all my paid-for duties, which you can check for yourself, and I sat with her in my own time as I didn't take full breaks. I've also worked double shifts because you're understaffed with a very high turnover. I don't have to do that.' To be honest, she has no idea what a second rate tyrant she is. Proper tyrants don't lose their cool like that."

A flutter stirred within Beth, although she could not say why. "What did she say?"

"Hate waves were coming off her. It was like she hadn't listened to a single world. Basically told me I wouldn't be allowed to mix with the residents at all from now on, as I couldn't be trusted. So now I've got the job of clearing out rooms on the top floor that were once servants' quarters. Apparently there are going to be double the number of residents in the near future, so all those rooms have got to be scrubbed – floors, windows, walls, the lot."

"On your own?"

"Looks like they don't want me talking to May, doesn't it?"

"I wonder why, though? How could they possibly connect May with you - a working class girl from wherever we said, was it Manchester? I really ought to know or I'll trip up."

"Stockport."

"Something's off. I mean, sitting on an old lady's bed for a chat hardly merits such an over the top reaction."

"She's really close to Freeman. He's always a good hour in her office, then he does a medical round as fast as a whippet." She pointed to her chest. "They both wear a brooch, like a pin with snakes and feathers on it. It's just occurred to me now. Might be nothing."

Beth nearly choked on her tea. "Ah, the caduceus!"

"What?"

"It could be medical but I'm not sure. Anyway, so she does what Freeman tells her to do, and it's him who wants you away from May."

Billy was hovering in the doorway with Spot in his arms. "You've got to look up what the caduceus is," he said.

"Why, though?" Jeannie asked. "And here's another thing - how did they know May confided in me? She whispered it all, Beth. And neither of them was on duty at the time because it was in the evening."

Beth shrugged. "I'm just wondering why Freeman picked you out. I have a feeling they're getting you followed..."

"Picked me out? Getting me followed? You're scaring me."

"No, don't be scared. We're on it. You're doing brilliantly, by the way. I'm really proud of you. And don't worry, don't be frightened. Think of it this way – you are a threat and that in itself begs the question why."

"I don't get it. Why what?"

"Well, Daphne French has effectively just informed us there's a connection between Crispin Freeman and May Morris, who was pretty much banned from writing about Allegra Mantel. See? Not every scary thing is a bad thing. Sometimes it reveals what we need to know."

Jeannie screwed up her face. "I'm part of something I don't understand, aren't I?"

"We all are," said Beth. "Perhaps especially people like Daphne French."

***

CHAPTER FOURTEEN

Joe Sully was waiting when she arrived at work next day. With the low winter sun directly behind her, he was rendered almost invisible in the oak-paneled lounge. She peered into the shadows, not seeing him until he stood and held out his hand.

"Gentleman from the establishment here to see you, Lily," Gareth boomed.

A row of heads turned around to stare, and for a moment Beth froze.

Oh no, he called me Lily!

She looked from one to the other. Gareth knew she preferred to be called Beth. Was her cover blown already?

Joe, however, seemed nonplussed. "Hi! Can I get you a coffee or would you prefer something else?"

Once again her face was burning. "Thank you, that'd be lovely."

As it turned out, the coffee made with Little Red Jester, chemical cream was anything but lovely.

"Is it okay?"

She wrinkled her nose. "Well, it's hot."

"That bad?"

"No worries. I'm going to try again to get Gareth to use proper milk. Apparently this is more economical."

"Not surprised. A box of that crap will last a whole year if no one wants it."

"True."

"So why did he call you Lily? I said I was waiting for Beth and he said you'd be along in a minute. Then he calls you Lily."

She pulled a face. "I use my middle name. Always have. Maybe he was being official?"

"I see."

"Anyway, what can I do to help? I take it you found your missing lady?"

He took a long drink from his pint and replaced the glass on the table before framing a reply. "Well, ideally I should be asking you first. Yesterday you were telling me you'd seen certain things. In a vision, I take it? And that it made you physically ill?"

"Yes."

"You also said you'd worked with the police back in Liverpool?"

"Yup."

"I'll cut to the chase. We could do with a bit of help because there's a lot not adding up." He took another long drink, almost emptying the pint glass. "Don't worry, I'm off duty now."

Beth bit her lip. "I'd like to but…"

He raised one eyebrow.

"Okay, well I just need to check if this could be kept off-record? It's just, you know, I don't want anyone here to know I'm a spiritual medium. I blurted it out when I saw you, probably because the images were fresh on my mind, but—"

He shook his head. "I've got to run everything by the boss."

Behind him, Billy was shaking his head.

"I'm really sorry, but I don't want to be on anything official. Sorry. Otherwise I would have done. I didn't realise…"

He frowned. "It wouldn't go any further." He indicated Gareth, who was lingering at the near end of the bar. "No one else would know except us in the department."

"No, I'm sorry. I'd rather not. I would have, you know, just tuned in and given you some impressions of what I think may have happened…that's all, really. I don't want to be known in the town as a medium. You have no idea how it affects my life."

Struggling with a feeling of deep unease, she began to stand up. This had been a mistake. Being recognised officially had never posed a problem before, and only now was it hitting her how difficult this was going to be. It didn't feel good not being a hundred percent above board with Joe, but needs must when the people who owned and ran the system could use it to trap her.

"All right," Joe said. "How about for now we keep it as a friendly conversation?"

She sat down again. "All right, yes. I'll certainly try to help."

"Thank you." He took a deep breath. "Basically things aren't adding up. There've been a lot of incidents on Mailing Street, as you may or may not know. It has what could be called a history. And now we have two separate violent deaths, one after the other and with no obvious connection, again on Mailing Street. Then I bump into you. So you said you had visions regarding number three on the night you walked past? I'm sure by now you've heard about what happened?"

She shook her head. "I don't read or watch mainstream news or listen to gossip. I tend to shut out third party accounts because they skew the messages... my messages..."

"Understood."

She told him what she'd been shown of the murder, and then the remote view of the car parked on the moors. "Gareth has since told me where the man was picked up, but just to relate what I saw before knowing that - I had a feeling the man was shocked and broken. He didn't give off any anger or vengeance and his aura was clean. I could imagine he'd acted in a moment of rage and then regretted it, but there was more to it than that. He seemed shattered, his mind blown to bits. I'll go a step further and say that whatever happened sent him insane. At least temporarily."

Joe was staring at her intently, and once again the sapphire blue of his eyes was highly disconcerting. After a moment or two he nodded, seemingly satisfied. "All right, I'll tell you something else now, Beth. And you need to keep this to yourself. We're in agreement on that, right?"

"Yes, of course."

"Good because I could do with your help. Every member of the team who's spent time in those houses has been unwell. One of my colleagues had a heart attack, although they're saying it's unrelated, and another is off sick with depression. No one lingered in there, no matter what they might say. Especially me. There's something else going on, an undercurrent I can't put my finger on it. Anyway, that's why I could do with some insight. I trust you. I don't know why but I just do."

She nodded. "Rest assured I'm not interested in knowing any more than I need to, and I'm happy to tell you what I can up front. Whatever helps, and frankly brings peace to those involved, the dead as well as the living. That's all I'm interested in."

"Well, you've definitely told me quite a bit up front."

Inwardly she grimaced. "Okay, well I'm going to need as much background information as possible. It means we can work out what we're dealing with. Spiritually, that is."

Gareth was still hovering and Joe lowered his voice. "The history of a building and so forth?"

She took a sip of coffee. "Ugh. Yes, and the land."

He nodded. "Sad place, Mailing Street. The couple were Eritrean. They'd only been in that dump a few months. And when we picked him up he was exactly like you described - dead-eyed, just staring blindly at the moors with his hands gripping the steering wheel. His body was that rigid with cold all they had to do was open the door and lift him out. The guy was helpless, absolutely helpless."

She nodded, watching that scene unfold.

"When he finally spoke next day, he kept saying this same thing over and over, 'I loved her.' Just that – 'I loved her!' Turned out he'd taken care of his lady all the way over here. They'd spent months in camps with her having miscarriage after miscarriage. It's not what people think, see? Not always. I'm not saying there aren't a lot of scammers and chancers. But a lot of innocents get caught in the net, and they'd handed over their life savings. Anyway, long story short, they regretted it almost as soon as they boarded the boat - realised they'd lost all their money."

For a second she faded out, recalling the dream, of the look passing between men and women on those dinghies, of wailing children, and the waves swelling ever higher.

"And somehow they end up on Mailing Street. Turns out they never felt settled. Soon after they were housed his wife started with nightmares, usually a man in a bloodstained apron pulling her out of bed by the feet. She'd be shouting in her sleep then wake covered in sweat, panting and terrified out of her wits. The kitchen would be swarming with flies even on a cold day. And they felt watched. Both said they'd seen a figure standing in the back yard staring in. A boy. They thought it was a boy. The house never got warm, either: mildew grew on the walls and it always stank of raw sewage. His wife went from being hard working and optimistic, to lying in bed all day, shaking, shivering, and muttering to herself."

"Poor things."

"Yeah, I know. Anyway, that particular night she'd made an effort because it was his birthday. After that he's a bit vague on detail, but he recalled that during the meal, which was in the kitchen, the television in the lounge flicked on and off by itself. They hadn't been able to afford a licence and he was worried, so he asked if she'd been watching it and was about to remind her they couldn't, when everything blacked out. And the next thing he knew he was holding her by the scruff of the neck."

Joe bit back the rest of what he knew he couldn't relate, but Beth filled in the missing words.

"He was slamming her forehead repeatedly onto the table."

He was staring at her, as with a jolt Beth fleetingly found herself in the murderer's skin once more, the bones of the woman's vertebrae snapping beneath fingers not her own. Her words came out in a rush. "He's got a knife in his right hand but can't recall how or when it got there. The back of his head hits the wall…He's sliding down….the knife falls….but it's what's in the other hand…his left hand. Oh! Oh my God…it's…" She clapped a hand over her mouth.

Joe was still staring. He had not told Beth a single detail of the murder.

"Go on."

"Her tongue."

Joe paled to the colour of boiled milk. "Fuck me, you're the real deal aren't you?"

She swallowed down a surge of nausea. "Oh, that was horrible. I didn't know until just now." She picked up the coffee and then put it down again, thinking better of it.

"And do you know what? He had no idea he'd done it. He said he knew he had to have done, but in all honesty he couldn't recall killing her or cutting out the tongue. All that happened in the interim between him mentioning the television and then hitting the wall in shock, was blank. He just kept saying, "I didn't do it. I loved her. I didn't do it. It was not me."

An icy flutter worked its way up her back, fanning out across her shoulders in feathery shivers.

"Obviously, he's guilty," Joe went on. "There was no one else there and I doubt the boss will see it any other way. But I just have this feeling, especially after meeting you…it's just…well, I'm wondering if something did happen to him in that house? Because now, as you well know, we have Molly." he shrugged. "I dunno, I'm probably barking up the wrong tree but–"

"Have you found Molly, then?"

"Yes."

"So you know what was done to her?"

He looked at her long and hard. "Yup."

"Do you want me to say what I saw?"

"Please."

"All right, well I don't know Molly except to look at, but what I was shown yesterday was a series of images. She had blonde hair with dark roots of about two or three inches, exactly as I last saw her here in the pub. But in the vision she was wearing a pink, faux fur coat, sitting in a bar that's not this one - a cheap joint with dull lighting. It looked like the end of an evening with not many people left, and she was on a bar stool with a young girl either side of her. They were all drunk but the girls weren't laughing as much as she was." She put her hands over her eyes. "I can still see it: a car with a taxi sticker on the dash, and a Perspex screen between the back and front seats. Someone's sick on the floor and they stumble out onto the pavement. They're hysterical and the front door's swaying."

"Okay."

"They're in a room that looks like it's downstairs because the curtains are open and there's a shadowy view of bins in a back yard, and a gate to an alleyway. The light is bluey grey outside, but candles are lit. Dozens of them. There's a heady smell of incense and it's mixed with a salty, putrid tang. The flames are flickering on the walls and the air's smoky. Very smoky, choking…"

She took a deep breath and clutched the edge of the table. "Sorry, it's replaying and I feel sick again. This is vile. There are flowers decorating a corpse laid out on a table, and there's a huge gaping hole in the body. When I first saw this I thought it was an operating table because the middle area, the abdomen, is all hollowed out… and…and…the insides are strewn all around the room with the flowers …I'm sorry, I've got to stop."

Beth held on fast to the table, focusing on keeping a steady inhale and exhale. Heat rose up in her head and the room began to spin. Vaguely she became aware of a hand splayed across her back and a gentle, soothing voice. "All right, take it easy. Nice deep breaths. I'm going to get you a glass of cold water, all right?"

She nodded.

She wears red feathers and a hooly-hooly skirt…she lives on just coconuts and fish from the sea….

Her eyes filled with tears as Gran's lullaby permeated the nightmare, one that was not hers and from which she must now unhook and let go. Silently, she thanked Gran, and opening her eyes again, also thanked Joe Sully for the glass of fresh water.

Taking a long drink, she eyed him over the rim as

he spoke.

"Spot on. Two teenage girls met her in a pub in Blackpool last weekend. The cabbie dropped the three of them off at Molly's house and it looked like they carried on drinking. Bit of a party, if you like. We've got them."

"Good."

"They're only bits of kids. And here's something else – like our Eritrean man, neither of them can recall a damn thing. And also like him, they cut out body parts exactly as you described. The difference with the girls though, was that what they did was more of a ritual. There were pages ripped out of a satanic bible and symbols daubed all over the walls in blood."

"Someone was watching."

"What? Who?"

"I don't know. A man, I think. Someone could see…an eye…an eye peeping!"

"Seriously?" He shook his head. "Okay. Blimey, you stun me."

She drained the water. "Ugh. Yuch. Why?"

"Tastes disgusting doesn't it? I filter mine these days. Well, because the guy who called us about the Eritrean couple was the one living in the middle house between number three and Molly's at number seven. He rang us saying he could hear roaring and growling like wild dogs in a fight. Not human. Anyway, he hanged himself shortly afterwards - the next night - so we didn't get to question him further. Thing is, the only reason he was in that house was because he was a paedophile on the sex offenders' register and he had to be housed somewhere. Sadly his habit of spying hadn't abated because there were little peep holes cut out in the adjoining walls."

A snapshot of a doughy face came to mind, of a man in a vest with sparse wisps of fair hair. The creak of a chain straining on joists echoed around him.

"They found him hanging on a chain in the back kitchen."

"Bloody hell, Beth. Yes."

"Everyone apparently, according to Gareth, knows there's a bad atmosphere on that street, but you'd like to know what's causing it?"

"Do you know?"

"I don't think anyone should be living there. People get houses evaluated for physical defects but no one pays any attention to the spiritual aspect: what you can't see doesn't exist, right? So houses are sold where people were brutally murdered and people don't expect a problem. And that street's riddled with them."

"If any of my colleagues could hear us talking they'd be shaking their heads, telling us we've lost it. So now you see why I agreed to this being off the record? Not one person in my department would give this the time of day, especially the boss. I knew, though. I just knew..."

We need to find who his boss is!

She nodded. "And I'm loopy loo. Yup, heard it all my life. Anyway, their opinions don't mean there isn't a serious problem at Mailing Street. There is."

"And no one in this town wants to live there, do they? I might ask the young lad in the office to dig around on its history." He looked at her. "Are you able to pick anything up about a place if we get you a key? I mean, to see if it's haunted or not? It'd have to be after work. I'm just thinking if I got Molly's key you could just let yourself in for a few minutes and–?"

"Molly's house is more than haunted. Why not go through the church?"

He shook his head. "Officialdom won't permit."

She frowned. "I could help through a local church, you see? All above board and no one would focus on me?"

"I'm telling you it won't get passed. And there isn't enough time for the paperwork. No, I think a quick scout round is our best hope."

She glanced at her watch. "Okay. Well look, I need to start work in a minute, but you're right to get the history. I think there's an issue with the site itself, with what the houses are built on. I'm pretty sure there was once an abattoir under there. I'm feeling something a bit off-kilter, too - a trick or foul play of some kind." She shook her head.

"That's interesting. I didn't know about the abattoir. I dunno. Maybe it was bulldozed after the war? And I don't know about foul play. Maybe you could enlighten me?"

Beth shook her head. "It's just a feeling. That something went wrong. There's something here that can't be seen, a hidden hand, and I don't know how it comes together yet."

"Okay."

"Sorry."

"No, you've been very helpful, confirmed a lot. Can I come back to you when we find what's underneath Mailing Street? I mean, I've got this thing that the place needs cleansing in some way. Would it be just bad energy or…? I mean, the girls and the ritual…it's more than just you know…?"

She nodded. "A haunting? Yes, they raised the demonic. And a place of pain and fear like that is a good place to do it. In my opinion the entire street needs to be razed to the ground, exorcised and blessed, then planted with trees."

He was shaking his head. "Freeman would never take that kind of a financial hit."

"Freeman?"

"Lord Freeman. He owns the land and most of the houses round here. His son's the local doctor. Carrie's father plays golf with him."

Joe's wife?

"Carrie?"

"Chief Superintendent. The boss."

She tried to keep her expression dead pan. "Ah!"

Crap…

***

CHAPTER FIFTEEN

That evening a sombre air lingered in The Lighthouse, the usual banter reduced to a few forced words. Most left food uneaten, drained their pints and went home early. Everyone, it seemed, now knew what had happened to Molly. Despite the way they'd whispered behind her back, calling her a lush or 'wasted,' or perhaps because of that, the news hit everyone hard. Mailing Street again!

After the last punter had gone, Gareth inclined his head towards the door. "Do you want to knock off early?"

Beth nodded. "Thanks."

Outside the wind had whipped up, and white horses broke on the waves. The crash and flow of the tide was hypnotic as she walked away from the harbour, the bracing air whipping back her hair welcome after such a closeted, depressing afternoon. The elements really did, she thought, blast away misery and grief.

She could not say what caused her to do it, but at the end of the promenade she stopped and looked back. The view had changed, time having fallen away to reveal a port from bygone days. Seagulls swooped and screeched over loaded trawlers, and along the quayside men in shirtsleeves shouted to each other, women filleted fish and stacked stalls, and barrow boys scurried at everyone's beck and call. The image was blurred and lasted but a few seconds, fading instantly at the splatter of a large wave breaking over the sea wall.

Beside her, Billy was deep in thought.

"I wonder what happened to turn this town from thriving to barren?" said Beth.

Because barren it most certainly was. Most of the boats now rotted in dry dock, paint peeling, rudders rusting. Only a handful of small vessels were afloat, chains creaking on the swell.

"We need to bring Jeannie on quickly," Billy said.

"Why? Has something happened?"

"No, but it's going to. She needs to be ready for what's coming and she's not."

"I thought we were making progress now she agreed to see this woman?"

He shook his head. "Come on, keep walking."

Puzzled, she headed for home, anticipating a hot bath and an early night, the scent of lavender in clouds of steam almost a reality, when on turning the corner of Portland Street, she stopped short and caught her breath.

"What the f…?"

Every house on the street was crawling with giant, black slugs. They oozed over the walls and squelched across roofs, antennae probing windows and chimneypots for entry. So too, the pavements pulsed with an oil-slick mass.

She looked over her shoulder. The buildings behind

were not infested. And high on the hill where the road led out to the moors, to where the nursing home stood bathed beneath amber streetlights, that also looked normal.

"But it's spread - from Mailing Street to us."

Billy nodded. "Look!"

In front of her eyes, the black shapes had started to divide and multiply like chopped worms.

"No, look at our house," said Billy.

While the rest of the terraces on Portland Street were covered in a jellied mass, there was nothing on theirs. Around the perimeter of the tiny, front garden and for several feet either side of the windows, the area was star bright and clear.

"They can't breach the seals."

And at the exact moment she was thinking about Jeannie and how it wouldn't be a great idea for her to walk home through all of this, a text pinged on her phone.

Jeannie. 'Just setting back. You ok?'

She texted back, "Are you on the main road coming down now?'

"Yeah, why? Thought you were still at work?'

'Will explain later. Can you go straight to the promenade? Will meet you there. Don't go home yet.'

'Why?'

'Laters. Important.'

'Ok. Will call at off-licence. Want anything?'

'Water, please. And baccy. '

'OK. See you in ten.'

Closing the phone, Beth looked askance at a channel of liquid blackness rushing down the pavement towards her feet like an incoming tide. Quickly she jumped back.

"She knows where we are, doesn't she?"

Billy nodded. And a knot of unease tightened in the pit of her stomach.

"Best get moving, then."

By the time Beth and Jeannie met, the sky had cleared and stars flickered in between passing bundles of clouds.

"There's a bus shelter a bit further along," Jeannie said, carrying a bag of packets and cans. "The girls at work told me about it. It's where they go to smoke."

"Okies."

As it turned out the shelter was seawater wet and strewn with graffiti, but at least it gave respite from the wind. Beth rolled a smoke while Jeannie unpacked her feast.

Handing her a bottle of still water and a packet of nuts, she laughed at Beth's unexcited face. "Well, you could have had chocolate. You could have had crisps. But you keep saying no sugar and no chemicals."

"I know. But I won't eat that crap. They don't, so why should we?"

"They?"

"The people who make billions out of selling it." She lit a roll-up and inhaled. "And I know, I know, don't comment. It's my only vice."

"Of course, Beth!" Jeannie laughed. "Anyway, how come you left work so early?"

"Another woman was murdered on Mailing Street. Everyone's a bit shocked. I think they just wanted to head home tonight."

"Oh my effin'–"

"Two teenage girls did it, apparently. The man who killed his wife's in a police cell so it definitely wasn't him."

Jeannie, who had a can of lager half way to her lips, put it down again. "Two girls? Serious? And on the same street? I knew it - soon as I saw the creatures on the roofs. This is what used to happen at Scarsdale. There'd be a run of incidents all supposedly coincidences, but everyone knew–"

"Mailing Street has a dark history." She took another drag of her cigarette then stamped it out on the concrete floor. "I won't have anymore. I'd rather have marijuana, if truth be known. It helps with the pain."

"What pain? Are you all right?"

"Yes, I'm okay. I had a lot of visions lately and I've been on the astral a lot. A hell of a lot. It takes it out of me – feels like I did a round with Mike Tyson."

"Do you feel lonely sometimes, Beth? I mean, neither of us have family, do we?"

She shook her head. "If I looked at it like that, I would. But I don't. I've always been on the outside looking in."

"Beth? Who are you?"

She opened a bottle of water. "Just on the merry-go-round like you, although I have a feeling it might be the last time for me."

"You mean re-incarnated? I've definitely been here before. There are those dreams for a start. I'm hoping Estelle will be able to sort out what's real and what isn't. I get confused."

"Wednesday you're going, isn't it?"

"Yeah."

"Anyway, the reason I asked you to meet up and not go down the street, is because those slimy things are all over the frickin' houses again tonight, and I didn't think you'd want to walk through them."

Jeannie stared at her. "I told you. She's found us."

"Mailing Street has a bad history like Scarsdale, and that's making it easy for whoever's projecting this. We need to protect ourselves but ideally the whole place should be cleansed. People have no idea what's under those streets. I think Joe Sully's going to be in for a shock too, when he finds out."

"He's your fancy policeman?"

"Not mine. Not fancy either. I've got to help, though. I mean, they're going to carry on housing people there. He said they just give it a lick of paint and move in another family even when there's been a murder. It just goes on and on, repeating and repeating."

"Also like Scarsdale."

"Yes, and generation after generation carries the karma. I'd rather they razed the whole street to the ground but apparently that isn't going to happen. The ground belongs to Lord Freeman."

"What? Hang on, back up a bit – so all of those houses are on land belonging to Lord Freeman. Crispin Freeman's dad?"

"And Lord Freeman plays golf with the police chief's father. Close mates from what I can gather."

"Oh crap, Beth! They'll check you out. I told you, didn't I? I'm not daft. You don't listen to me. We need to get out of here. You don't know this Sully bloke."

"Nope. Not getting scared off that easily. Remember, it's all tricks and lies and we have God on our side. We're protected, we're guided, and we're here to break this thing. Both of us. You're important."

Beth flicked a glance at Billy, who was inspecting the graffiti. "What are you reading, soft lad?"

"Melissa Carter is a slapper! And….Jemima Cropper sucks all the boys'–"

"All right, we get it!"

When she'd finished laughing, Beth looked up to find Gran Grace sitting next to Jeannie, who was wide eyed.

"I haven't laughed as much as that in ages," Gran said.

"It is funny. Teens make me laugh."

Jeannie's eyes widened further.

"Did you just hear Gran speak?"

"No, but I can see you talking to people I can't see. And this side of my face has gone icy cold like I'm standing with a fridge door open." Turning her head, she sniffed the air. "There's a scent of lilac."

Gran Grace smiled and nodded. Yardley's Lilac had been a favourite.

"That's brilliant. I knew you could do it. And this is you in a low vibe."

Jeannie had the look of someone who'd just been slapped on the back of the head with a cricket bat.

"It's real, isn't it? Spirit?" She looked around her. "I sort of… I mean…can they see me? Why can't I hear or see anything? I thought being haunted was a bad thing. But I don't feel scared. Why don't I feel scared? I mean, I did in the cottage back in Curbeck and I do in the nursing home–"

"Spirits won't hurt you and spirit guides will never ever scare you. The only thing that definitely intends to scare the crap out of you is the demonic. You'll really bloody know about it if that turns up."

"Stop!"

"What?"

Jeannie clutched her temples. "Oh, sorry. There was this flash in my head when you said that about the demonic. It was the same thing: standing on one side of that door in the turret. A key's turned in the lock and there's a creak just before it starts to open. Oh, that was horrible, like vertigo."

"Sorry."

"It's okay. It's gone. I just know one day it'll open and I'll see. I'm scared of going insane. I have a really bad feeling about what's in that room."

At the far end of the shelter, a small, neat looking woman had appeared behind Jeannie. Dressed in a cloak, her complexion was pale, her hair snowy white and tightly curled.

"Do you want to step forwards?" Beth asked.

Jeannie whipped round. "Who? What? Is someone there?"

Beth spoke again. "What's your name? Can you come forwards?"

Jeannie stared intently at the same spot. Her colour had drained away and her hands were shaking. "Beth, I'm not sure…"

The image began to fade. "It's all right. She's your spirit guide and she's around you a lot. But she won't appear to you until you're ready. Our guides never ever want to scare us, that's what I'm saying. Just know she's an older lady and she loves you very much."

Jeannie crushed the empty can and began to bag up the rubbish. "I'm so tired of being scared, Beth."

"Then don't be. It's a choice. And it doesn't help, like I said. What's coming's coming and we've got to face it or we go under."

***

CHAPTER SIXTEEN

"Anyway, let's shuffle back. Gran says the street's clear now. That kind of intense energy doesn't last for long. It takes a lot, you know? They can't keep it going."

Jeannie zipped her jacket up to the top. "Good, it's freezing and I'm knackered. I don't know why but I always feel safer outside than shut in a room."

They started to walk. "By the way, I've got something freaky to tell you. See what you make of this. Remember Daphne French told me to clean out the upper floors on my own?"

"Yes."

"Well, those rooms are crammed with heavy oak furniture and I have to lug it round, scrub the floorboards and wash down the walls. It's really hard work and there's no extra money, either."

"Almost like they want you to leave?"

"Yep, and I could have done except I don't want to go through more admin checks or interviews. And most importantly I don't want to desert May Morris, which is what I think they're really after."

"I wonder why? I mean, what can the old lady possibly do? What can you do, come to think of it?"

"I know. Anyway, let me tell you this. I was moving a bed in this room at the back of the house when my ears started ringing and I had to stop. It was like a tuning fork vibrating through my brain and I almost blacked out. Then at that exact moment a ray of light slanted through the glass and lit up a pillar of dust. And through a million dancing, swirling motes, I found myself looking into the dressing table mirror by the window. It's one of those three way mirrors, so you can see yourself from all angles? We had one in the old cottage at Curbeck."

Beth nodded. Knew what was coming, what Jeannie had seen. And as Jeannie finished describing what happened, the image was conveyed.

"And I was staring at my own face, another one flashed in the wing on the right. My reflection was in the middle. But this was a different one - staring directly at me from the shadows in the back of the room."

They continued walking in silence for a minute, the sound of crashing waves fading as they levelled with the houses.

"I know, it sounds crazy. I'm questioning it myself. And it only lasted for a fraction of a second. I mean, it might not have happened at all, I don't know. But what I do remember is the feeling. Because as soon as that face appeared, the light faded - daylight to dusk in a heartbeat – and a shiver ran up my back. All I knew was I had to get out of the room or... I don't know...something...it...would walk right through me like a cold wind."

Recalling the length and darkness of the shadow following Jeannie home a few nights ago, Beth grabbed hold of her arm as they turned the corner onto Portland Street. "Stop a minute."

"You're worried, aren't you? It's her, isn't it?"

"She can't astral travel. But others can."

"Who?"

Those already dead...

Beth took off her own tourmaline and black obsidian necklace, and Gran's bracelet of opalite and turquoise. "Wear these under your clothes."

"What are they?"

"For protection, and also these will connect you to Gran and Billy until you can speak directly with your own spirit guide. She'll always be there but until you're ready, you won't be able to communicate. This way I'll know what's happening and where to find you."

Jeannie looked into her eyes. "Am I in danger?"

"No, you're protected. But—"

"You saw something in the mirror, didn't you? What? I need to know. Oh my God! What?"

"You saw it, too. You didn't process it but it will come back to you. You will have seen him. I think what we have is an adept, but I don't know how he connects to the Mantels or to you; or to what's happening."

"He? Doctor Freeman?"

She shook her head. "Not from your description, no. To be honest, I couldn't make out the features and I still can't, it's odd."

"Young or old?"

"Again, I'm not sure. All I can remember is he was wearing a black hat and coat, and that the eyes were, I don't know, blank, empty. And there was no aura. The energy was...missing... I'd have to see him again. Come on, let's get home, it's perishing."

"I wonder who it is and why me?"

Beth shook her head. "Oh, I know what I mean to ask - what's the house at the very end? The one next door to the nursing home? It doesn't have a street light, so it's completely unlit."

"Beth, something's just come to me."

"What?"

"No, it's gone again. Erm, yeah, the place next door. It's boarded up. Actually though, now you come to mention it, I did see someone once. It was late at night after I'd finished an evening shift. He was walking round to the back and I'd have thought it was a squatter or a burglar except he was..." She stopped short just as they got home. "Fuck!"

"What?"

"The image in the mirror. You said a black coat and hat?"

"Yes–"

"The man walking around the back of the house next door was dressed in a long black coat and hat. A fedora type hat..."

"Did you see his face?"

"No, he had his back to me," said Jeannie. "But...oh, that's it! It flitted in and out of my mind, but that's exactly it!"

"What?"

"The face in the mirror and the man in black...both vanished when I blinked."

***

CHAPTER SEVENTEEN

The urge to uncover Crewby's history outweighed the need to sleep that night, and Beth sat up in bed tapping searches into her phone. Moorlands Road was intriguing. All the houses were huge Victorian piles, presumably for the wealthy merchants and businessmen of the day. So why would the street lights stop short before the end house, leaving that one in darkness? Or had it been removed? Was it even relevant?

Frowning in concentration, she decided to keep searching for something, anything that might connect history to present day. Something would click.

As was often the case, there were archives of historical photos, and the first set she came across had been proudly uploaded by the grandaughter of a local fisherman. Having already had the vision of the harbour as it used to be, looking at the photographs now was kind of like déjà-vu, she thought, flicking through. Sepia-washed and faded, the quay was alive with barrow boys, men in shirtsleeves, and one or two merchants in suits and top hats. A woman in a long, full skirt and cape, wearing a hat with a flower pinned to it, stood in the doorway of The Lighthouse pub. With her hands folded neatly in front, her face was immortalised in the camera flash, features blanched. Additional photographs captured the essence of the day – a fisherman holding up his catch on a hook, and women chatting over stalls of mussels and whelks. In the background, the glimmering bay was empty save for a line of rowing boats. She examined the scene closer. A large ship was anchored further out, and the boats, weighted down with heavy cargo, seemed to emanate from there.

"Why can't the ship dock in the harbour?"

Billy was hovering, keeping vigil at the window.

"Shallow water."

"Okay." She thought again. "But this is just a fishing village. Why would a large ship offload here? Wouldn't bigger business be done at the main ports?"

"Not all of it."

She narrowed her eyes. "I'm looking at this though, and it seems odd. I don't know. Maybe not. But these little dinghies are nearly sinking with the weight of massive crates. It doesn't look like a great idea. I mean if the sea was rough they'd…well…it looks like a risk. Okay, I don't know what I'm talking about. I feel like I'm looking for something that isn't there. I don't know. Help me out, Billy!"

He smiled, and she raised her glance to the ceiling. He couldn't do the work for her, but it was annoying if he knew.

"Keep looking," was all he'd say.

Most of the photographs were of the harbour area, but some had been taken of the hills and moors behind. One that drew her eye showed a white Morgan driven by a man in a high-necked shirt, and a suit with a waistcoat. His passenger was a lady in a ruffle-necked dress, who was holding onto her hat as they headed up what was undoubtedly Moorlands Road. Beth lingered on the image. There was a feeling the pair was not as carefree as the image projected, that the man was decades older than the woman. Her expression seemed forced, features strained. His daughter? She shook her head. No, not his daughter... Without names ascribed to them it was impossible to say. And again there was really nothing much to go on, apart from the oddest feeling all was not as it seemed.

The other shots of Moorlands Road showed dozens of horses with fully loaded carts, trekking out of town on what was still essentially a dirt road. There weren't any close-up pictures of the houses, though. It would have been interesting to have had a look at that last one, the house without a light outside. Sadly, the only things visible were gateposts and chimneypots glimpsed behind foliage, and the occasional stone facade.

She sighed, mumbling to herself. "Okay, let's have a look at Crispin Freeman and his father, then."

Crispin wasn't difficult to find, although his background information was scanty, and there were no social media profiles. The only reference to his childhood was a single shot of him at a private boarding school. Marked out from a class of others by a circle drawn around his face, there was absolutely nothing physically remarkable about Crispin, who was indistinguishable from the others. The only son of Lord Arthur Freeman, his bio stated he had practiced as a doctor overseas and now worked as a surgeon. Mr Crispin Freeman had a private surgery, an interest in psychiatry, and also owned Moorlands Nursing Home in Crewby. Unmarried, he lived quietly on the outskirts of town and enjoyed sailing, art collecting and golf.

His avatar depicted a clean-shaven face with emotionless, pale eyes behind silver-rimmed spectacles. Although the photograph was black and white, it was obvious he was fair of both hair and skin, and bodily he was what Gran Grace would describe as puny. Beth closed her eyes, tuning into the essence, the signature…Small boned but strong and sinewy with grasping fingers. She saw neat hands…the same ones winding in ropes on a yacht that also sliced a lancet through skin…Crispin Freeman, she knew, was unlikely to have been the school's cricket or rugby captain, his skills never pitched against a straight opponent. But those hands were powerful, belonging to a man whose strengths lay largely hidden.

Who was he? What was it about him? She looked more carefully at his photograph, and as she did so, his mouth suddenly cracked open to reveal a set of sharp, pointed teeth. And at the precise moment she realised what was happening, a rush of black ink shot up her forearms out of the keyboard, and reeling back she threw down the phone.

What the freak was that?

She looked at her hands. Normal colour. Okay, not real!

After a minute or two, once her heart had settled back into its normal beat, she picked up the phone again and exited the site.

A warning?

Okay, quickly then - who was Lord Freeman? There

was a reason Crispin didn't want Jeannie talking to May Morris, yet neither woman was a threat. So what was this? How the hell did this add up? Art? Shipping? Darn it, she was getting tired and ratty.

Her eyelids began to weigh heavy. There was precious little information on Lord Freeman. And why were people called Lords? It seemed…

"Odd," she answered herself. "It doesn't sound right to me – princes, dukes and lords - oh, I don't know."

He was certainly proving to be a tough search. She stabbed at the keys, weary and impatient. There was, however, only the one result. He'd long since retired from the House of Lords due to ill health. But, and here her eyebrows lifted, Lord Arthur Carlisle Freeman was the son of a Swiss art dealer and the grandson of a Bavarian count. A grainy photograph stared out from over the top of a sycophantic biography. He had an unusually large, bald head, somewhat elongated and age-spotted. The facial bones were angular, and like his son, the complexion was pale, eyes expressionless. But it was what was pinned to his tie that made her eyebrows almost reach the hairline. The man was an art dealer and landowner. So why then, was he wearing a caduceus pin? Wasn't that medical?

"Joe Sully needs to speak to you," said Billy.

"Eh?"

"He's just had a moment of epiphany."

"How d'you mean?"

Billy rocked his hand from side to side. "A spiritual one. It's just hit him hard that we're real."

"He already knew."

"Yes, but now he really knows. Not just an open

mind but…"

"The full punch in the gut?"

"Yup."

***

CHAPTER EIGHTEEN

Joe, Beth decided, would ring when he was ready. Likely he'd need time to gather his thoughts and feelings, and just as likely he'd need a bit of help. As Gran Grace would say, 'softly does it.' It took until Wednesday.

At work, conversations ping-ponged between Gareth and his customers: how terrible to hear about Molly, how fondly she was remembered, what the very last thing she'd said to them had been, and how they'd never imagined it would be the last time they saw her – there on that very bar stool. No longer a lush, now she was a woman with a good heart, loved by all, and whose memory would be that of one who'd endured a hard life but always had a smile.

The banter echoed around the bar that morning, with Beth only catching the gist when the door to the kitchen opened.

"Will you be sorting out the funeral, Gareth, or will it be one of the others? You won't be the famous five anymore now, will you?"

It took a conscious effort to block out the image of the woman's gaping mouth as it had been cruelly left -

knifed from ear to ear, sprigs of flowers decorating the yawning orifice. The very essence of Molly lingered here, as if she'd considered the pub more of a home than her own. And Molly, it seemed, did not want to move on after death.

Beth…Beth…

Whispers flew into her head unbidden, and the odour of stale nicotine, wine-soaked skin and decaying flesh repeatedly assaulted her senses. To complicate matters the pub had a nefarious history all its own. Sometimes the back door would whip open to a scuffle of litter on a sea breeze. No particular spirit lingered in the building, but in the corner of her eye a man in a long military coat would occasionally appear in the arch of the doorway, his shadow flitting across the back yard.

Beth…Beth…Listen…

She tried to make out clear words, but nothing came through except what sounded like the tinkling, chiming bell of a carriage clock.

Beth…Beth…Listen…

What was Molly trying to convey?

It wasn't until she was packing up on Wednesday afternoon, however, that Joe rang.

"Hi, Beth!"

"You all right?"

"Yes, you?"

"Yes, good. So, what can I help you with?"

"You rang me, Beth."

"No, you just rang and I picked up. I've only this minute finished washing down the kitchen."

"I swear you rang me. Hang on a sec and I'll show you."

He rang off and her glance flicked to Billy, who was sitting on the kitchen table, grinning. "You used my phone, didn't you?"

"You two need to speak."

A moment later the phone pinged with a text and there was the screen shot. Yup, her phone had indeed rung Joe's.

Shaking her head, she answered as soon as Joe called back. Billy and Gran had learned to use the phones and send texts. Why was she even surprised? No one would believe this stuff in a thousand years and yet it happened to her as a matter of course. No wonder people like her were consigned to psychiatric units – this was so hard to explain. Should she even try to tell Joe?

Deciding against it, she laughed it off and put it down to, 'being a bit ditsy today'.

"Well, as it turns out you were next on my list to speak to," said Joe. "So it's just as well you rang."

"Okay."

"What time do you finish?"

"I'm done now actually, although I'd prefer to nip home. I stink of cooking–"

"Can you get to Mailing Street in about twenty minutes? I'd like to do this before dark if possible. Number seven is the one I've got access to."

"Molly's?" An image reared up of the red setter she'd seen previously, hanging lifelessly on a chain in the yard.

"Yes."

She glanced outside. It was going dark already. "Okay, well as long as you don't mind me stinking like a chip shop, I'll meet you in ten."

Many things were on her mind as she grabbed her

coat from the hook and hurried through the now empty aisles of the market place. High up on Moorlands Road, Jeannie would still be at the nursing home, shadows already creeping under the doors and lengthening across the walls. Briefly Beth saw her friend's face as she washed a cup out in the downstairs kitchen, the solitary walk home down Moorlands Road already haunting her thoughts… the journey still to come…

And then there was Gareth, his glance constantly flicking towards the bar stool where Molly used to sit - every afternoon, every evening, month in, month out. It was almost as if he'd lost a part of himself, some facet now missing.

You won't be the famous five anymore…

By four-fifteen the light was rapidly tipping into dusk, and the February sky was already spitting rain. She bent her head against the prevailing wind, aware of the hard stone of reluctance lodged in her stomach on nearing Mailing Street. There was such a desolate feeling around it, a howling pit of emptiness that could never be filled. No one, she knew, could ever settle there and make it home.

On reaching the street corner more quickly than expected, or wanted, she stood for a moment, surveying the four adjoining end terraces.

Built of dark stone with front bay windows, each had a low front wall separating them from the pavement, plus a yard at the back. Numbers three, five and seven were currently unoccupied, standing hollow-roomed yet somehow watchful, as if the very fabric of the buildings had taken on intelligent form. Taking a deep breath she began to walk towards them, instinctively casting a quick glance up at the window of number five. And as before, a shadow slipped away behind the nets. Didn't Joe say the man who lived there was the one who'd called the police and then hanged himself? The man who'd been housed there because he was a sex offender, the one who had holes in the walls…peepholes…through to both sides?

As she levelled with number seven, a knock on glass brought her up sharp and only then did she notice Joe in the parked car outside. Clearly he didn't want to go in the house alone, then!

"Thanks for coming over," he said as they walked up a path cracked with weeds. The meagre front garden between house and wall was strewn with crushed cans, cigarette butts and fast-food cartons. "It's just, well…I wanted to see if you picked up any erm…presences. If you can, you know…" He fiddled with a ring of keys "Hope I've got the right one or it could be tad embarrassing. I don't think I'll get another chance either. This is well off…ah, here we go."

The key turned.

Behind them a seagull shrieked as it was blown across a blustery sky.

"No worries," said Beth. "Blimey, it's going dark quickly today."

"Aye, I know." He flicked the light switch in the hallway. It sparked blue and died. "Crap!"

"They cut the electric quickly."

"Freeman again. I'll tell you one thing – the rich don't get rich by giving it away. This was supposed to be left on 'til we'd finished."

His words, however, trailed away and she barely

heard them.

A rush of freezing, stale air had escaped as the door creaked open, and before she had even entered the hallway she knew she ought to leave immediately. The house buzzed with static, the stench of cloying incense and decay overpowering.

Billy's energy wrapped around her own.

Out loud she said, "God is my armour. Christ is my shield. I am God's child."

Joe hung back as she put a foot inside.

"I'm not staying long," she said. "It's not safe."

As soon as the words left her lips a deafening screech pierced her ears. She lunged for the newel post and held on tight. The door to the main room was ajar. A draft wafted it further open. And the horror of the recent trauma, trapped and imprinted, replayed.

On the table a corpse lay spread-eagled, and out of the hole gouged into the abdomen, was a flower arrangement similar to the one in the mouth. Flowers had been strewn everywhere - cut stems with lolling heads. The scene fused onto Beth's mind in a static blur as the screech amplified. She put her hands over her ears. An upside down cross had been placed on the mutilated chest. In a room lit by dozens and dozens of candles.

"A ritual! They had a ritual."

As abruptly as it started, the piercing screech stopped.

"You okay?" Joe's voice came from far, far away.

She couldn't speak. Staring at her from the sofa were two girls holding a book, trilling verses from it in singsong, child-like voices. As she acknowledged their presence, the one with long black hair looked up and smiled.

Beneath her feet, the floor began to buck and sway, the air becoming thick and oppressive.

The light of Joe's torch was bobbing down the hall as he walked past her towards the kitchen. "You all right, Beth?"

Forcing herself to let go of the post she followed, but the kitchen felt even worse and it was difficult now to breathe. In the shadows of the yard there was an outline of a dog hanging from a chain and she whipped around, heading for the stairs.

"I'm having the very quickest of looks up here, just to get the gist, and then I'm going."

The atmosphere in the house was akin to the aftermath of a bomb explosion. The static crackled with evil, only lessening slightly on walking into the front bedroom.

"Steady on," Joe said, clambering up after her. "I dunno, I thought you'd take your time, tuning in and such…"

The front bedroom afforded a good view of the hills and the streetlamps winding up Moorlands Road.

"My friend works at the nursing home up there," said Beth, trying to quell the feeling of abject panic.

I have to get out.

Joe hovered in the doorway. "Crispin Freeman's place?"

"Yes. I just wondered about the last house, the one next to it. According to Jea…er, Maria, it's empty. Do you know what it is, only…?"

Alas, she could not stay for the answer. It was no

good. The walls were fluid, collapsing inwardly. The veils of time were dissolving, the floor falling into an abyss of howling pain and confusion. And above it all, malicious laughter echoed through the ages, along with the tinkling of a carriage clock.

Gran Grace suddenly appeared by the window with her arms folded. "Beth! What are you doing?"

Ignoring Joe's questioning stare, she bolted from the room. "Sorry, I have to get out."

***

CHAPTER NINETEEN

She shot downstairs at bullet speed straight out of the front door and onto the street.

Dark now, rain and sleet fizzed around the streetlights as she crumpled onto the low front wall in a daze. The pavement was a sea swell of black tar and already the slugs were oozing up the walls of the houses. As she looked at the house opposite, one of the creatures collapsed into itself, then unfolded and spread out like a jellyfish across an upstairs window. This was the most diabolical place she'd ever come across, amplified for one such as her who could actually see it.

Out of breath, Joe burst out a second later, his face coated with a ghastly sheen of cold sweat. "Excuse my French but that was fuckin' 'orrible. I feel sick." He bent double. "It's like I had ten pints on an empty stomach. Sorry, I'm going to puke."

She watched him walk smartly down the road towards number three, and averted her gaze when he suddenly bent over a garden wall and retched.

After a while he came back mopping his brow, and sat next to her.

"You okay?"

"Never better."

She managed a smile, still swallowing down her own nausea. "Okay, you know this is all real now, don't you? You know the demonic exists and you know that's what we're up against?"

He nodded. "I heard something in there."

"Did you?"

"You won't believe this—"

She almost laughed. "Try me."

"I heard my name. I swear to God something said my name. It was whispered in a cold breath down the back of my neck." He rubbed his face up and down again with a handkerchief. "Told me I was a scared little arse-wipe. And instantly I got this memory of being in the school playground and walking past a kid getting the crap beaten out of him. I could have helped, I could have...but I didn't, Beth. And I didn't because I was scared."

"That's how it works, Joe. The enemy is sly. And to weaken you, to take the focus of itself, it will pick your deepest secrets - every embarrassment and every flaw. You just have to get there first. Do the shadow work yourself and face it. That way there'll be nothing to disarm you later."

He stared down the street so she couldn't see his face.

"I work for God. I work for Christ. Most people don't see the battle, but it's there all the time, all around us. Look at the arguments, the drink, the selfishness, the greed, the porn, the apathy. Like I said, the enemy is sly. We're supposed to be the best we can be, to evolve, but look around. Ask yourself what kind of energy that is."

"I don't have a religion."

"Me neither." She thought of her good friend, Father Greg. "That doesn't mean there aren't highly gifted, spiritual people in the church, it's just I don't affiliate with any particular one."

He nodded. "Too many rules, too much exclusion."

"In my opinion there is infiltration everywhere, but it doesn't mean there aren't good men and women in those places because there are. A lot. Anyway, are you feeling better now?"

"Yeah." He shoved his hands deep into his pockets and shivered. "Cold, though."

"Joe, I can't go back into that house again on my own. If you felt bad can you imagine what it was like for me? That's how possession happens and I'm like a radio transmitter–"

"Stop. That really does freak me out!"

Out of the corner of her eye she could see them: the slugs had swollen to the size of sated snakes, gorging on the loosh of fear pulsing out of the houses and from under the paving slabs. The squelching noise was like food being macerated in a saliva filled mouth.

She nodded towards his car. "Any chance we could sit in your car for a bit, maybe just park on the prom or something?"

The evening was as dead and black as the interior of a cave, the amber glow of the streetlights barely reaching the edges of the road.

"It's not a good place to be."

"Absolutely."

He flicked the remote and they jumped in, remaining silent until he parked alongside the coast a few minutes later. When he buzzed down the window, a rush of seaweed-laced fresh air blasted in and they both sat breathing deeply for a few minutes.

"Ah, life again!" said Beth. "I love the smell of the sea."

She glanced at his profile.

"Look, I want to help," she said. "But it's too dangerous for me, full stop."

"It's okay, you don't have to—"

"I'm a trained exorcist, Joe. I learned from the best, the real deal, the absolutely incorruptible ones who know what's going on in this world and what the battle is. And I can tell you now their faith is unshakeable, as is mine."

"Okay."

"I went on the course – for mostly nuns, monks and priests - and out of twenty of us there were only three left by coffee break. This is not to brag. I'm just telling you I don't scare easily and I don't baulk at the job. I'm a spiritual medium and a healer. Mostly we, my guides and I…" She flicked a glance over her shoulder at Billy on the back seat. "We help clear poltergeist infestations and move on lost spirits. Sometimes it's more complicated than that, though. To be fair it's very rare to come across the diabolical. Raising demons is usually kept to particular inside groups such as satanic covens or secret societies, and frankly it's an extremely dangerous game to play because the tables can and do turn. Anyway, it only works because it's hidden. Think about it – who's going to believe this goes on?"

"Not so powerful when it's out in the open, is it?"

"They'd be locked up for real if it was. The

diabolical secrets are what bind them together. Thing is, I only just left a place where that's what they were doing, and I can't help feeling there's a connection with what's going on here, and that the network is so much wider than I thought."

"And that's why you changed your name?"

She grimaced. "Tweaked it."

He sighed. "I'm supposed to work by the book and–"

"I know! But those who make the rule books do not abide by them. They're just for us, and if I'm not free I can't help anyone. I have to get you to understand that those of us who do this kind of work will be stopped from doing it at all costs. So this is the question - do you want this situation to continue? Do you want the next lot of poor saps to move into that place as it is now? More murders? What if they have kids?"

He nodded.

"I can trust you, Joe?"

"Yes. I mean, looking at this logically, it's not like you get anything out of it, is it?"

"No, the opposite. I risk my physical and mental health every single time. And I have nothing to my name. Nothing."

"Sorry. Look, on a purely human level we do need your help. Is there anything you can do?"

She nodded. "We can try. First I need the history, not just of Mailing Street but the whole town, and also some geographic information. And I need support from others who can do what I do. There is no way I can attempt to do this one alone. I had to under the Hall because of the children–"

"What?"

"Not live ones."

"Oh."

"And there's a lot of preparation that needs to be done. Is there any way you can put Freeman off moving new people into those houses yet?"

"Not a chance. The boss has already told us to wrap it up by Saturday so they can get the painters in on Sunday. It's going to be that quick."

"Crap."

"But you can do something, yes? They're going to put families in there. Apparently, there's a list as long as your arm that need urgent housing. We can't say they're haunted, it won't wash."

From the back seat, Billy said, "Ask him about the abattoir."

She nodded "Um, did your officer find out what was underneath Mailing Street?"

"An abattoir, Beth. Like you said."

"Any other information?"

"Yes, it went by the name of, 'Freeman's Livestock and Shipping Corporation.'"

"So he owned that, as well. Probably his family has always owned the land here."

"Yes, he was the original lord of the land, as they say – family goes back hundreds of years. Might be the maternal side. I'm not from Crewby, I'm from Manchester originally."

"Don't suppose you know what kind of soil it is? Clay? Sandstone? Quartz?"

"Sandstone, I think. I only know that because the missus insisted on a new build."

"Ley lines?" She looked to the east. If we drove

directly east from here we'd go over the Pennines and arrive in Yorkshire, yes?"

"Yes."

"You know that to summon the demonic they need to harness the lowest energy vibrations? So that would be fear, terror, misery, anger, pain—"

"Er, Beth—"

"It's a contract, a deal with a particular named entity. And there has to be blood. You can't be satanic without sacrificing—"

""Beth—"

"If the demon has infested someone weak or they get the upper hand from a conjuror, then they have control. If however, the one who did the summoning is in control then they have to supply more and more and more blood as part of the pact, if you will. Blackmailing never stops or the tables reverse."

"Okay?"

"So I think the one doing the summoning is the same one who's controlling what's happening here. And she recently lost some power. She would have felt that."

A freak gust of wind off the ocean gripped and shook the car, rocking it visibly at the same time a sea horse of water reared over the barrier wall and sprayed across the bonnet.

"And so she must retrieve the power lost or she loses the upper hand. Think portrait in the attic, because these people sold out…"

Joe was staring out of the windscreen as if he'd accidentally started watching one of the worst horror films imaginable but couldn't tear himself away.

Beth turned to face him. "I know this doesn't make

sense to you but somehow it's all interlinked. I've been getting visions of tunnels and crates. She has to feed whatever she's raising with—"

Joe's eyes were now as wide as dinner plates.

"Sacrifices didn't die out with the Aztecs, you know? Dark magic still goes on, but like most people you think it's rare."

"No, we've had a few cases. And I've seen possession. I know it's real. We had a drug dealer and his brother brought in for selling crystal meth. They used to take non-payers onto the moors and pull their teeth out with pliers. Anyhow, we got him in for questioning, and when he looked at me across the table his eyes were totally black, full of pure hate. I can't describe it except it was like a sickly thump in the chest. And the other thing was, while his eyes were boring into mine, his whole face cracked into a grin. It threw me back physically. The feeling was nearly as bad as it was in there." He indicated the houses behind them. "I had nightmares for a long time after that."

Beth nodded. "It's a line crossed."

"I once saw this addict slithering across the floor like a snake. I've been aware of this stuff for a while, Beth."

"Those would be the victims, the infested. My belief is that the drug trade is orchestrated at the highest levels, but I can't prove it. What I can say for sure is there were sacrifices made on or under Mailing Street, and that the demonic was raised with full intent. And the abattoir had no moral standards. Someone incredibly cruel worked there and was put there deliberately. I can feel madness, malignant glee at another's suffering—"

"And this is linked to that place in Yorkshire?"

"A stately home."

"Which?"

"Those two girls who killed Molly - who are they? I don't mean their names and addresses, I just mean what's the story?"

Joe shrugged. "As far as we know they're two lasses who got chatting to Molly that night and neither of them can remember a thing. One's a thin little waif who won't look you in the face; the other's blank, as in eyeballs you right back, won't speak, no emotions."

"Are the psychologists involved yet?"

"Main unit's in Blackpool but apparently there's an adolescent unit here. I haven't met the psychiatrist yet. I'm going over tomorrow."

She nodded, deep in thought, already planning to drop into the local churches next day, to see if any help could be sought.

Joe's voice cut in. "I still feel a bit sick, to be honest. Not relishing the thought of going back in that house again any time soon, but I suppose–"

"You're not protected at all."

His aura was blue, a clear narrow band of aquamarine.

"Are there any trees near you, like a park or some woods?"

"Yeah, where my allotment is. It's where I take the dog out."

"Okay, well when you next take him–"

"Her. Rita."

She smiled. "When you take Rita out this evening try and get into nature. And if you can, go barefoot so your feet connect with the earth, no rubber soles. Open up all your chakra points like flowers opening up to the sun. You want to drain the grey, smoky negativity into the earth. This will be your fear, anxiety, stress... Channel it down one leg, turn it to light, and bring up the light through the other. Bring in blinding gold-white light from above your head and chase the murky energy down, okay? Picture the whole of your body full of light so you're lit up within, and spread it around you until you have a surrounding bubble of it. The emotions you're after are gratitude, love, truth, feeling connected to Source, to God."

She stopped. This was where most people blanked.

"Like a circuit board."

"Exactly. Yes, it's all about energy."

"Nature always makes me feel better. You know..." He shook his head. "I always felt there was something else to this world, something we couldn't see. I'd get hunches I couldn't explain, and there've been one or two things that would make most people's hair stand on end. The only people I mentioned it to looked at me like I was nuts. Anyway, I've got to go and take Rita out or she'll bust."

"Oh yes, you must."

"Shall I drop you outside yours? Portland Street, isn't it?"

"Thanks." Her phone beeped just as he started up the ignition.

It was Father Greg and her heart leapt. Just when she needed him.

The text read, 'I'm in North Thailand. Spot of trouble. Don't try to contact me. Will be in touch when

I can.'

Sighing, she texted back, 'If you do pick this up, please tune in over the next few days. We need A LOT of help. Beth x'

***

CHAPTER TWENTY

Two days to prepare wasn't long. Still, it was only five o'clock. The night was young.

After waving Joe off, Beth stood looking at her car. One of the tyres didn't look too good and she knew for a fact the tank was nearly empty. However, the urge to go for a drive was a strong one.

"We need to take a proper look at Crewby," said Billy.

"I know. And we've got to find a vicar or a priest."

What to do? She bit her lip and looked up at the house. Today was the day Jeannie was seeing Estelle, which meant she probably wouldn't be home for hours yet.

"I could probably kill two birds with one stone?"

Billy nodded and she sighed. It wasn't him who'd have to walk to a garage in the dark if they broke down. Still, there wasn't much time to play with.

"Garage and then church? Okay, well here goes."

She jumped in and turned the ignition key. The engine screeched with the kind of metallic grind that set teeth on edge. She tried again. This time it chugged valiantly, briefly, before dying out completely.

"Okay one last go." With her foot flat to the floor she turned the key extra hard and chivvied the car along while bouncing in the seat. "Come on!" Amazingly it sparked into life and she laughed. "Hurray! Right," she explained to the Peugeot. "Looks like we'd better get you a drink and pump up this tyre or we won't be going anywhere ever again, will we?" Setting off, she continued to coax the car as if it was a living thing. "I'm sure there's a garage just beyond the retail park. Not far, so do your best to make it."

"What?" Billy, on the back seat, was shaking his head with laughter.

"It worked, didn't it?"

Ignoring the permanent red light on the petrol gauge, she trundled onto the dual carriageway at the lowest possible speed without inciting road rage. The plan was to fix up the car pretty quickly before visiting at least one church this evening. So hopefully…she flicked a glance in the rear view mirror at a set of headlights tailgating… the car would make it. The journey seemed to take forever. How long was this dual carriageway? Fast food outlets came and went, then office blocks, another retail park… but no garage. She glanced down at the petrol gauge and grimaced as they passed signs for the motorway junction. Oh no, there had to be a garage along here somewhere. There used to be!

The tailgater blasted his horn just as the very last roundabout came into view, yards before it became a fast route to the motorway. And there on the left was a neon sign for the garage she knew was there.

"Thank you God!"

They should make it.

The tailgater was now almost on the back seat and once again he blared the horn.

"What's wrong with people?"

The right lane was clear. Why didn't he overtake? If the Peugeot gave out or she tapped the brakes there'd be a collision. The horn blast from behind was now constant, the interior of her car floodlit.

"What's his problem?"

She might have known. Should have guessed it was an omen. But in her confusion and panic at missing the garage and being forced onto the one-way system, it didn't register at the time. Approaching the roundabout in a cacophony of horn-blasting and dazzling lights, she saw the forecourt only at the very last second, and swerved in just as the tyre slumped to flat and the tailgater shot past with a hair's breadth to spare.

Her heart was thumping so fast a sweat had broken out. What on earth was that all about? The car was parked sideways, slightly blocking the exit, but it had given its all and there was no more left to give. Still shaking, she walked into what was a small cabin tacked onto the side of a workshop, thankfully open until six.

After booking in for a new tyre, she added, "Oh, and there's no petrol in it. Sorry, I just had to leave it where it landed. Sorry, I–"

Without any mistake the man in overalls behind the counter, definitely said, "For fucks sake,' under his breath.

"Sorry. Do you want me to get a can and–?"

"It'll have to be next week now."

She nodded. "Next week? For a tyre?"

"Needs aligning. Take it or leave it, we're busy."

Her gaze flicked to the noticeboard behind him. Out of around forty or fifty hooks, only one had a set of keys hanging from it, and she couldn't help noticing the open logbook containing barely half a dozen entries.

"I see. Okay, well I guess I can do what I need to do on foot. Thank you."

"Leave the key."

She smiled despite the waves of resentment coming off the man. "Much appreciated. I'll be back next Wednesday, then. I'm on a–"

"You'll have to ring first. We're very busy. I can't promise anything."

"Will do. Thanks."

A minute later, back on the forecourt, she glanced back at the heavyweight man in overalls now staring out unseeingly from his fluorescent cubicle. 'All of them are lost', she thought. 'Souls trapped in little boxes all over the country…all over the world…disconnected…'

Cars and lorries fizzled past, spraying rain across the pavement, and she pulled up her collar, preparing to walk home. This was the built-up part of Crewby – a mesh of sprawling housing estates, office complexes and business parks – and definitely not a place of history. No churches, either. About to cross the road, however, a sign indicating the nearby hospital caught her attention. Funny, she hadn't noticed or even thought about the hospital until Joe mentioned the adolescent psychiatric unit earlier.

It was half-five. Should she take a look?

Billy was nodding.

She hesitated.

"You're here now," said Billy. "Such a history to hospitals. Have you ever thought about it?"

A fresh gust of wind whipped around her ankles, and after a moment she nodded and turned back. What would it take? Ten minutes?

The hospital was at the far end of a 1970s housing estate on the outskirts of town. Mostly semis with a few detached, the houses were built of brick and had large gardens, the pavements tree-lined. Passing a school playing field with a line of shops opposite, a brief memory flared up of the semi she grew up in on the outskirts of Liverpool: 'London Calling' was blasting out of the family kitchen on a Saturday afternoon, everyone singing to it. And suddenly all that seemed such a long, long time ago. 'All these moments,' she thought, 'floating away in time like soap bubbles in the wind...nothing lasting, nothing solid.'

Maybe she'd smiled to herself, but striding towards her a couple of girls were eyeing her with the most insolent of stares.

Clones of each other in baseball caps, leggings and skintight tops, one muttered as they levelled, "Past it."

"Yeah," said the other, more loudly. "Well past it."

"Bitchy girls," came Gran Grace's tut-tut voice, and Beth laughed inside. Some things didn't change.

Shows I've still got it, Gran!

Eventually the estate ended, and the road dimmed to rustling evergreens and the bare branches of February. Ahead was a blaze of lights. Ah, the hospital.

Suddenly tired, her feet began to drag on nearing. Here the wind whistled off the moors and from the darkness of the surrounding fields, a dog fox barked.

Despite the place being busy by necessity day and night, there was something desolate about it, and by the time she got to the main gates that feeling had intensified.

The main building was three storey red brick, linked by covered walkways to various annexes and prefabs. All pretty humdrum. She walked around the perimeter, skirting a near-empty car park. At the back was staff accommodation along with a boiler room and various laboratories. Interestingly, there was also an old stone building behind the main red brick one, smaller, and likely the original.

"So before the housing estate was built, this would have been quite a way out of town, several miles from the harbour?" she said to Billy. "Was it originally an isolation hospital?"

She looked up at the moors, then back at the older hospital, and closed her eyes for a second.

Billy was next to her. "Do you feel the energy? It's really strong."

She staggered slightly "Whoa! Did they bury people here, as well? There's a feeling underneath…"

A surge of energy was pushing upwards from within the earth, similar to Mailing Street but not as aggressive or violent. This seemed older, more miserable and ingrained.

"A graveyard?"

She glanced up at the wards and saw them: people lying in the full glare of fluorescent lights, labelled and gowned, hooked to drains and drips, vaguely aware of the hiss of oxygen and the beep-beep of machines around their heads.

The buzz underfoot was tingling, powerful. "This is

on a major ley line, isn't it? That's it, isn't it? Oh my God. Crewby is on a ley line axis, with the water on one side and the hills on the other. And why do I feel people were buried here? Directly underneath a hospital? Or did they build the hospital on top of a cemetery?"

"Did you notice the psychiatric unit?"

"What? No."

Inside the complex at the rear of the old hospital, the signposts were unlit. Cranking open a wrought iron gate, Beth walked along the path in the direction of the medical residences. And there it was. Sandwiched between the labs and the laundry, in the shadow of what had once been the isolation hospital but was now a women's health unit, stood a single storey building that resembled an old prisoner of war camp.

"Fucking hell!" She slammed a hand to her mouth. "Crap. That's a shock."

On a plaque gratefully acknowledging him for generous financial backing, were the words, 'The Lord Freeman Mental Health Unit.'

The feeling here was decidedly off-kilter, and over and above the noise of the generator, came the much closer sound of the dog fox – one bark every few seconds.

"I've had enough of today. Come on, let's go."

The walk back through the housing estate was a fast one. Panting for breath, her mind chattering ten to the dozen, Beth then sprinted across the dual carriageway and cut through the back of the retail park onto Mailing Street, which was where, just as she remembered that Joe Sully had actually replied about the house next to the nursing home, she saw Jeannie.

She was getting out of a four wheel drive vehicle, thanking the driver.

Locked into her own warren of thoughts, it took Beth a few seconds to fully register the face of the driver as she accelerated past. Yet it would imprint on her memory - alabaster skin, delicate features, ice-blue eyes - along with the scent of pear drops.

***

CHAPTER TWENTY-ONE

Time was running out, but with the next day a working one Beth had no option but to get through it. That morning she'd visited the local churches. The vicar at the largest one, situated on the High Street, had been cool and evasive when she'd introduced herself. She was welcome to join the congregation and contribute to the flowers and cleaning rota, but when it came to questions surrounding Mailing Street, suddenly time waited for no man and he all but shooed her out. Another had been boarded up and there was no answer at the mosque. One however, held promise, and that was a small Methodist chapel. Almost hidden from view behind a factory, Beth had walked straight in. Its wooden pews gleamed, fresh flowers scented an atmosphere exuding calm, and the minister, Christine, had the most beautiful aura of violet and rose-gold.

While chopping, frying and stirring in the kitchen later that day, she turned over the chat she'd had with Christine about Mailing Street, and in particular about Molly. Compassionate and all-encompassing, Christine was definitely the one who would help with the coming ordeal. It wasn't always about numbers, but the power of belief and conviction, and Beth thanked God she'd found her.

Her thoughts, after a while though, drifted back to Jeannie. The transformation after meeting Estelle was nothing short of jaw-dropping. Jeannie had been euphoric. Not since the day they left Curbeck had she looked so animated. Estelle, it seemed, was the perfect choice. So…Beth shook her head…why the creeping unease, then? She had chosen Estelle Vickers herself!

No, it was fine. Her disquiet was about the history of the town, not her friend. Jeannie was happy and that in itself was wonderful to see. She now had a professional she liked and trusted to help her through the trauma. It was good. All good.

On noticing Beth walking home the previous evening, Jeannie had waited for her to catch up. "Oh, it's you! I thought it was. What're you doing here?"

Beth explained about the car. "So, was that Estelle? Did it go okay?"

"Yeah."

"It was nice of her to give you a lift back."

"Yeah."

"So she lives in Crewby?"

"Moorlands Road, of all places."

"Wow! One of the big houses? And it went well, I take it? You're happy with everything?"

"Definitely. In fact it went better than expected. When I first got there she said we'd be about an hour while she took notes, and after that there'd be a course of treatment depending on what we agreed. Anyway, she took two hours. She's really, really nice. And very highly qualified – everything from psychotherapy and hypnosis, to past life regressions and counselling - whatever's needed basically."

"Great."

"I was the last client of the day, so that's why she said she'd give me a lift seeing as we live in the same town. Anyway, she took ages with me, Beth. And the whole thing's recorded. So at the end of the treatment programme I can replay it and listen whenever I want."

"Good idea, yes. So do you mind me asking – what did she suggest? Counselling or psychotherapy or–?"

"At the moment it's just talking. She said it sounded like there was a lot of confusion, so first we need to go through my history. And we discussed doing past life regression later down the line. The thing is, I felt like I could tell her everything, and I mean absolutely everything. And she really understood. Apparently, she's been through similar things herself and that's why she does what she does. So you know, she's just like me?"

They'd reached the front door and Beth had the key in the lock, Jeannie standing behind her. "Been through what?"

"She just said victim of abuse."

Victim of abuse…

Again the cold grip of unease.

As Beth worked in the kitchen, she briefly tuned into Jeannie as she was now, today, in her blue and white striped uniform with a mop and a bucket of grimy water. Although she worked alone in those upstairs back rooms, and dust motes drifted in the air, she was humming to herself, and her eyes had a faraway dreamy look…What was that song? Darn it, on the fringes of her mind….

"Look sharp, Lily!"

Beth carried on rinsing lettuce, still thinking about the name of the song Jeannie was humming, when the voice cut in again.

"Lily! Hellooo… anyone home?"

It had taken a second too long and she jumped at the realisation. How many reminders did it take? She'd told Gareth she answered to Beth. Why then, did he insist otherwise? Nevertheless, it had caught her out. Again.

"Sorry." She wiped her hands on her apron, wishing her cheeks didn't flame so easily. "No one calls me Lily, Gareth. I told you - I'm Beth to everyone. Sorry, I was genuinely miles away."

Every move you make…every breath you take…

"Thanks, Gran!"

"What?"

"Sorry, sorry. Talking to myself again. What can I do for you?"

He stared at her for so long it became embarrassing.

"What can I do for you?" she repeated.

Shaking his head slowly from side to side, he shoved an order slip on the spike before leaving her to it. "Steak and chips twice. Extra rare."

Watching his back as he retreated down the hall to the bar, Beth stood motionless, paralysed. Something was coming, was about to happen…

There's going to be an escalation of events now. You must keep watch…

On autopilot, amid a sense of everything being unreal and of time slowing, she turned to take the required steaks out of the fridge. And when she looked down they were bleeding. Transfixed, she watched in horror as veins rose from the slabs of muscle in rubbery tubes that now began to throb and pulse as if alive. A pool of blood quickly spread out towards the rim of the plate and began to swill like soup. She slammed shut the fridge door and threw the plate onto the kitchen table, holding fast to the back of a chair as a great heaviness suddenly took hold, weighting her down. Neither one leg nor the other would move. And from the faint line of ocean seen through the kitchen window, to the pans and jars on the units, to the cooking range, everything at once blurred in a fusion of wobbling, vibrating colour.

It was over in a second.

She sat down.

"I can't eat meat anymore. I can't eat animals or even cook them. And I'm a chef."

The impact was huge and for a while she sat motionless, stunned. She had been shown without any doubt whatsoever that for her, it was time to stop eating meat. She took on the pain and trauma of the animals, so that was that. The message was unmistakeable and to go against such strong guidance would not be wise. Especially not with the task that lay ahead on Mailing Street.

She regarded the steaks in a way she never had before. Garnet in colour, a sheen as globular and fresh as if the arteries had only just been slashed now glossed the surface, the last flood of an aortic pulse having washed through the tissues mere moments ago.

"I'm gonna be sick."

In the staff toilets upstairs, she held her hair back from her face and let the tears stream as she retched. All these years and cooking meat had never bothered her. But now it must stop. Immediately. Eventually she dried her eyes and washed her face, sat on the toilet lid and closed her eyes.

"Sometimes we're forced into changing," said Gran Grace, appearing on the wicker chair by the sink. "It feels like a slammed door, but that can be what it takes to move you on, child. Sometimes you have to be made uncomfortable enough to change. Another will open."

She nodded.

"You can't keep chasing pay packets. Sooner or later you must step into your own boots and do what you came here to do. Full time. Larger scale. You have no idea how important your role is going to be."

"I've got to pay the rent."

"Trust God. Trust us. Tomorrow will propel you into a new life. And when this experience is over... you will not be the same again."

***

Part Three

'Oh, what a tangled web we weave when we practice to deceive.'
William Shakespeare.

Chapter Twenty-Two

The time had come. Beth and Joe were standing next to his car, contemplating Molly's old house on Mailing Street. A constant train of traffic trundled past on the main road, and overhead seagulls swooped and cried on darkening winds.

Billy and Gran Grace had already gone inside to prepare for the task ahead, vanishing beyond the dark stone walls.

"Thank you for doing this," said Joe.

"You okay?"

Joe was pale about the gills, constantly fiddling with a bunch of keys. "Forensics have gone. These three houses get cleaned tomorrow, so I'm just hanging onto the key to number seven for a bit." He looked at her and shrugged.

"Three new families are moving in on Monday?"

"Yup."

"Look, I didn't have much time to prepare. The main C. of E. vicar was a closed shop. I got the impression he was happy to discuss messy churches and white weddings but not, definitely not, exorcisms."

"Thought Jesus cast out demons?"

She nodded. "I know. Fortunately they don't all shy away, though. The Methodist minister, Christine, actually invited me in for coffee. Turned out she knew Molly as a kid. She was orphaned, did you know?"

"I knew there weren't any living parents. No family, either."

"Molly grew up in a children's home. Anyway, it turns out she went to see Christine a lot over the years. Obviously Christine wouldn't betray confidences, but I got the feeling Molly was very troubled and had been for a long time. All she said was that things were not as they seemed, and when I told her about the atmosphere in the house, she already knew."

"Knew what?"

"That Mailing Street was, to use her own words, 'infested with dark spirits.' She'd been praying for Molly, and all the others, for years. We had quite a long chat and Christine will be praying with us today. She's not like me exactly, but she did ask who the woman in the turquoise shawl and topaz brooch was sitting next to me. She said, 'She's just left the side of an old lady in a nursing home and now she's here with us.'"

"Turquoise shawl?"

"My great grandma, Gran Grace. Gran and Billy are my spirit guides, and the point is that Christine saw Gran. So Christine is the real deal. She understands there is dark and light, that the battle exists, and she's not afraid. She's authentic and she's powerful."

"Glad she's on the team, then."

"Exactly. I'll tell you something else while I remember, too. I think Molly knew something, as in something that would have landed her in a lot of trouble if she spoke out. I may be wrong, but I don't think she was drinking out of grief for the lost husband. I think it was to escape–"

"The horrible house?"

Beth shook her head. "Then why didn't she move out? I know she was on benefits but she could still have–"

"She was in a bad way for a long time, apparently. I mean a serious alcoholic. And there's a housing shortage, as well. Maybe she just got stuck?"

"Maybe. Anyway, we need to get started." She held up a vial. "I've got some holy water, and… just a minute…" She rooted around in her bag. "Holy oil."

"And this is going to work?"

"I can't guarantee anything. By rights this would normally take days, possibly weeks, plus a whole team of committed people in constant prayer. Our faith, however, is absolute. And both Christine and Father Greg are with us in spirit, so we will do our best."

"Father Greg?"

"He's not in Crewby, but distance doesn't always matter. I can feel his presence."

As she spoke the air became slightly grainy like a television set with a poor signal.

"I wish I knew more about the two girls and what ritual they were doing. We're going to use tribal banishment–"

"Actually, I've got some info on the girls. One of them, Toyah, the one with the dead eyes who stonewalled every line of questioning, spent three years on the psyche unit here in her early teens. So that's between you and me and I'm not privy to anything more. Crispin Freeman gave me quite the lecture. I wasn't allowed to see either of them."

Lord Freeman's Mental Health Unit?

"Crispin Freeman being in charge of adolescent psychiatry?"

"Associate psychiatrist, apparently. Yes."

"Indeed." She frowned. "Okay." She checked her watch. "Well, time isn't on our side so we'd best go in and start peeling back the layers. We may not be successful today, you do realise that? It's such a pity we don't have more time. Are you sure you can't–?"

"Nope. Carrie said we have to wrap up today. I've wangled things as it is."

"She doesn't know about me?"

"No way. And if she found out I'd kept a key I'd have a hell of a lot of explaining to do."

Instinctively, Beth looked up at the windows. There was a sense the house was waiting, watching, anticipating. "Thank you for doing the right thing. A lesser man would not have taken the risk."

"Do I need to erm…I mean, do you need me to come in with you or–?"

"No, you won't be able to. You mustn't be anywhere near. Fear makes it worse."

He coloured slightly. "I'm not scared. I've told you. We had another murder last night. The guy was one of the gang leaders I was telling you about the other day. Him and his gang took their victim to a disused factory yard and kicked him to death. Then they chopped off his hands. It's like these guys crossed the line a long, long time ago and that's where they live now."

"With the enemy."

"Yes. Look into those totally black eyes too long and you feel like you'd fall down a tunnel, that you'd never be able to get out again. I'm telling you I never saw this on such a scale 'til fairly recently - the last ten years or so. Anyway, I'm not in fear."

"He stares at you, doesn't answer questions, mocks you?"

Joe nodded. "His legal's ill, too. She's been handling these cases for a while now and she's only a young lass. Saw her last night and she was ghastly pale with dark rings under her eyes. Said she wasn't sleeping well, kept waking up in the early hours after dreaming she was in her own street or back yard with a gang waiting for her. Kind of like being trapped in a twilight zone, only stuck in dreams and not able to wake up."

"The lower astral. It's where people like those gangsters stay even after they've passed into spirit. It's pretty much what hell is."

"So that's where she ended up in her dreams?"

"It's where fear put her. One day she'll get to the point where she's ready to face it."

"Poor Trish."

"Yes, she's going to need some help."

He nodded.

They walked up the path to the front door and as he put the key in the lock, Beth said, "If you see her again tell her she has the answers inside." She pointed to his heart. "Tell her all she has to do is ask and help will be given."

"She'll think I'm nuts."

"Maybe we need to stop caring about that and just give the message. Sorry. Anyway, I need to get on with the job in hand. It'll be dark soon."

He opened the door then handed over the key.

"Shall I give you a knock later or–?"

"No, can you just keep an eye out for however long it takes? We must not be disturbed under any circumstances whatsoever, or the whole thing could go badly wrong. It's really important. Just be right outside and don't try to enter the premises. You'll be rebuffed anyway."

He paled further. "Sure thing."

"Just don't leave me unguarded. Okay, we need you to go now."

The street was still empty with no parked cars in the vicinity. Such a strangely deserted place…and as Joe walked back down the path it occurred to her to wonder where those dead-eyed gangsters lived.

She waited until the sound of his footsteps faded and the car door opened and closed. A sharp gust blew down the adjacent alleyway. And only then did she walk inside, shut the door behind her and turn the key.

***

CHAPTER TWENTY-THREE

The gloomy interior reeked of bad drains, and from within the yawning cavern of silence came the echo of a child's laughter, followed by the rattle of a blind in the front room.

She stood motionless, apprehension clutching at her heart, when the phone pinged.

Father Greg: 'I'm with you!'

They were connected, and she thanked him for tuning in: 'Starting now.'

Christine was also kneeling in prayer, her head bent in a shaft of light streaming through a stained glass window. Silently Beth thanked her, too.

She switched off the phone.

"Billy?"

Having gone on ahead with Gran to probe the layers of energy, the power of his protection now encircled her auric field as she stood on the threshold. Most sensitives, Beth thought, would instantly feel deeply uneasy here, but they would not see what she could see - the defiant young boy standing on the stairs, staring back with a smirk on his face. Nor would they be able to hear the clatter inside the cupboard underneath the stairs. The boy flicked a glance in the direction of the cupboard, before turning tail to run back up. Somewhere along the landing a door slammed. And then once more the air stilled and silence reigned. Almost as if whatever possessed the darkness, whatever greedily devoured the fear and misery here, had played a card and now awaited her next move. She could almost hear it salivating.

"God is my armour. Christ is my shield. I am blessed by the blood of the lamb. He is my light."

A low snickering echoed around the hallway as slowly she ventured in. The sound of her own pulse throbbed in her ears, the click of her footsteps reverberating through the house as she headed for the front room and pushed open the door. No light filtered through the blinds, the air thick and stagnant. Turning around, she regarded the cupboard under the stairs.

The energies were disorientating, and a reel of grainy images began to flash in her mind at the same time as what sounded like a microphone malfunction screeching inside her head.

"Beth!"

Gran's voice brought her up sharp. They couldn't safely start until an effective framework was in place. And if there was a seal here it must be found and broken.

Pulled towards the mirror over the hearth, she took it down. On the back was a sigil inscribed in blood. She turned it this way and that, but from every angle it looked the same. She sensed Billy was as puzzled as she was. Certainly it was nothing they had come across before. It had, she thought, the feel of being ancient, possibly never documented. Walking smartly to the kitchen door she ripped off the back and burnt it in the yard, then sprinkled the mirror with holy water and scooped the ashes into her tin.

A scout around the rest of the house produced no other signs or symbols left behind, although there was a feeling some were painted beneath layers of wallpaper, notably in the back bedroom. She didn't linger. The sight of the stained mattress and tide marks of damp was enough. Besides, the nucleus of energy was downstairs. And once more she was drawn to the cupboard.

It was empty, the floorboards bare, paint peeling.

Was the seal underneath?

As she was peering into the cupboard, the air in the hall behind began to thicken, and the feeling the boy was watching intensified.

Quickly she set to work, placing carnelian, hematite, amethyst and quartz crystals at the four cardinal points. This formed a web or net, which should locate a buried seal. One went into the kitchen, one at the back of the cupboard under the stairs, one at the outer wall of the front room, and one beneath the bay window. Then the border of the area she would be working in was lined with salt.

At this point Beth became aware that more of the soul family than usual were in attendance, and the faint sound of tribal drumming had begun. Gran and Billy had already been working on disrupting the densest energies and were now starting to build up the light. The power was growing. She stood in the centre of the salt ring, calling on both the Children of the Light and Archangel Michael. Deep in meditative prayer, she tuned into both Father Greg and Christine, aware of both praying with intent and conviction. Also present were both of Gran's sisters, the tribe healer, the elders, and the one who had been present under Scarsdale Hall. She had only seen him once, and still did not know who he was or from what dimension, only that he did not take physical form and appeared as a soot-black, glittering mass of energy. This time, however, she was aware of his presence and sent out waves of gratitude.

While the spirit guides worked on holding back dark energies and building up the light, Beth began to probe the layers of time. Again the atmosphere was akin to the aftermath of a bomb, a prickly feeling of immortalised shock. She began to push through the vibrations. Then instantly hit a barrier - a head-splitting screech along with disorientating vertigo.

She paused before trying again. This time a roar of distorted sound rushed out, the pent-up force released so powerful it sent her reeling backwards in surprise. Stumbling, she clutched at the edge of the dining table to stop the fall. Dirty yellow smoke was now rising in plumes through the floorboards. A thought filtered into her mind that a thousand bodies or more were about to erupt from a mass grave. And half expecting to see the floorboards splinter and crack apart, it was then she had the sudden feeling that she was Molly.

A carriage clock tinkled.

Molly was about to transfer her final moments.

It occurred in a single flash: a memory trapped and relinquished in the blink of an eye.

The room was candlelit. Molly's chest hurt as if she'd been pushed roughly onto the sofa. It smelled of vomit and her head banged in time with her pulse. A girl with stringy, black hair was straddling her, a girl whose leering mouth had stretched joker-wide to reveal blackened teeth at the back. What was wrong with her eyes? Something had changed in her eyes…yellow…cold…

No!

Absolute shock now jackhammered into Molly's heart, as with one final aortic thump her life force gushed freely out of her stomach in an unstoppable torrent. Her pulse accelerated….bang-bang-bang-bang-faster-bang-bang-bang…Her thighs were warm…syrup spreading over them…as she stared at the gash of a red-soaked mouth, and the flick of a tongue.

The flash died to grey, and Beth immediately pushed it from her mind, even as singsong voices filled the room. The experience was not her own, the emotions not hers.

Recovering quickly, she got to her feet. "Thank you for showing me, Molly. That's enough. I don't need any more."

There was work to do. Carefully she pulled apart the energies. The image was unclear and off kilter, but there were two girls, both young and thin with curtains of dark hair. The blue light of a television screen lit the room as they carried out their gruesome task, singing and humming, absorbed with cutting and snipping as deftly as surgeons. A chorus repeated. She tried to capture the words but they made no sense. Latin or…? Ah! The understanding clicked. The words were backwards. Reverse Latin.

She began the exorcism.

"Father have mercy on us. Christ have mercy on us."

The prayers being said from a distance now intensified, and the drumming became louder as the spirits pushed back increasingly heavy energies. As the scene of the two girls faded, brown fog began to fill the room, and the smoke rising through the floorboards grew thicker. The pressure was compressing her lungs, making it more and more difficult to breathe, to think.

Suddenly the temperature plummeted and high-pitched screeching pierced her eardrums again.

Beth, continuing the prayers of exorcism, glanced across at Billy, who now had a pillar of light in place. Like a ray of sun breaking through a hole in the ceiling of a broken barn, it shone with laser precision into the dusty room below. Opening up her heart chakra to God, she now became a conduit. Pure love channelled through her. There was one chance to help these trapped souls out of the hell they had endured for decades, if not centuries. Help was here. They were the ones these souls had been waiting for.

The air was now icy. The dull light of a late winter afternoon tipped into dusk. And the bare lightbulb hanging from a flex in the middle of the ceiling began to flip back and forth like a lantern in a high wind.

All of their voices chimed harmoniously in prayer – from near and far, across the airwaves, a nexus of connected light forms. Love poured in from the divine. They kept going, building up power and momentum without stopping, while suffocating dense energies rolled in like a bonfire out of control. The pressure squeezed the breath from her lungs, threatening to engulf her, spectres of darkness began to amass in every corner, and rage thundered beneath the boards.

Screeching screamed into her brain.

"Father have mercy on us.

Christ have mercy on us.

Father have mercy on us. Christ have mercy on us."

As they prayed, more layers were being stripped away, revealing the horrors imprinted in time. A series of events had been stamped onto the ether, forever locked into the consciousness of those still there, souls endlessly re-living their nightmares with no escape. It was as if a dark mirror had them trapped inside it, their torment condensed and eternal, with nothing else existing to dilute, distract or negate. No light. And it was that concentration of pain and fear which fed the demonic.

Relinquish those souls to the light, however, and it ceased to exist.

Focusing on the feeling of absolute faith and absolute love, with the heavy energies held back, Beth began to see through the veils.

A dingy bedroom with flocked wallpaper had appeared. It looked old-fashioned, maybe post-war. Something moved in the pattern of the wallpaper and she honed in. There it was again. The flicker of an eye! Easily missed amid the busy design, the eye movement darted here and there, and thus the observer became the observed.

A couple was lying in bed, and the woman suddenly sat bolt upright, clutching the sheets to her throat. "He's bloody there again! Do something!"

Naked, the man jumped out of bed, grabbed a screwdriver and began to stab at the eye. Did he miss? His knuckles hit the wall, the tip of the implement vanished, and black clouds of rage burst from the man's mouth.

The scene then fell quickly away to reveal someone crouching in a dark cupboard. A woman with a fist in her mouth as if to stop herself from breathing, the heart rate fast, the feeling sickly. She was looking up at a silhouette of grey light around the perimeter of a door maybe only two feet high. The one under the stairs? The image was grainy, but suddenly the door was flung open from the outside. She was being dragged out by the arm, and it felt as if the scramble for life now drained out of her; all the running and fighting was over. Thrown headlong into the kitchen, there was a clean snap like that of a wishbone. Her head cracked on the corner of a table, and in slow motion she fell amid a rack of greying vests and sheets. Her body slumped onto the linoleum, expression cut to dead.

The man's face was puce, the expression glittering with contempt as with the back of his hand he wiped away a line of spittle dripping from his mouth.

Beth was still saying a prayer for the woman as the scene faded. A disembodied scream was locked and crystallised as more and more layers fell away, blurred moments of cruelty on repeat....an old lady flailing against a pillow over her face while a woman in the kitchen downstairs baked a cake...a child shivering under the covers as her bedroom door inched open and the silhouette of a man loomed across the wall...

Until once more she was looking at the boy. The boy on the stairs. And the rapid fire of images paused.

Dressed in grey woollen trousers and a hand-knitted sweater, he looked maybe nine or ten years old, with short, sandy brown hair, and he was sitting on a bed reading. Gently rocking to and fro, his finger was tracing each line as he read aloud to himself. But there was something wrong with the book. The moment caught and registered.

Ah, the book was upside down. And just as Beth acknowledged that information, he peeked over the top and smiled.

Hello, Beth! Welcome to the house of the Dark Lord...I am the gatekeeper...

From far away the tribal drumbeat permeated her shock, and praying now with renewed vigour, she concentrated on the thread of brilliant light filtering into the murky depths she now found herself in. Flickers of silver darted into the darkness like electric sparks, and Father Greg's powerful, constant prayers resounded in her head. Energy flowed through her in a channel like sun permeating the surface of the ocean, and Christine's energy reached down like loving arms, raising her into more buoyant waters, along with the faster vibrations of the drums.

The power of God filled her as she faced the enemy. Everything here was mocking and illusory.

Your lover fucked his sister...Oh, didn't you know? Travis fucked–

"Oh, I know that."

Light blasted through and she soared on the currents of pure love and unshakeable faith. The entire soul family resonated in prayer. He was not real. It was a trick.

"You can't get me with that one," she added, as his image began to weaken and fade.

The journey continued at lightning speed. Years of encapsulated moments now whipped by, a dizzying whirl of lives lived. Each soul, each conscious moment of thought had to be acknowledged, and the time and space continuums separated from a tangled knot of confusion. So much fear here: people lying in bed wide eyed, listening to every creak of the house, scratching in the walls, the pitter-patter of rodents on lino, lights flickering on and off, a television set switching itself on downstairs…

There was a sense of falling, of being in rubble, and then a concrete yard, to a place before the houses had even been built.

The journey ended at the muddy yard she had been shown before, the one with animals being herded off carts - the abattoir they knew for certain, had existed.

This was what lay beneath; the foundations on which all that misery had been built. But there was something peculiarly malevolent here, and it was far beyond the act of habitual slaughter. A faint echo of maniacal laugher rippled through the air. She stood as if in the middle of an abyss, having descended to the deepest point of a cave. And immediately the same panic gripped her as it had the animals. A feeling had caught and spread among them like wild fire, a fast-mounting dread igniting blind terror, as they neared the line being whipped into narrow, filthy corridors.

I can't turn round, I can't get out. There's pure evil at the end!

The hilarity of a madman now emerged: the image of a man laughing hysterically, as haphazardly he swung an axe, chopping and hacking at soft, furred flesh…

"Beth! It's not real. It's the past. Stay neutral."

As with the boy, the moment had been a split second, but her heart was pumping hard as Gran Grace's words filtered through. Immediately she resumed prayer, holding the immense love channelling through her, fixing her sight on the light sparkling high above on the surface. The prayers were constant from Billy and Gran, Gran's sisters, the tribal healer, Christine and Father Greg. And now they rose in volume as if an entire congregation had joined them. The Children of the Light, who she had never physically seen before, now appeared as a huge wall of blinding whiteness and the sight of them took her breath away. Every single one of these animal's souls must be turned to light. All darkness must alchemise and be returned to the light, and the task filled her with honour at being chosen to do this.

There could be no thoughts of revenge or feelings of judgement or anger. No blemishes, no smudges to the power of light. Whatever lay at the root of this would taunt, provoke and goad her into exactly that if she let it.

Beth forced herself to the head of the queue of animals. To the man waiting for them at the end with a blunt axe, the one she instinctively knew was referred to locally as, 'The Butcher.' Yet no one had done a thing about it. And made herself look at who he was.

Without hesitation the man lunged forwards and tried to jump into her skin.

Billy leapt between them.

Yellow-green eyes gleamed with soulless joy as the dead man stared into her head. With hair scraped back into a greasy, steel-grey ponytail, his jagged teeth had long since rotted into the gums. Saliva dripped from his mouth as he stood inches from her face, mid-swing of the axe.

"Give me your name, demon. In the name of Christ I command you give me your name."

A garbled spew fell from a mouth twisted with malice. He oscillated between hilarity and rage, the yellow eyes darting from left to right. And she saw then that he was completely insane. Not a shred of humanity remained, and whatever had taken hold of the vessel possessed it totally. Look at it too long and it would send her insane, too. Demons, as she had repeatedly told those who insisted on dabbling, did and would, jump.

"In the name of the Christ I command you say your name."

Waves of filthy smoke filled the air and her chest was beginning to physically hurt. It moved in like smog, and unintelligible words now flew at her from every direction in a garble of shouts, roars, screams and sobs: one behind her, one to the left, a crowd above… below…

Time stood still. The atmosphere thickened like treacle. She could barely breathe. It wanted to consume her, disorientate, and crush.

"Archangel Michael, we call on your assistance. Archangel Michael, we call on you for help. Father have mercy on us. Christ have mercy…Father have mercy…"

From far away she heard the unceasing prayers of her soul family. More silver and gold light flitted into being, sparking like tiny forks of lightning. The drumbeats grew louder and faster, overriding the discordant screeching. And golden rays pushed through the cracks of what she could now see was a broken corrugated iron roof, reaching down to a pit of blood-soaked sawdust and smeared warehouse walls.

Her heart filled at the sight of the Children of the Light who now dominated the scene. Far taller and more voluminous than imagined, their powerful, dazzling white beings were almost too much to look at. And joyous beyond words she took a deep breath and knew the light had won. God wins. Always.

And so it is done.

"I command you...."

Without warning, the madman sprang directly into her face in a blur of knuckles and bared teeth, his once human features contorted into a monstrous stretched mouth, the jugular and carotid veins raised to purple, the eyes poker red. With one swift movement he drew back the axe...

A myriad of doors opened up around her, howling drains of blackness pulling her in all directions; and then just as had happened beneath Scarsdale Hall, the glittering metallic being appeared. And guillotine chopped the scene to nothing.

The madman was uncreated.

He simply ceased to be.

"Look," said Billy.

She glanced down. The crystal grid she'd set up had located its prize, and the magnetic pull beneath her feet told her where it was. Embedded in the dirt floor where the possessed man had stood not a second before, was a glinting piece of black crystal the size of penny. The seal. Forming a fist she reached down through the energy layers. Pain shot up her arm. But she held on.

A single, black obsidian mirror. More dangerous than any Ouija board, it had absorbed black mass after black mass of demonic energy over decades, possibly centuries.

"Break it!"

The pain was a deep ache but she pulled it through the energy layers and threw it at the hearth, the sound of its fracture into a myriad of shards an ugly raucous scream. Immediately the pressure popped like a cork. White light flooded the room. And a cathedral choir of a thousand voices broke out in a King of Kings chorus, heavenly voices lifting the rafters as hundreds upon hundreds of animal souls now burst free from a tightly matted coil. In a roar of sound they rose and disappeared into the many columns of light waiting to take them home, back to Source. And vanished.

Like the breaking of a storm, a strike of lightning, or the rapture of summer rain after a drought, the air now cleared, bringing with it the sweet scent of wet grass and rose petals, and Beth sank to her knees in prayer.

Billy and Gran Grace were leading all the trapped souls into the light as one by one the witnessed scenes dissipated, and the tormented were released. Breathing rhythmically, crystallising the blissful moment, she watched silver and gold filaments dart around as all of the imprints in time – the woman hiding under the stairs, another in a hairnet scrubbing shirt collars with a wire brush - all trailed like ribbons streaming on the wind, waiting to be untangled. Wiping her eyes, she carefully began to unpick them all, just as she had once separated strands of wool for Gran Grace all those years ago, until they fluttered quite separately…spent, colourless, history…gone.

Finally, at well past seven o'clock, she noticed the time. Apart from a streak of amber across the floor, it was completely dark.

She looked at that streak of amber again.

These were not floorboards.

Instead, for a mere fragment of a second, she was surrounded by elemental beings – wood sprites and fae - in a wildflower meadow caressed by a spring breeze, and the coppery shimmer of trees.

This was a sacred hollow. A magical ring.

So, an ancient sacred site had been defiled and an abattoir built on top!

***

CHAPTER TWENTY-FOUR

Beth jumped to her feet and peeped through the blinds, noting with relief that his car was still there. Thank God!

The street was empty, as usual. But there was a difference now – the streetlights illuminated the pavement enough to cast shadows – the gloom had lifted. She smiled, exhausted. Joe would no doubt be fed up waiting, but there was still a bit more work to do. No openings could be left.

While Gran Grace probed the other houses for residual energies, persuading those now freed to go to the light, Billy stood next to her.

"That was one of the worst we've ever done."

"I get the feeling the girls were sent here deliberately."

"One of the girls."

"The one with yellow eyes, the older one?"

"Yes, she painted the back of the mirror. The other's her servant. "

"Maybe they met in the psychiatric unit? I wonder who they answer to. Freeman? But how would they meet someone like Lord Freeman unless it's through a cult?"

Billy shrugged.

"The abattoir was his, and I'm guessing whoever employed the madman knew exactly what they were doing."

"He was mad before he got the job."

"So we're back to the psychiatric unit again?"

"They use the insane or they send them insane. And the dead. They don't let go of the dead, as you've seen."

"I think this whole area was once magical, as in white magic hundreds if not thousands of years ago…" She put her fingers to her temples. "I said some kind of trick or foul play, didn't I? I can see now…a circle of stones, and a well…something taken…Oh, I don't know. I'm too tired to think."

"Molly knew," said Billy, wandering over to the window again.

Molly's spirit was on the very edge of her awareness.

"You are free, Molly. You've shown me what happened. The ritual was undone when we broke the seal. You're free and there is nothing to fear." The woman's presence was now faint, and it occurred to Beth she was desperate to depart. Yet still she lingered.

"She knew something about the bigger picture, the root of all this, didn't she?"

Billy nodded.

"Maybe that's why she was drinking – to make herself look harmless? She knew they wouldn't let her go, even in death."

"Just like Curbeck."

She nodded. "They got her in the end, though. The ritual was meant to bind her here."

The atmosphere in the room was now fresh and although cold, it just felt like an empty house would normally feel if it was unheated and unloved.

"Did you hear that, Molly?" Beth said. "They meant to bind your soul, but you're absolutely free. All you need to do is understand that!" She waited for a flash, like that of a photo booth, to signal Molly had gone to the light, but it didn't happen. Instead, the essence of pear drops drifted on the air.

"She has more to tell us," said Billy.

Beth cast him a sidelong glance. *Why pear drops?*

"Okay, well I can't think anymore. Got to go or I'll pass out. Come on, let's wrap up and then put Joe out of his misery."

Each room throughout the house had to be anointed with holy oil and fire, and healing vibrations sent with thanks, praise and prayer. The last job was to scoop the broken obsidian into a tin, along with that of the back of the mirror, sweep away the salt and collect the seals of Soloman.

Joe was sitting in his car, cold as stone, when she tapped on the window half an hour later.

She handed back the key. "Hi! Well, whoever moves in now will be able to put their own stamp on the place."

"I need to tell you–"

"There was a pressure cooker of bad energy underneath those houses, like a vortex. But we've managed to shift it. It's gone."

"Beth, I have to–"

"I think the abattoir was built on top of an ancient sacred site. This is a place of immense telluric energy. In fact, the whole area is on a ley line axis, a real power point. And I think it was once all woodland. There was a ring of stones in a copse, used for the good, to connect to the Divine. There might have been a church built on top of it, over a well or water, I'm not sure. But it was defiled. And something was moved, stolen…I'm not clear–"

"Jump in, love. You must be freezing."

"No, you're all right. I need to be outside for a bit. Anyway, I'll just explain quickly - this area is a convergence of ley lines, so you have a major one running west to east, but the town itself is a natural energy grid, a network. And there's possibly a system of tunnels underneath that connects certain places. I'm drawn to the old hospital, or it could be under whatever you said that house was next to the nursing home–"

"Energy grid?"

"You know, ley lines? The aborigines had a word - spirit trails. People could feel the pulsing earth energy through bare feet and it led them to sacred places like forest glades or wells. So that's where your major castles, cathedrals or lodges would be now. On those."

"Okay."

"So you have the old hospital at the southerly point, this is west, and that house at the opposite end of town is at the northerly point, forming a triangle? So anyway, sorry, I know you told me the name of it, but what's that last one called next to the Nursing Home. The name instantly went out of my head the other night. We were standing in that upstairs room–"

His eyes were bloodshot. "What? Slow down, you talk at the bloody speed of light, Woman. Do you mean The Gatehouse? It's empty. Boarded up, front door blocked with stone. Apparently, it belongs to a holding company once used for storing art collections. Probably why it's still got a barbed wire fence and CCTV. Expensive stuff."

"Really?"

"Listen, I've got to tell you something important and I need the heater on even if you don't." He started up the engine. "Do you want a lift back?"

She shook her head. "No, I need the walk." She looked down the street. One or two lamps were on in people's front rooms and the chimneypots were clearly silhouetted against a starlit sky. "Nice and clear here now. I really wasn't sure we were going to be able to do that in one session, although to be honest it's only a small part of the prob–"

Joe poked his head out of the window. "I said I had to tell you something," he hissed. "I don't want to speak any louder but I can't get a bloody word in."

"What?"

"We had a visitor while you were in there. He saw me but not before I copped a look at him. Anyway, long dark coat and black fedora."

"Man in black? Oh, I think I–"

"No face."

"What?"

"No frickin' face. I kid you not. What should have been a face was flour-white and totally blank. No features. I blinked and looked again. But he'd gone. I thought it might have been a dream, like a waking nightmare but–"

"It wasn't," said Beth.

***

CHAPTER TWENTY-FIVE

Who was the man in the black fedora? It felt as if time was running out, but what lead did she follow next? The Gatehouse was boarded up and Joe had no access to the psychiatric unit.

Gran Grace's voice tugged at her inside, "Don't overthink it, Beth."

And then there was the not insignificant problem of being a chef no longer able to cook meat. Over the last few days she'd managed to fend Gareth off by forgetting this week's meat order, and accidentally spoiling what was left in the freezer. But the situation couldn't last forever.

I won't be here much longer!

"You will remember next week though, won't you?" Gareth was saying. "Only people do like a nice fillet steak. Me, I like mine rare. Just show it the pan and smack its arse. That'll do me. Preferably still pumping blood – nice bit of sauce to dip your chips in."

She kept her back to him, busying about the kitchen. "Don't worry, yes. Anyway, there's a great fish menu." At least she could still cook fish.

On the work unit, however, a row of mackerel was

lined up. She eyed them now as they eyed her. Each mouth gaped with a hook puncturing the fine silvery skin… And suddenly a needle pierced her own lower lip. There was a pop as it emerged through the other side… Pain shot through a nerve…and then came the rush of a salty wave, a catapult into the air, the futility of a furious, desperate fight, of flailing inside a net…no way out…

"You all right?"

Gareth was once again looking at her as if she'd had a frontal lobotomy.

"What? Yes, sorry."

At a guess there was another week at best before she'd have to 'fess up, because there was quite simply no way on God's earth she could do this anymore. Where once it had been simply 'meat', now, in the blink of an eye, it was a living creature, a murder as raw as if she had been the one to commit it.

After Gareth returned to the bar, once again shaking his head, forced to deal with a lunatic, she stood at the sink. Clouds breezed across the window and an odd lurch inside her stomach caught her off guard. Nothing felt stable, tethered. The world was shifting.

"You've gone up a notch," said Billy, standing beside her. "And you met Max in the library the other night, do you remember?"

Max? She shook her head. That was the thing. Although she was recalling more and more of her time spent on the astral, much of it remained a mystery - most especially the astral library. Usually the visits there happened after a soul family meeting in the forest, and sometimes the information replayed later. Mostly though, she simply could not remember. Which was frustrating because the astral library was where all answers to all questions was kept."

"Don't you remember the talk we had on the beach after you left Curbeck? You asked me who he was when he appeared underneath the hall. And he was with us at Mailing Street, too."

"Ah! The glittering one? And that's his name? Wow! But he's not a spirit guide, is he? So what is he? I mean, how does he do what he does?"

"He's here for you, to protect you. And no, he's not like us. I can't tell you anymore and there won't be any verbal interaction with him. But he will be there when we need him, and he can do what we can't."

She nodded, knowing better than to question further. There were a million mysteries, and what was needed would be conveyed at the right time in the right way. "Why do I feel so odd, so disconnected?" She held onto her stomach. "You know how on a fairground ride where your stomach gets left behind for a second? It's like that. All the time. My insides keep lurching."

Billy sighed.

"Oh sorry, you've never been on one, have you?"

"No."

"I remember at Scarborough, you loved looking round the fairground. Sorry, I keep forgetting. Anyway, why do I feel like I jumped without a parachute…?" She grimaced. "Oops, you didn't have parachutes, either…"

Billy laughed. "And you haven't galloped bareback or taken out prey with a single arrow. Clean, no trauma, no suffering."

"True. It's just that we're like brother and sister and

it's easy to forget we're in totally different time zones."

"Answer is you're evolving. Faster vibrations, that's why."

"I thought it was panic. I mean, getting back to the job in hand - where do I go from here? I can't see what to do next. I'm worried about Jeannie and I can't be a chef much longer. I've hardly any money left, the car's going to cost an arm and a leg and I don't know how to–"

"Trust God. You know you're guided."

"Yes, I know. Sorry. It's just that it's hard."

Billy nodded. "Try not to overthink. Use your heart instead. Follow the energies and pay attention to your dreams. You were thinking about the man in the black fedora before Gareth came in."

Slumping down at the kitchen table, she put her hands over her eyes and tuned into her higher self.

Show me…

Following the exorcism on Mailing Street, her entire body had ached and needed healing. But after the walk home and a soak in the bath, the minute her head hit the pillow she was pulled onto the astral.

There'd been a sense of floating in a room where a familiar photograph was propped up on a bookcase. Why familiar? Old-fashioned, taken decades ago, it was of a couple in a white Morgan motorcar - the driver in a smart suit, his young passenger clutching her hat. The room was full of books, a pair of spectacles on the arm of a chair…and a sweet smell…pear drops…

Molly had conveyed pear drops, too. Why?

She shook her head. Another viewing was coming back to her. She'd been gazing through a window, looking down on a man in a long black coat and hat. A solitary figure, he was walking slowly and methodically around the corner of a building. The house, too, was familiar. Where was it? She held the moment in her mind's eye, focusing on detail. Ahead was a view of the hills, and behind her, in the centre of the room, was a discarded wheelchair. This was the nursing home? So the man was walking around the back of the house Joe had said was boarded up. The Gatehouse?

The knowledge thudded into her heart. And with it came a low hum.

Billy had been with her as they perused the outside of the house seeking a way in. Just as Joe had said, it was physically impossible to enter. And it was also impossible on the astral. No remote viewings, then? The feeling had been queasy and off-kilter, and every time she drew near the humming had grown louder. She was as powerfully repelled as having walked into a brick wall.

The viewings had ended with the blinding whiteness of the astral library, and the many questions she knew she'd asked, but alas, could not remember.

Sighing, she opened her eyes. "I don't know why I feel uneasy. It's just, I don't know…I can't see ahead…"

"Keep the faith. Remember your faith," came Gran's voice. "And pay attention. We've told you things will escalate, so be ready."

After a glass of water, she began the mundane but comforting task of cutting vegetables and washing salad leaves.

"Jeannie's worrying me. She's been avoiding me for a week. I know I'm missing something." After a quick glance at the doorway to check Gareth wasn't listening, she added, "And I've got this feeling about Estelle. I mean, I know I was drawn to her. I actually chose her…Ooh!" She stopped chopping. "Something just flashed into my head."

"Gran's gone to pay her a visit."

"So there is something wrong with Estelle? Oh my God."

"She's been every day," said Billy.

"Who? Gran?"

"No, Jeannie."

"Jeannie's been to see Estelle every day? Why didn't you tell me? I thought her appointments were once a week? So how can she afford that?"

"Who are you talking to?" said Gareth.

She swung round. "Oh!" A flush swept up her neck into her cheeks. "Sorry, I nearly jumped out of my skin. Didn't see you there."

He continued staring at her.

"I was muttering away to myself, sorry. You know how it is? Imaginary confrontations!" She laughed.

"Right."

"It's the girl who rents out the other room in the house. I'm a bit worried about her, so I was kind of you, know, role-playing? Wondering how to broach a few subjects?"

"Oh aye?"

"I haven't seen her in a few days."

"I get you."

He was loitering again and she bristled. "So then, how is everyone after what happened to Molly? It looks like things are getting back to normal. They're not all walking around looking shell-shocked, anyway."

"Yeah, we're all getting there. There'll be an inquest but life has to go on, doesn't it? And I see the immigrants have moved in already." He shook his head.

"Life does have to go on, yes."

"She was an odd case, our Molly. Married one of the lads from 'Silverdown.' Carl died soon after, which was very sudden, very sad. He was only in his twenties when a truck hit him. They'd just got the place on Mailing Street, as well. She was devastated and never recovered. That's how it happens." He shook his head. "Poor old lass."

A black cloud passed over her mind.

Molly knew something…

"You all right? You've gone a bit blank."

"What? Yes, sorry."

He gave her a sidelong glance as he prepared to move off. "Anyway, two cod and chips needed. With peas." He rammed the order note onto a spike. "When you're ready."

At quarter to four the kitchen was washed down. She untied her apron, made a cup of coffee and jotted down a few notes. 'Molly and Carl. Silverdown? Moorlands Road, Morgan car, Estelle Vickers, pear drops, The Gatehouse, Freemans psyche unit, tunnels…'

With a heavy sigh, she looked across the table at Billy. "Not making sense."

"We need to talk to Jeannie."

"My brain hurts and I'm tired." She picked up her mobile and sent a text. "Are you ok? Can we talk? B x"

After ten minutes with no reply she switched it off

and packed up for home, grabbing her coat and shouting to Gareth she was off.

It was a brisk walk and once again the house was empty. While she made tea and washed up, thoughts turned over about the last few months and what now seemed like a bizarre and frantic escape from Curbeck. It was nothing short of miraculous that Jeannie had managed to elude the mind control that had captured the others. She thought back to their conversation.

"I spent a lot of time daydreaming, I suppose," Jeannie had said.

"So you just didn't listen to the teacher?"

"I think they wrote me off as backward, so maybe I slipped under the radar, too stupid to be a threat?"

While Jeannie was talking, a spirit lady with white bubble curls had settled behind her, nodding.

"Or your intuition was strong?"

Jeannie shrugged. "I never thought about it except to keep out of the way. Keep my head down. Anyone who answered back got a right hard time. Anyway, soon as you turned up I knew I had to grab the chance. Don't ask me how. Looking back, all I remember is how dark it used to be. All through summer and even with the lights on, it was permanently gloomy in those cottages. It's odd really, like the whole thing was just a strange, bad dream."

Standing now in the empty kitchen, silence sang in Beth's ears. Was Estelle giving Jeannie the help she needed? The clock showed ten o'clock. She really ought to be home by now.

She wandered into the front room and peered through the blinds. The street outside was deserted, the pavement shiny dark with rain. It slanted sideways in front of the streetlights. Which was when she saw him. Standing directly opposite the house. A man in a long black coat and fedora. With a shock-white featureless face.

She blinked. Looked again. He was still there.

Who are you?

***

CHAPTER TWENTY-SIX

Half an hour later Jeannie still wasn't home.

What to do? With no answer to her calls, Beth left another voice message and another text. She'd definitely been back here each day because there'd been the customary mountain of dirty dishes in the sink. Not exactly a missing person. What then, was she doing?

I need to go see…

After a soak in the bath, Beth slipped into meditation, and as soon as she closed her eyes a soft mist caressed her face and the solid weight of Yukon settled onto the bed. Within seconds she was looking down at May Morris in the nursing home.

The old lady's breathing was unnaturally laboured to the point of Cheyne Stokes. Alarming to the observer, every time it seemed she would not draw another breath, minutes later her flaccid, frail body arched with a desperate gasp for air before slumping back onto the mattress like a rag doll. The sound of a film peppered with shouts, screams and gunshots, permeated the still night air from a nearby television, the bedroom door slightly ajar to a fully lit hallway. The curtains had been left half drawn, the room eerily bathed in moonlight. And in the centre a wheelchair had been left with a soiled towel on it, the smell of urine lingering.

May's arms, withered and bruised, were exposed on top of the sheets.

She's so cold.

A brief glimpse into May's past came then: her head bent over a typewriter in a college or university, the window arched and lead-paned. A middle-aged man was standing over her, the sinews of his face tight, eyeballs bulbous beneath wiry brows. He was holding a sheath of papers, shaking them at her. And the young May Morris was cowering, cringing, murmuring words of appeasement. Beth didn't need to be told – every fibre of May's being was willing the man far, far away.

May's fingers began to grasp and clutch at thin air, and a whimper escaped her lips.

"Shh…" Beth whispered softly to her in her dreams. "It's all in the past, all over…"

The vision fast-forwarded. Only this time Beth was not a third party observer but seeing through May's eyes. Instantly there was a feeling of déjà-vu. The scene was from here in this room. She was peering through a gap in the curtains, looking down at a man in a long, black coat and hat walking around to the back of the house next door. May was stock-still, holding her breath…

The man had paused, his body stiffened.

May stepped back.

As slowly, oh so slowly, his neck began to creak around on its stem.

Then suddenly, in the slam of a heartbeat, the entire

scene blanked. Not only was the astral visit curtailed without warning, but Beth was repelled as violently if she'd been physically thrown out of a nightclub.

Stunned, she found herself staring close range at the front door. Well, that was a shock! Yes, she'd been blocked from remote viewing before and had to dart from a chase, especially when in military situations, but never had she been ejected backwards through the ether.

"I did it," said Gran Grace. "It's too dangerous and we need to talk, Beth."

She looked around. Mist hovered over the lawns, the area deserted - no cars trundling past, and no streetlights were on.

And when she turned around again, the door was not as it had been a moment ago. Although, it was the same generously proportioned, stone porch with a stained glass window set into the door, the gold-embossed sign, 'Moorlands Nursing Home' had vanished. Now the door was ruby red, and etched into the stonework on the arch above was a caduceus. Standing as proudly as a coat of arms, it was a beautifully crafted piece of painted masonry: a downwards-plunging silver sword with a small pinecone atop the handle, from out of which spread enormous eagle wings. Two silver snakes coiled around the gleaming blade, each possessed of a flicking viper tongue, golden eyes fixed on whoever stood below.

For a while she inspected the symbol in all its intricate detail, wondering why the sight of it should cause such deep unease. Behind her, a phantasmagoria of sea mist coated a garden laid to lawn, the drive bordered with rhododendrons. The scene was as dormant as a snowy, winters night, the rush of the distant ocean tide muffled, hypnotic, as gradually her attention switched to the house at the far end. The one standing in darkness.

Intrigued, she took a closer look.

The Gatehouse stood brooding behind wrought iron gates that were chained and padlocked. The front door, as Joe said, had indeed been filled in with stone, and the windows boarded. And just like before, as soon as she drew close the humming started, clouding the senses and confusing thought.

What was inside? Was it deserted? If so, then who was the man in black and how did he get in?

The place was secured with wire netting, and a barrier of holly and spiky pyracantha added an inside layer to the surrounding laurels and conifers. To the rear, adjacent to a steep slope leading to fields and moorland, was a wall at least fifteen feet high. All of that made it off-putting for casual trespassers, but even a professional could not gain access to a property blocked up with stone. She had a good look around the periphery. Nope, there was absolutely no access to that building.

The longer she lingered, however, the louder the hum, and every time she moved closer the static increased. Again she tried to push through the energy wall and again was rebuffed.

There had to be a way…

"You will not gain entrance," said a cut glass voice behind. "You will never get in."

Billy's light wrapped around her own.

"You won't win, either."

She did not turn around. "What's your name?"

"You should leave."

"I'm not leaving here until God says I leave, not you."

"I don't mean the town. I mean the earth. We have orders to escort you off."

***

CHAPTER TWENTY-SEVEN

In the drowsy state between lucid dreaming and wakefulness, the photograph of the white Morgan toyed with her mind. Framed in silver on a floor-to-ceiling bookcase stacked with files, yes mostly files, it belonged to a woman sitting nearby…spectacles on the arm of a sofa…the smell of pear drops…Estelle! It was Estelle…but how did Molly connect to Estelle Vickers?

Beth turned over, mumbling to herself, drifting back into sleep.

"Beth?"

Her heart jolted at the sound of her name.

Jeannie was sitting on the side of the bed holding a mug of tea. "You were calling out. You must have been dreaming."

"Was I?"

"Yes. Anyway, it's gone nine so I brought you some tea before I go."

"What?"

"Sorry, you're not with it yet, are you? I said it's gone nine. Anyway, I'm off now–"

Beth struggled to sit up. "Gone nine? Aren't you either too late or too early? I mean, your shift–?"

"No work today. I'm going to Estelle's."

She took the tea. "Thanks for this. Actually, I waited up for you last night. I must have nodded off. I was getting worried - haven't seen you since last week when she dropped you off. Are you getting the bus to Fleet?"

"No, I go up to her house on Moorlands Road. Her office is in Fleet, but she knows it's a long trip for me so I see her here now. I take the first or last appointment each day."

"Each day?"

Jeannie chewed at her fingernails. "Yeah, Estelle recommended several intense sessions. So basically I've done a lot of talking, and um...yeah...it's all on tape. It's good. I feel better."

"Wow."

"I don't remember a thing afterwards, but like I say it's all on tape so we can discuss it later."

"I see. Well, that sounds encouraging."

Jeannie smiled. Behind her, sitting on the window sill, was the old lady with white curls who had appeared before. She was shaking her head.

Beth motioned to her. "Would you like to step forwards this time?"

The old lady nodded.

"What is your name?"

Jeannie looked over her shoulder. "Who are you talking to? Is she there again? I keep feeling a cold draft on my face. I'm not sure I'm ready for this...I mean I feel a bit..."

The answer came in a whisper, high pitched as if from a long, long way. "Elise."

Jeannie stopped mid-sentence and her face drained

of colour.

"Did you hear that?" Beth asked.

"I just got shivers on my back. I'm scared, Beth."

"No need. She will never ever frighten you, but she does need to connect." She looked past Jeannie. "Hello, Elise."

Jeannie swung around to face the wall behind her. "Elise? Elise Lockwood?"

Beth tried to tune in but could not make out the words. "Slow down. Elise, can you help us with information about Estelle?"

Jeannie swung back. "Oh no, I don't like this."

"It's all right, she won't hurt you–"

"You're making it up. I must've told you once about my past. There's no one there. You can't use this to say stuff about Estelle."

"What? Wow! No, I–"

"She's the most wonderful friend I ever had and she hasn't charged me a bean since the first session. As soon as I told her my circumstances she waved all charges, and sometimes the sessions are three hours long."

"I didn't realise."

"All she wants to do is help me. Apparently, I sometimes lie there without saying anything for an hour or more. I just lose time but she doesn't mind." Her eyes filled with tears. "Beth, you've got to believe me - she's lovely. She came from a children's home where they were abused and it's her life's mission to help others. She said the money didn't matter a jot and not to worry about it, that some things are more important."

"That's good, it really is. I'm sorry." She bit her lip.

Elise was fading now but she'd been shaking her head, lips pursed like a despairing mother. Despite Jeannie's convictions, the feeling persisted that something wasn't quite right. And yet she had chosen this therapist herself.

Jeannie stood up. "No sweat. Right, well I'd best get going. We did the last recording session late last night, so today's the day we start a course of treatment. This is honestly the best thing that's ever happened to me."

"Jeannie, I didn't mean to cast aspersions. It's just that your spirit guide clearly wanted to speak to you and—"

"Elise was my great-grandma. I probably told you about her? She was the one who made up stories about mice families living in the daisy fields. She had a thing about them. She was a seamstress and made all the staff uniforms and children's clothing. I think they left her alone a lot to work in the laundry, so she probably made these stories up to keep us kids amused."

Or to give you a fantasy escape route, an alternative world.

"Anyway, there's no need to worry. Estelle's amazing. She's honestly the best thing that's ever happened to me."

A tiny part of her died inside, but Beth smiled back encouragingly. Maybe her misgivings were wrong?

And Elise? Was she wrong, too?

"That's great then. Sorry."

"It's okay. Anyway, one thing I should forewarn you about is the possibility I could be admitted to the psychiatric unit for a few days. She wants to run a few tests to rule out other causes for my symptoms before starting therapy. She does everything by the book, no stone unturned."

Beth shook her head. "Symptoms?"

"Well, apart from imagining things that aren't there like being followed by shadows, there are things I've said under hypnosis that couldn't possibly have happened." Jeannie looked at a point over the top of Beth's head as she spoke. "She said I was talking about reptilian shapes looming over people, so obviously that's bonkers. Anyway, it could be schizophrenia. Even a brain tumour. I mean, this isn't to frighten either of us, but these things have to be ruled out, don't they?"

"She told you that?"

Every hair on Beth's body seemed to lift from its follicle, and a rash of gooseflesh spread up her spine, crawling up to the scalp. She could see it - Lord Freeman's Mental Health Unit at the back of the old hospital. Didn't Joe say one of the teenagers who'd killed Molly had spent time there? Three years? That she and her friend were there now? Fleetingly, the image of the yellow-eyed girl astride her victim flashed before her. And wasn't Crispin Freeman the associate psychiatrist? Joe has said something about that, too….

She stared back at Jeannie, not knowing quite what to say.

"I've known you for over four months and you've never once showed any signs of needing to be hospitalised–"

Jeannie stood up. "Well you're not a doctor, are you? Or a therapist."

"No, but I thought you were adamant you'd never go into a psychiatric hospital after what happened to your sister and–"

"That's at Curbeck not here in Crewby. This is a civilised town. And it's only to run some tests, there's a world of difference. You know, Estelle said I shouldn't talk about it and I can see now she was right. I was really happy about the way things were going, and that I'd found someone I could trust who could help me. Anyway–"

"Jeannie, don't be upset with me. It's just that you were coming along great guns. You got a job and made this place, such as it is, a home, and–"

"I was terrified out of my wits, Beth. All the frickin' time. There were shadows following me home and I felt watched. It's only now I can see how ill I was. One night this bloke stepped out in front of me just as I left the nursing home. It was on the drive, about half way down where it's dark. He was the one I told you I'd seen before, the one in the black coat and fedora type hat. But this is the thing, right? He had no face! No features and no face. I screamed and ran home as fast as I could. That's illness, Beth. Something like that cannot exist so how could it be anything other than what Estelle said – schizophrenia? And not only that, but the nightmares of being in the turret or stuck in the tunnels never stop. I live and re-live them constantly. I could not sleep. You said yourself – sort fact from fiction? So that's what we're doing."

"But you aren't delusional. I've seen the man in black, too. And so has Joe! All I wanted to do, the aim of asking you to consider therapy, was to help you cope with ancestral trauma and a very scary, highly unnatural childhood. I mean, do you really think you should be admitted into–?"

Jeannie was shaking her head. "Got to go, I'm late. Anyway, don't worry about it. And don't worry about Estelle, either. She really is the most lovely person imaginable. And she's well respected, got loads of clients. I'm lucky to have had so much time and attention."

"Sure. Okay, I'm probably worrying over nothing."

I found Estelle… I was drawn to her…

"But Jeannie, please don't allow yourself to go into a psychiatric unit. You're fine. You're well. It's just a case of–"

"I'll do what the professional thinks is best. Actually, if you gave her half a chance I think you'd like her. You could benefit, too. She said she'd love to meet you."

"You told her about me?"

"Yes, I've told her every last thing. How we came to meet, how we escaped from Curbeck, and that you can see ghosts. I've told her everything. It would be great for you to meet."

After the front door had slammed shut, Beth pushed back the covers and went to the window, watching Jeannie's back until she disappeared into the genal.

"It's called free will," said Billy.

"I know. And after all we achieved in getting her away from Curbeck. I really wish I'd never pushed the idea of therapy. I don't know, maybe it will be all right and Estelle really is being kind?"

The scent of pear drops wafted on the air.

"Estelle's recorded all the information," said Billy. "Including your alias names."

"Yeah, that is a worry. Although, logically why

should it be if she's a private therapist and keeps everything confidential?"

Doubts churned inside. No way did Jeannie need admitting. A scan could be done with an out-patient appointment.

"No, I don't like it. But she was hell-bent and bloody determined to do whatever Estelle said."

Her gaze moved to the windswept moors, blurry with the fog of a wintry morning. "I feel I've let her down so badly. I was the one who sent her to this woman."

"It was meant to be. You'll see. Sometimes we have to bait the fish or they don't pop their heads above water. Estelle is showing herself. They all are. Trust us."

Beth's spirits plunged into her boots.

"How does Jeannie going into a mental health unit help with anything, though?"

The weight of darkness hung over her, along with the taunting whispers of the enemy. *You're stupid, useless, why don't you kill yourself, she hates you, they all hate you, your family hate you...they hated you in London...You don't know anything...penniless loser...pathetic...*

Instantly she snapped out of the trance and spoke out loud. "Christ is my shield. God is my armour. I am God's child. And you are not welcome."

Sometimes it was easy to forget the golden rule of not getting enmeshed. An eagle, Gran told her many times, did not fight the snake in its pit. Instead it snatched it from the ground and swooped high, letting the serpent flail around in mid-air.

"Circle high," came Gran's voice. "See the aerial

view. Bigger picture. And don't let it out of your sight."

She nodded as one of Gran's favourite pick-me-up tunes now played in her head. 'Let's go fly a kite, up to the highest height…'

"Thanks, Gran!"

Something huge was circling, closing in as stealthily and silently as a prowling panther. It was time to get a lot smarter. Full armour on.

"I'm going to ring Joe," she said. "At least to cross-link all the information we've got so far, because if anything happens to Jeannie I'll never forgive myself."

"Or you. If anything happens to you."

She stared back at Billy. "Estelle works with Crispin Freeman. Lord Freeman is bound to be connected to Countess Mantel. How the hell has this happened?"

They stood looking across the roofs of terraces. A bank of cloud was chasing shadows down from the moors, sweeping them over the town in a cloak of darkness. And as the light plunged to gloom she saw it. High above the moors, circling, squealing…a single sparrow hawk.

She's here…she's here…

***

CHAPTER TWENTY-EIGHT

It was only after Jeannie had gone that Beth remembered the car.

"Crap! It's been at the garage for a week. I completely forgot."

Reaching for her mobile she stared in dismay. No battery. Damn. In that case, she'd walk down and hope for the best. The plan beginning to form was to drive up to Moorlands Road before work. Which house was Estelle's? And then what? Knock on the door? Come up with some emergency to get Jeannie out of there? Her stomach tied itself into a fast knot at the thought of her friend willingly being admitted to Freeman's psychiatric unit. Incredibly, in Jeannie's mind it was reasonable.

Think, Beth! Think!

Estelle had grown up in a children's home. And Gareth said Molly had, too. Same one?

Silverdown!

Something clicked into place. The name on the ruby red door with the caduceus above hadn't said, 'Moorlands Nursing Home' anymore. Had the plaque said, 'Silverdown'? She shook her head. Couldn't be sure. And the couple in the photograph of the Morgan -

were they connected to the children's home in some way, too? Who owned that house now?

She plugged in the phone, showered and made coffee. Without doubt all roads led to Lord Freeman. The links were there, albeit as hidden as a cobweb in a glory hole. And Lord Freeman's international dealings in fine art, was possibly not fine art at all. She kept coming back to the crates and the children in cages underground…the foreign port…the people on boats…And Scarsdale Hall. But every time she attempted to fit the pieces together, a mind-numbing hum filled her head, blocking all further thought.

Half way through combing her wet hair, she paused and turned to look at Billy, who was standing in the doorway. "Why do I keep seeing Estelle's face as she drove past me last week? It was after she'd dropped Jeannie off, and I remember her staring straight ahead like a mannequin or a Stepford Wife or something. I know I'd have noticed a woman waving to Jeannie, but she didn't. She just shot past looking neither left nor right. And then there was Molly out of her head with drink. Both were brought up in the same place."

He nodded.

"Well, what if the couple in the photograph of the Morgan was Lord Freeman and his wife? And the children from the home grew up to find doors opening for them in key positions? You know, rewarded if they do what they're told with regard to his international business, or maybe threatened with some kind of exposure or…" The dull thud of understanding plunged into the depths of her soul. "Or they tried to break away like Carl and Molly?"

He was only in his twenties when a truck hit him. They'd just got the place on Mailing Street…

"Sleeper cells," said Billy.

She picked up the hairdryer. "The scale of this is really beginning to hit home. I'm beginning to see what happened at Curbeck happening everywhere. So could key positions include therapists?"

"Particularly therapists."

"Social services, police, psychiatrists, nurses…all the people an abused child needs to talk to and have on their side?"

"Media, charities, church, teachers…"

"I keep thinking how bad things, absolutely diabolical things, get to happen. Because someone has to do the kidnapping, unload the crates, ignore complaints, get rid of witnesses, fail to report…"

She put down the hairdryer and covered her face with her hands. The enormity of it all came rushing towards her in a tidal wave. How widespread was this? Images flashed of the people in boats on the high seas, the heat haze of a foreign port, the hollow eyes of those locked in underground cages, the women staring straight ahead in single file at Curbeck…Just as Estelle had done…

Do what you're told and you get to live?

So what happened to those who stumbled on the truth? What could they do when it all sounded so insane - too evil to be believed? Who would listen to someone like herself? All she had were visions and an undocumented and totally unsubstantiated recent history at Scarsdale Hall. No proof of anything. And now Jeannie was willingly being admitted to Freeman's

Mental Health Unit. What happened to the kids in there? Did they have parents? And when they grew up, what professions did they enter? Did potentially incriminating information hold them in check? How easy would it be to smear and dispose of those diagnosed with psychosis, especially if they'd been deemed violent, should they ever blow the whistle?

Jeannie.

Check mate.

Fuck!

How many mind-controlled individuals do people like Allegra Mantel and Lord Freeman employ?

Still processing rapid fire thoughts, Beth finished drying her hair, dressed, and added pendants of shungite and obsidian. After putting on some make-up she finally felt ready to face the world, despite a mind in turmoil. So many questions and so few answers. Yet it felt as if one answer would suffice. As if the answer, in fact, was very simple even though it currently remained elusive.

"One thing at a time," came Gran Grace's voice inside her head. "Don't rush at it, child. You cannot do it all. You cannot save the whole world."

She nodded. Okay, so first things first - why would Estelle Vickers choose to live on the same road as the children's home she'd grown up in? And surely therapists didn't make enough money to afford one of those enormous mansions on Moorlands Road? Especially in addition to a private practice in Fleet.

She didn't charge me a bean....

Grabbing her winter coat, Beth shot a glance at Billy sitting on the stairs playing with Spot, the ghost cat. "She was put there, that's why. But tell me why I picked

225

her out and recommended her? I know you said she was a fish popping up but I don't like this. I don't like it one bit. I feel really guilty - more than guilty - scared for Jeannie."

Billy nodded. "There's a reason."

"Yeah, but…"

She hurried down Portland Street towards the dual carriageway and the garage, wishing now it wasn't so far. Time was knocking on and a fine drizzle was setting in. Fragmented thoughts darted in and out of her head as she walked. May Morris was going to die. Prematurely. And Joe's boss, what was her name? Carrie Gordon, yes, she was niggling away at her, too. And those girls who had murdered Molly…and…

The sight of her car parked on the garage forecourt wiped all further speculation clean away, and she hurried across the road.

This time a blond woman sat behind the desk. She took several slurps of tea before looking up from a computer screen. "Yes?"

"Hi! I left my car here last week for a—"

"Reg. number?"

She told her.

A piece of paper was pushed over. "Four hundred and thirty-eight pounds, fifty pence."

What the fuck?

She picked up the invoice and stared at the print. Quick calculation: this meant if she gave notice at the end of the week, working a week in hand, there'd be precisely nothing left, a big fat round zero, at the end of the month.

And yet they must leave here. Soon.

Jeannie had gone and told Estelle bloody everything. Not only about herself but Beth, too! All sense of self-preservation had gone out of the proverbial window, hurtling them both towards a dangerous place. Yet this was every bit as much her fault as Jeannie's.

A reason, eh? Well, for the life of me I can't fucking well see one!

Everything was a blur. Her hands were shaking. Gareth had paid cash each week as agreed, and she'd managed to save just enough to pay this bill, although it was supposed to have been for emergency use. For the passage out of here when the time came...

The blond woman eyed her steadily. "Is it cash or card?"

"What? Oh erm, cheque."

"I'll just see if that's all right with Ron." She stabbed at the intercom. "You'll have to put the address on the back."

It was only after she'd written out the cheque, while the woman took dozens of little slurps of tea, that the truly perilous nature of the situation hit her. That was the thing with a psychic attack: it crept up unseen, came on many levels, and from all angles. No one else knew it existed and there would be not a shred of evidence. Thus, with only her intuition for guidance, the conviction that Allegra Mantel was about to close in grew stronger by the minute.

Joe! She had to tell Joe Sully about Jeannie; that she would not have wanted to be admitted to a psychiatric hospital and it was totally out of character.

Why have I got this feeling if she goes in there she'll never come out?

Dashing out to the car, Beth whipped off the plastic sheeting from the seats and jumped in. She had to find Estelle's house. Somehow persuade Jeannie not to do this. Pressing Joe's number on speed dial, she left the phone on loud speaker while reversing out of the parking bay.

The rain had intensified and a solid bank of battleship grey loomed over the town. Glancing up in the direction of Moorlands Road, Beth wondered which one of those dozen or so stone mansions would be Estelle's. Maybe there would be a plaque? A ruby red door came to mind but she pushed it away.

Silverdown!

The phone rang and rang.

"Come on Joe, answer!"

She pictured Jeannie discussing the recordings, nodding in agreement, and was just nosing the car onto the main road when he finally picked up.

"Hello?"

She looked right. Two clear lanes. Not a car in sight. And pulled out.

"Joe, hi! Sorry to bother–"

It was the last thing she said before a black SUV shot out of nowhere. With a gasp of shock she winged the steering wheel around, crashed up the kerb, through a fence and smashed sideways into a wall.

The world blanked out.

***

CHAPTER TWENTY-NINE

When Beth opened her eyes it was to find a crowd of people around her bed, a throng elbowing each other aside for a closer look. She shut them again. The ceiling was spinning and the bed was floating. A swell of sick rose in her throat and she swallowed it down.

Where was this?

A vague recollection of being wheeled along a dimly lit corridor breezed through her mind, cold air rushing into her face, the clanking of a lift gate, and flirtatious laughter... Everything afterwards drew a blank.

Hospital? Was this a hospital?

With a start she opened her eyes again. The crowd was still there. They seemed expectant, excited, as if waiting for her to wake and see them.

"Touch her...You touch her..."

A putrid stench laced the air, of septic wounds and incontinence. Long, gnarled fingers reached out and she tried to pull back but could not, noting in horror the weeping sores and nails ingrained with dirt.

They're not alive.

And not only were these people not alive but they far outnumbered those who were. A babble of voices now rose in a crescendo as if the group had burst through an invisible veil, the noise similar to sitting in a shopping mall on a Saturday afternoon – nothing coherent or distinctive – just a mass of jumbled sound. Coming closer, they began to stroke her arms and pull at her hair.

"No!"

Rank breath wafted into her face. Their flesh smelled sour, the stink of decay gag-making. She tried to call out but they had swelled in number to such an extent her voice was lost. One began to tug at the sheets.

"No!"

A strong pair of hands grabbed her ankles and yanked her down the bed.

"I said, no!"

In a sedated daze of confusion she called out for Billy, and then for Gran.

Where were they?

"No. I do not consent. I do not consent."

She squeezed her eyes shut, blocking out the images coming thick and fast as each face loomed into her third eye, determined to be seen. The bed was swirling around on a whirlpool.

Drugs...sedation? What have I had? It will wear off. Breathe...it's okay...

"Christ is my shield. God is my armour. I am God's child. I am loved. My father will protect me in the dark."

Calming down, she began the process of protection, cloaking herself, praying, until she drifted into sleep again. Time fell away.

And when she next opened her eyes, although the

long sash window on the right was still there, her bed was facing a long row of others. Maybe twenty faced another twenty. Each bed had been made up with starched sheets and every patient was female, dressed identically in a white nightgown and cap.

She sat up and looked around. This was a long way back in time. What – a hundred years? More?

Feeling scrutinised, Beth turned to face the patient on her right. And as she watched, the woman started to peel down the top sheet, holding Beth's gaze as she rolled it further and further down...*are you looking*...before stopping at what she clearly wanted Beth to see: a huge abdominal cavity. The wound was so deep that the layers of globular, yellow fat around the sides resembled a honeycomb wall, much of it necrotic, the tissue oozing with pus.

This was not real. It was history. Not happening now.

She turned to the other side. The skin covering the woman's skull was little more than a grey sheen. She stared at Beth from sockets bruised purple, her expression dull and empty. And although the sheet was fastened tightly, it came up only as far as her chest, which was covered in festering sores.

Beth's eyes widened.

The sores were full, pulsing, lifting, and popping...

Wake up Beth! Wake up!

This was not real! It had happened long ago. She struggled to sit up, to switch off the nightmare, but could do neither. All the beds, she saw now, were occupied by deathly visions of skeletal women. Ceramic pots on the floor contained the contents of brownish bodily fluids draining out through pipes, some of which had begun to overflow. And the windows were not only closed but nailed shut, the stench inside suffocating.

She looked again at the patients. Many appeared to be post-surgery, some pulling away bandages saturated with blood and secretions, poking with dirty fingers at gaping wounds. Groans mingled with opiate-induced, macabre laughter…a surround sound… as with dismay Beth realised they were getting out of bed and gravitating towards her.

She closed her eyes. "Gran! Gran!"

Someone mimicked her cry, taunting in a singsong playground voice. "Graaan…Graaaan…I'm a big baby and I need my graaaany…"

"No. I don't want to see this. I do not."

Eyes tightly shut, she began to pray once more, tapping into the highest vibrations of love and the swell of the heart she knew so well.

"Our Father, who art in heaven,

hallowed be thy name;

thy kingdom come;

thy will be done;

on earth as it is in heaven."

Perhaps she drifted in and out of sleep, she couldn't say. But when next she opened her eyes, the nightingale ward had been replaced by a modern six-bed unit. And the woman in the opposite bed had her arms folded and lips pressed together as if she'd been waiting far too long for Beth to notice her. Dressed in a floral nightdress, her ruddy-cheeked face was topped with a henna-dyed, bubble perm.

Possibly it was because the scene was more recent,

less gruesome, that Beth relaxed a little, only realising her mistake when she met the woman's eyes. Tiny, black beads pushed into the fleshy face like currants in dough, they danced with malice. Too late Beth tried to pull away, to not see, just as the woman's mouth dropped open to reveal a brown-toothed smile. She licked blood-red lips. And then out came the snipe, "Travis fucked his sister, didn't he? You didn't even know. She used to keep an eye on you in the kitchen….they were laughing at you the whole time!"

The lights began to flicker on and off and Beth called out, "Billy! Gran!"

A faint touch on the top of her head reassured her they were there. But why could she not connect? Why did she feel so sick? So dizzy and disorientated?

Slowly, slowly, the disjointed time lines flickered in and out of frequency like an old television set, until they settled into the present again, along with her thoughts. Crewby. Yes, she was here in Crewby hospital.

The memory of standing outside it resurfaced as she struggled to stay conscious. Yes, the women's unit…once the old isolation hospital for infectious diseases…must be here…There had been many contagious diseases in the past…Nothing unusual… just imprints in time…

Perhaps she fell asleep again.

Yet it was so cold.

Outside in a field. Why am I outside? Aren't I in the hospital anymore?

The air was icy, a bitter wind sweeping overhead. An ocean hissed and crashed in the distance, and closer, much closer, a roar rushed through trees. A valley? Was she lying in a valley?

Tuning in, she tried to make sense of the information.

What's that noise? What is it?

There was something that sounded like an animal splintering bones...chomping, gnawing, eating... Drifting away again, a shock of freezing air brought her round once more. This time a dog fox was barking and something was snatching at her foot. She kicked it away.

Let me sleep!

Yet it persisted. Fingers. A hand. A hand had a firm grip on her ankle, digging into the flesh, tugging and pulling. She felt herself beginning to slip, the first hand now joined by another and then another, gaining purchase on her shin and then her thigh, pulling her down, down, down...into what? Her body was sliding on mud, the descent gathering momentum. An overwhelming stink of disease and decay caught in her throat.

"Wake the fuck up, Beth!"

Billy never swore, not ever. Was it her own voice? Was she shouting at herself? Because only now did it become clear what she was sinking into.

They were dead mostly. Hundreds if not thousands of bodies in various stages of decay, lay piled on top of each other. One or two escaping moans suggested some were still alive, as with horror she realised foxes and rats were tearing at their flesh, dead or not, stripping tissue off bone, gnawing and crunching through faces, sinews and tendons.

Paralysed with horror she found herself staring at a mass grave full of entwined corpses. Frantically kicking off grasping hands, she scrabbled for the edge of the pit. The long dead were now only bones and matted hair, skull faces turned blindly upwards. Those still clinging to life were feebly trying to fend off rats that burrowed into their orifices and gnawed at their eyes. Black tar blisters gleamed in the pearl of moonlight, great buboes still pulsing and growing.

It's a plague pit...I'm in a fucking plague pit...

She grabbed at the soil, fighting to get out, even as the rumble began underneath, the ground shook and great cracks opened like jaws....

A claiming...

And when the mass grave rose in a tidal swell, she sat bolt upright and screamed at the top of her lungs.

***

CHAPTER THIRTY

"Ah, the sleeper awakes!" A nurse stood over her, filling a syringe from a vial. "Did you have a bit of a nightmare, Lily?"

Sheathed in cold sweat, Beth nodded, her heart still in near fibrillation.

"I'm just going to give you something for the pain, love."

"No!"

A frown passed over the nurse's face. "It needs to be every six to eight hours and you've gone nearly eight."

"I don't have any pain. I want to go home."

"I know you do. Everyone wants to go home, but you can't yet. We need to keep an eye on you. You've had a nasty accident. A head injury."

Beth tried her best not to look, but behind the nurse a young girl was spinning in the middle of the room - whirling around and around, the white of her hospital gown a blur, dark hair whipping around a ghostly face.

"You were complaining of pain. Don't you remember your accident?"

"Yes," she lied.

The nurse, young and fair-haired with a pleasant if

vacant expression, nodded as she tapped at air bubbles in the syringe. "This won't hurt."

"I don't want the injection, thank you. Honestly, I'm fine." She struggled to prop herself up against the pillows, but each movement was met with another surge of nausea and the bone ache of concussion.

Whipping the curtain around, the nurse began to tug down the sheet.

Beth pulled the sheet back up. "No, really. I'm serious. I don't want any more painkillers. I don't need them."

"Doctor said you're to have it."

"I don't want it. Thank you. Please." She was holding the sheet rigid like a battle shield. Suddenly aware of that, and embarrassed, she softened her stance. "Look, I know it's not your fault but I don't want any more drugs. You don't know what it does to—"

"Come on now, let's not be silly. Doctor said—"

She squinted at the nurse's badge. "What's your name?"

"Carol."

"Hi, Carol. Please listen to me. I don't want any more injections. I'm sorry but that's an end to it. They're knocking me out and I get…I mean I see…I mean they're making me feel sick. Can't you just squirt it into a plant and sign it off?"

Carol frowned.

"What is it, anyway? Can I see the vial?"

"Um…"

There was a tiny hesitation and a flush crept into Carol's pale-skinned cheeks.

It isn't an analgesic, is it?

The nurse's face swam before her and her image wobbled.

The vibrations were changing again and Beth's stomach lurched, as with no warning an odour of decay crept in and static began to crackle. Through a gap in the curtains she noticed the patient in the bed opposite. The woman wore an oxygen mask and her eyes were closed. But as soon as Beth's attention focused on her the eyes snapped open. Ulcers began to surface, rising in a pox that spread, blistered and burst, splattering blood and pus all over the woman's hands, arms and face. Her mouth then sagged and gaped, and from out of an orifice of congealing black blood, a succession of swollen clots oozed down her chin.

Beth clamped a hand over her mouth and scrabbled to get out of bed.

"I can't stay here another minute. You have no idea what it's like."

Carol caught her by the elbow. "No, you'll fall. Lily, you have to calm down. It's all right. You've had an accident and we're just keeping you in for observation."

"I'm not Lily. How long have I been here?"

She glanced at a hazy image of a clock on the far wall, and from somewhere in the distance a phone was ringing. Her head felt like a goldfish bowl swilling with water.

"Three days."

"Pardon?"

"You've had concussion."

"Three days?"

Carol nodded. "I only came on duty yesterday, but they said you'd been knocked unconscious in your car.

And that we had to keep going with your meds."

It was Beth's turn to frown. Vague memories of being helped into an ambulance now filtered in. "Come again? Keep going with my meds? What meds exactly?"

"For…" Carol lowered her voice. "You know, for your schizophrenia."

"Pardon? But I don't have schizophrenia, Carol."

A paralysing shock of fear plunged into her gut. Everything else faded out. Once, a long time ago back in her teens, she'd been hauled off to a psychiatrist because her schoolteacher had noticed her 'talking to people who weren't there.' Those weeks spent on medication had been the only time she'd been unable to connect with Billy and Gran. How long as a teen had she lain on a bed unable to move, with the strangest people appearing, stroking her hair, pushing up her dress? And the man, the older one with the grey beard stained yellow…lips as red as a campfire in the bush…had laughed when she told him. 'Now, now, don't be silly. What's all the fuss about?' And then he had tried to touch her, too. In his office with its green couch and dappled sun on the lawn outside. 'No one will believe you, so we'll not say anything, will we? You wouldn't want to never get out of here, would you? No one likes liars, Beth…'

Blinded by panic, Beth pushed back the sheets. "I have to leave. I'm sorry but you'll have to get rid of that stuff. I'm not having it."

Carol's voice tightened. "It's part of your illness to deny you're ill. You don't know you're ill."

Beth locked eyes with her. "I'm not ill and you have no right to keep me here. I'm not having medication for anything. I wasn't on anything. I can prove it and I'm leaving."

To her amazement, the nurse put the syringe down and swished the curtain back. "I'll finish the round and then I think we need to get the doctor back."

Think, Beth! Think! Why won't my brain work? Where are you, Billy? Gran?

Like a bloodless ballerina in a never-ending pirouette, the young girl in the middle of the room was still spinning. No way was she staying here and no way was she waiting to see who the doctor was.

A name flitted into her mind and then out again.

"I'm checking out."

"Let's calm down a minute," said Carol, easing her gently back against the pillows. "Why don't you lie back and relax? Supper will be here soon and then maybe after a good night's sleep you can ask about going home in the morning?"

Beth lay rigidly. Panic had seized her whole body. Almost imperceptibly she managed to nod, her eyelids like lead weights.

Mustn't fall asleep…

"Good. Okay, just take it easy and try to take nice deep breaths. I'll finish up here and then we can have a chat."

"Okay."

As soon as Carol moved onto the next patient, Beth took a better look at the spinning girl. Also watching the girl was the ghostly imprint of a nurse. She wore an ankle-length grey dress with a red cross pinned to her white apron. Her dark hair had been tied severely back beneath a fussy white hat, her face a mixture of austerity and concern.

She comes back from Spirit to help her lost patients find their way home.

As soon as Gran's voice floated into her mind, Beth's body sagged with relief. Every single muscle relaxed and her heart soared.

"Gran! Thank God!"

Carol shot a quick glance over one shoulder, staring one second too long.

Beth smiled. "I said, 'Grand!' As in grand day." She indicated the rain spattering against the window panes.

Carol raised her eyebrows, the long, "Okaaay," sounding anything but convincing.

The second she left the room, however, Beth nodded to the ghostly nurse and sent her a message telepathically. "Hello."

She nodded back, and a tinny, high voice came over the airwaves. "Can you help Tilly? Tell her to pray. She's a simple soul. They kept operating on her brain. They just kept...operating...on all of them."

Beth settled back against the pillows and opened up her heart chakra, using all her energy to send waves of love towards the spinning girl, picturing ripples of aqua water flowing through the ether. It wasn't simply the words used, which could be brief, but a vibration of pure love and whether or not that resonated with the lost soul. She could see Billy now and Gran's voice was in her head.

The occupants in the opposite beds were drowsy behind oxygen masks, and the bed next to her was empty. After a quick glance to check no one was looking, Beth whispered, "Tilly, can you hear me?"

The girl began to slow down a little, the blur of her spinning image clarifying, until eventually puzzled brown eyes met her own. "You are now in spirit, Tilly. You don't want to be here on a hospital ward surrounded by sick people anymore, do you?"

Tilly stared back.

"My name's Beth. I'm a spiritual medium and I can see you. Hello."

Next to Tilly was a pillar of light, and Beth smiled at the sight of Billy standing beside it.

"Let's pray together. Can you remember the words?"

Tilly began to blurt out the Lord's Prayer, which transmitted like a crackling radio.

The other patients thankfully remained dozing beneath the hiss of oxygen masks, and even more thankfully, they looked normal.

"Our father, who art in heaven….Our father, who art in heaven…"

As she cited the only words she could remember, Tilly floated closer to Beth's bed until she was standing directly over her, constantly repeating the first line. And as she did so Beth noticed there was something highly abnormal about her head. It looked as if a chunk of the cranium had been removed. As a result the skin had caved in, like the canvas of a tent without pegs.

Silently she prayed, as did Billy and Gran. And so did the old-fashioned nurse, who now led the child to the pillar of light. Being innocent and pure, the girl would simply return to Source, to God, and Beth smiled as the nurse looked over her shoulder and mouthed the words, "Thank you."

The love had reached her.

"Thank you, God."

Hospitals, Beth thought, were full of tortured souls. Maybe it was because people died suddenly, or were in a state of drugged confusion? Or was it because the energy was so dense, so negative, their souls could not ascend and remained trapped? No sooner had she uttered a prayer of thanks, however, than the horror of her own situation struck her anew: Carol said she was on medication for schizophrenia! But how the hell would anyone here know she had once been on that? For one thing they were calling her, Lily. And Lily did not exist on any medical records.

Beth racked her brains. Lily was supposed to have been treated as an overnight emergency. Yet it had been three days and they said she had schizophrenia. Was her real identity known and those childhood notes unearthed?

Conversations that had floated around her during the past few days, now replayed, along with an echoing voice, in the coolness of a room close to an open door…a noisy group hovering outside a flowery curtain with a gap in it …The casualty department?

'Doctor Freeman said to move her!'

Doctor Freeman?

Crispin Freeman, the surgeon who owned a nursing home and was also an associate psychiatrist? But this was not a surgical ward and it was not a psychiatric unit. So how come he was in charge of her care?

What the fuck?

Well, there wasn't a cat in hell's chance she was staying here another night. She swung her legs over the side and jumped down. Then realising the gown gaped at the back, clutched it tightly and walked barefoot over to the nurses' station. It was not conducive, she thought, to personal empowerment when forced to wear a hospital gown open at the back, a plastic wristband, and your face was a shiny, make-up free mess. Where were her clothes? And her phone, keys and bag?

I have to get out. What if I can't? What if I can't get out?

A wash of nervous sweat surfaced as she stood waiting for the nurse at the desk to look up from a computer screen.

"Excuse me."

Their eyes met.

The nurse in charge was a woman of middle-age with a severe, black-fringed bob and a gash of red across her lips. A badge on her navy tunic labelled her as, 'D. French. Senior Nurse Manager.'

Instantly Beth recoiled.

Seen her before. Where?

That there wouldn't be one iota of help from this woman, was already a given. Still, there was no way she was spending another night here, so that was that.

Beth drew herself up to full height, trying not to sway or too obviously hold onto the desk. "Hi. I'm B...I mean, Lily. I'd like to go home now, please. Can you arrange a taxi and tell me where my clothes are? I was only supposed to be in overnight but it's been three days."

The dawn frost of a chill settled between them.

"That will be for Doctor to decide." With emphasis on the word, 'Doctor,' the senior nurse manager eyeballed her with an expression devoid of emotion. "He'll be back in the morning. You'll have to wait until then."

"No, actually it's for me to decide, and I will not be here in the morning. I don't mean to be rude but–"

"But you are."

"Sorry? Look, I'm going home and I'd like my belongings, please."

"Lily, you are not fit to go home." She tapped at the computer. "You have a head injury, you've been heavily sedated, and as such it is not advisable for you to leave our care. This is for your own safety."

Beth looked around. Only one other member of staff was around and she had a drug trolley open. Carol couldn't leave that trolley without taking a minute to lock it. She hesitated. What to do? How to handle this? If she kicked up a fuss they could build on the schizophrenia diagnosis, say she was delusional, paranoid, even have her sectioned.

They know who I am…they know…but how? How the hell do they know?

She gripped the desk. "Um, actually I refused the shot seeing as I had no pain, so I'm not heavily sedated." She smiled. "Look, I know you mean well and thank you for your impeccable care, but it's been three days and I want to go home now. I'm definitely discharging myself. So, if you could retrieve my belongings?"

"I'll just call the doctor and check."

Beth raised her voice. "I do not need a doctor, thank you."

He must be busy, he can't come that quickly. She'd have to make me wait.

She drew herself up again. "And for the last time,

please get my belongings! I have told you I don't want any further treatment and I am not having any."

As the woman's fingers hovered over the phone, Beth's glance flicked to her name badge again.

French.

D. French.

Comprehension filtered in slowly through her still drug-addled mind, at the same time she noticed the little gold pin on Daphne French's lapel. A caduceus.

She raised her eyes to Daphne's.

The hum of the computer and the clatter of a supper trolley trundling from the lift encapsulated what seemed to be the longest moment in time, while images of Daphne French wearing bondage gear floated before her. Subservient was the word that came to mind, not for Daphne but for the blindfolded man she was horsewhipping – the one who was naked except for a giant nappy, whimpering on his hands and knees.

Beth grinned. "My clothes?"

"I hardly think–"

"Right, listen I've had enough now. I'm not going to ask aga–"

"Everything all right, Beth?"

She whizzed around so quickly she almost fell over.

He caught her just in time.

"Joe. Thank God."

***

CHAPTER THIRTY-ONE

"It's pure coincidence I found you," said Joe, pulling out of the hospital carpark. "Uncanny, in fact."

"I did wonder." She leaned back, concentrating on keeping her head absolutely still. Dusk merged with the glare of oncoming headlights, Joe's voice unnaturally loud as sleep dragged her down again.

"Yeah, well it was Gareth, actually–"

She jerked fully awake. "Oh, no! I've just remembered - I was on my way to work after picking up the car - no one told Gareth!" Instantly regretting the sudden movement, she swallowed down a fresh wave of nausea. "And Jeannie! Oh my God!"

On approaching the roundabout, Joe flicked on the indicator and the car lurched as he changed down a gear.

"Whoa!"

"You okay?"

She nodded. "Just. Not really. But I can't go home. I need to find Jeannie. Sorry if I sound like I'm speaking from a long way off, by the way."

"You don't."

"Feels like I'm talking underwater."

He pulled over. "Am I not turning left here, then?"

"Sorry. I'm trying to keep calm but I've had three days of being drugged into a stupor. And it's only just hit me now: the morning I had the crash when Jeannie went to Estelle's, and she said she might be admitted and...sorry, tell me how you knew where I was? Sorry, it's just that—"

"Take a deep breath, lass. Take it easy."

She did as he said. It was all she could do to breathe steadily as the last conversation she'd had with Jeannie resurfaced. She'd been on her way to Moorlands Road before going to work... The sweet scent of pear drops wafted on the air, the car heater suddenly suffocating.

"Bit better?"

She nodded. "A bit."

"Jeannie's your friend, the one you share a house with?"

"Yes."

"Okay, well this might be making a bit more sense now. After you rang and then cut me off—"

"Did I?"

"Yeah. Anyway, a couple of days later I went to The Lighthouse hoping for a chat because I'd had some erm...nightly visitors, should we say? Faceless demons in long black coats and hats, bit unnerving, like that character I thought I saw outside Mailing Street when you did the exorcism, but a gang of them?"

"Nightmares?"

"More real than that. It's got quite bad, to be honest. Anyway, I haven't much time so long story short, Gareth told me you'd had a car crash. Maureen at the garage told his wife, who told him. Then he went on to rant about you not being who you said you were. Not Lily Beth Kitlowski at all, but Beth Harper. And word's out you have a psychiatric history. Gareth knew it all along, of course – saw you talking to yourself on more than one occasion."

"What?"

"The coppers checked your reg."

"Yeah, but psychiatric history? Where the hell did that come from?"

"I don't know. But you've certainly given them a packet load of gossip to chew over."

"My God, that was all decades ago….And Jeannie and I had to change our names because of a situation that was downright dangerous. I can tell you the whole story but it'll take hours and I feel sick, drugged, thirsty, and filthy with hospital stink."

"You do pong a bit."

"Thanks. Look, I am definitely Beth Harper, and I have a valid driving licence and a CV as long as your arm to prove it. But we hadn't got a bean between us after escaping that place and she…" She sighed. "I promise I'll fill you in, and actually it does tie up with what's happening here, so it's going to be important."

"Do you mean the Mailing Street murders?"

She buzzed down the window and inhaled a gust of fresh sea air. "It's so beautiful here, you know? Well, it is if you look at the harbour and the coast. Isn't it funny how old houses and buildings blended with the landscape, but modern ones are plain? Or even ugly? I dunno–"

"I know what you mean."

"Sorry, I digress."

"All right, well the thing is, Beth – and this is where things get a bit odd - after I left the pub and was thinking about visiting you at the hospital, I got a call from Colin, a mate I've worked with a few times. He'd phoned about something else entirely, but here's the thing - he was on his way to an incident at the psychiatric unit involving a woman called Maria Kitlowski, the surname I'd only just heard of. Apparently, one of the staff had been attacked."

"So she is there! Oh my God!"

"Looks like it."

"But attacked someone? No, Jeannie wouldn't do that."

"And here's the other odd thing - when I asked Colin about it later, he wouldn't discuss it, completely clammed up. Said it was nothing. Case closed."

"What's happened to Jeannie, then?"

"I don't know. It was purely by chance I made the connection at all."

"I have to see Estelle Vickers."

"Estelle? Carrie's sister? Why?"

"Sister?"

"Half-sisters, I think. They share a dad, Eric Vickers, the one who plays golf with Lord Freeman, remember?"

"Ah! So who's Mr Gordon? Carrie's husband, I mean. What does he do?"

"Judge Gordon. Mervyn."

"My, my, what a tangled web we weave."

"You've lost me."

"Me too, except all of these people are connected so…"

Had the police check included pulling medical information from her childhood and deliberately been released into the gossip pool? But who would have done that and why?

She looked out across the twinkling water of the bay. "Right under our noses. All so normal, so out of the way…as to be invisible…"

"Beth?"

"Sorry, you asked me why I need to see Estelle. It's because she was the last person Jeannie saw before ending up in that psychiatric unit under the name of Maria Kitlowski. And Estelle knew her real name because she recorded everything. It was Estelle, as her therapist, who said she might need to be admitted. And Joe?"

"What?"

"She was terrified of those places. I've known her nearly six months and we've talked about this in depth. She was one hundred percent adamant she'd never be admitted to a psychiatric unit, then after a few intense sessions with Estelle she did a total U-turn and was suddenly fine with it. I'd planned to follow her up there the day I crashed the car. I was going to try and find the Vickers' house and wait for her to come out. I'm telling you something is not right. She was acting totally out of character."

"This isn't a case I can open, Beth. You'd have to go through the proper channels."

"Yes, and all that will happen is they'll turn it round and get a shed load of information on me instead. Sorry, but I can't play by those rules. We only just got her out of Curbeck and now look! Jeannie is in real danger."

Aware her voice was rising she stopped and took another deep breath. "Sorry, it's not your problem. You've done more than enough, and I'm really grateful you turned up today. Thank you. Anyway, you have things to do, so I'll go pay Estelle a visit, I think."

He nodded and started up the engine. "Come on, let's get you home first."

"Thanks."

"Is your car all right, by the way?"

"I don't know. It had only just been fixed and the bill cleaned me out. Now this!"

"I'll go see."

"Really? Oh, thank you."

"I've got a mate who's a mechanic," he said, turning onto Portland Street. "So we'll get it moved and take a look. It's the least I can do after what you did at Mailing Street. Two new families moved in on Monday, did I say? I drove past yesterday and they were chatting outside. And you know how that place always sapped the light? Well it didn't. It just looked…normal."

"Wonderful. That's really good news." She bit her lip. "You know, I hope the other driver's okay, the one in the truck or whatever it was. Think it was an SUV. I suppose I'll hear if he presses charges. But honestly, he shot out of nowhere and there was nothing there at all. Both lanes totally clear, I swear. I was actually looking right when I pulled out and–"

"Beth?"

"Yeah?"

He parked outside her house and switched off the engine. "No other car was involved. There was no other vehicle there of any description. That's what Maureen told everyone. She watched you pull out onto an empty road and then violently swing the car round and crash into the barriers. There's a CCTV on the forecourt to back that up. So it was just as you said – the road was completely clear and you were the only one there."

She turned her face away so he couldn't see the flush of confusion."

"Right, you get yourself sorted and then we'll go pay Estelle a visit. Nice lady."

"Oh, you've met her?"

"Only briefly. She was at a local charity event a year ago now. Pretty much the whole town was there: Carrie, Daphne French – the one you just had a run-in with - and Gareth. Oh, and Molly."

You won't be the famous five anymore, will you?

He switched on the ignition again and she started as if electrocuted. Every sound popped like a firecracker, every colour too bright. Whatever had they given her these last few days? Chlorpromazine? Because the last time this happened was after leaving the psychiatric unit as a teen. They'd told her to stay on the tablets but she'd spat them out later. Boy though, the rebound!

"Anyway, I'll pop back in about an hour, got a few bits to do. Then I'll give you a lift over to Silverdown."

Silverdown?

She'd been about to open the passenger door. "What? That's EstelleVickers' address?"

"It must be."

"So you knew? I mean…" She shook her head. "I thought you said you'd only met briefly, so…?"

It was his turn to flush. His mouth opened and closed. "Beth, this is weird. The name just flew into my head. It came out of nowhere. I honestly had no idea you even wanted to go up there before you told me a couple of minutes ago, and I definitely didn't know the name of her house." He rubbed his face with one hand, as if to swipe away the confusion, then shook his head. "Bloody Nora. I don't know what made me say it. Bloody Nora!"

Beth nodded. "I'll tell you what else is weird: I saw that nameplate in a dream. I thought it was the nursing home before it was converted." She shrugged. "But all those houses look similar."

"To be fair, it's not an uncommon name round here. I could have seen it anywhere recently and that's why it flew off my tongue."

"Don't miss synchronicity, Joe."

"No, but it's true. It is common round here."

She nodded and made to get out of the car, then hesitated again. "Why? Why is it common?"

He was staring at her as if the fabric of his world was unravelling. "When I first came here I did a lot of hiking, and one of the guys gave me an old ordinance survey map. Looked like his grandad had bought it – yellowing pages and all – anyway, where most of the retail parks and estates are now, that was once all woodland. Silverdown. Not much of it left…" His voice trailed away.

"An ancient woodland covered this whole area, then? Remember, I told you there was a sacred site beneath the abattoir under Mailing Street? And some kind of foul play? Something moved? Something stolen?"

Even as she spoke the images swirled: of boulders

being lifted, the piecemeal dismantling of a building, followed by the discordant crash of a huge pipe organ.

***

CHAPTER THIRTY-TWO

The vision, when it happened, was both unexpected and shocking. Beth was standing under the shower less than five minutes after getting home.

Never had it happened this way before. No meditation. No preparation. One moment she was lathering up wondering if there was anything edible in the kitchen, the next she was looking down as if from a CCTV camera high on the wall, at the figure of an exceptionally tall, reed-thin man. The first thing she noticed was his unusually elongated bald head, age-spotted like a speckled egg.

Seen you before…who…where?

An aura of cold isolation emanated from him as he walked purposefully along a dimly lit corridor, tap-tap-tapping with the aid of an ebony cane. Instinctively she cloaked her presence, snuffing out any signs of light that might attract attention; and continued to observe. His appearance was that of a man from a bygone age, dressed in a funereal frock coat over narrow black trousers. And as he passed directly underneath she noted a high collar, waistcoat, and a flash of silver on his lapel. Her eyes now became accustomed to the gloom and the details of the corridor itself, which had curved, dark stone walls similar to parts of the London Underground. As if to emphasise that impression, it sounded as if a tube train was passing nearby, although the rumbling seemed to come from above not below.

His back was to her now as he came to the end of the corridor and an arched doorway fronted by a wrought iron gate. Here he pulled out a long key of elaborate design and a gate swung open to reveal a steel inner door. He stabbed at a combination lock with fingers unnaturally long, and as he did so her attention was drawn to the masonry on the arch above his head.

The carving of the caduceus was identical to the one above the door at Silverdown.

Had her shock resonated?

At once he paused as if he sensed the presence of another. Almost indiscernibly, his back had stiffened and his head cocked to one side. A blackbird listening for a worm.

Don't look up!

The moment was loaded. She held her breath, aware of both Billy and Gran poised and ready. The shower drummed down on her head, a tropical rainstorm, and she became aware of being in two places at one time.

Already the vision was fading. And when he pressed the last digit on the combination lock and slipped deftly inside, the clunk of closing steel behind him was as heavy and final as that of a bank vault.

The whole episode had lasted but a few seconds, yet it left her shaken. The air felt charged, different, her senses heightened to brilliant detail. Quickly, she shampooed her hair.

Where was that? Who was he?

It was only after she'd wrapped herself in towels that she remembered Lord Freeman's online biography and photograph…It flashed before her - the unusually large, bald head, elongated and age-spotted; and the caduceus pin.

So that was him!

She hurried down to the kitchen, mind on overdrive. Boy, it was good to feel clean again after being glued to a plastic mattress for three days. But what was in that vault? Why had she been shown Lord Freeman and where was it? Beneath the London Underground? Was there a system below the Victorian one? She had always found tube stations eerie – the tiled walls, trains vanishing into black tunnels amid a rush of cold air, the swaying silent passengers…

But was there another network underneath?

Deep in thought, the attack caught her off-guard, despite Yukon's low growl of warning. She should have known, and later would thoroughly berate herself. The man was not only steeped in the dark arts but a senior occultist. At his level he would have a legion of minions.

It started with a low hum. Shadows rapidly accumulated on the walls and fatigue dragged at her limbs. Not thinking clearly, assuming the fogginess was due to the drugs, she switched on the kettle and took a mug out of the cupboard. It was only when the lights dimmed, buzzed and flickered that she stopped.

Billy stepped into her aura and Yukon's growl became a protective snarl.

She stood in the middle of the kitchen.

"I am God's child. God is my armour. Christ is my

shield. My father will protect me in the dark and you are not welcome."

The atmosphere fizzed with static.

On instinct she whipped back upstairs and rooted in the wardrobe for her bag. Everything needed for spiritual protection was always kept together, always there ready. As a precaution she lit some white sage sticks and got them smoking, then salted the bedroom and the thresholds of the house.

"Be gone. I do not consent to the presence of the dark. I do not consent to the negative. I will not acknowledge again. In the name of Christ be gone! I am a child of God. Be gone."

It was to be expected. She had focused, albeit briefly, on the dark side and felt the accompanying malice. That Freeman was as dark as all hell and served the demonic, there was no doubt.

"Have I been followed, Billy?"

Billy shook his head.

No, it had been but a trace of the man's peripheral energy and nothing more.

"We'll make sure," said Billy, vanishing.

She carried the coffee upstairs, deliberately clearing her mind of Freeman's image, and switched her thoughts. What colour lipstick to wear? What shape was her car in? What was there to eat? But as she sat at the dresser to blow dry her hair, May Morris came to her on the stale smell of neglect. Beth saw in that moment the laboured intermittent rise of May's bird-bone chest as she gasped for life; an undignified end for a dignified, intelligent lady. The image of May, as she had last seen her, lingered. And shortly afterwards, as Beth was getting dressed, a sigh sounded in the corners of the room. May had passed over.

Filled with compassion, Beth bent her head in prayer. Silver and gold filaments were flickering around the old woman's soul even as her emaciated, soiled body was being unceremoniously rolled onto a gurney, the paperwork signed off with the sweep of a pen.

You opened Pandora's Box, May. And we will shine a light on what's inside! Nothing will remain hidden, you know that. What you've done has been remarkable. We know so much because of you. Thank you. God bless.

May, she knew, had been well prepared for her passing and was happy to fly away. But there was something which needed to be told, and which could wrong a right. Beth tried to hear, to see, to understand the silky whispers, but could not quite grasp anything other than the name, 'Jeannie.'

She began to tie up her hair, watching in the dressing table mirror as sparks of light mingled and danced with the greyness of dusk. Strange an old lady should be such a threat? Surely stuck in that home she was utterly powerless? Plus her work was out there already and had been for decades. So why on earth had it been a problem when Jeannie befriended her?

Jeannie...

Aware of the time, she forced herself now to prepare mentally for what immediately lay ahead. How best to approach Estelle? Did Estelle have a husband? Maybe if she just said she was worried about her friend, and did Estelle know where she was? Something like that?

Dear God, please let Jeannie be all right! She's been through so much.

Glancing at the clock, she applied a flick of mascara and a dab of powder, then scooted downstairs for a sandwich. There was just time.

In the lounge, amber streetlights lent a glow to the unlit lounge as she sat wolfing down stale bread smeared with jam. Not the best, she thought, licking her fingers. At least it calmed the awful swilling feeling inside. Probably starvation – nothing but drugs and water for three days – no wonder she felt sick. At the sound of sleety rain smattering on the windows, she grimaced. It was a night to turn in early and pull the covers up, not head out again, especially feeling like this. The bread had already turned to concrete in a stomach made sensitive. What was the bet Crispin Freeman had prescribed the chlorpromazine she'd had thirty years ago? An old anti-psychotic, it had given her lousy side effects as a youngster and this felt the same – shaky, trembling limbs and a sandpaper-dry mouth? Probably he'd added an opiate too. Why did no one question him? Who was there to question him?

Alarm swept up the bones of her spine. What if he and Carrie Gordon had her arrested and sectioned on some pretence or other? How long could they do that for? A month? Six months? She might never get out again. What if Daphne said she'd been violent?

She forced down the last hard lump of sandwich.

Was that what happened to Jeannie? A false event now documented?

Car headlights swept across the room and she jumped up. Joe! Thank God for Joe. Rushing upstairs, she quickly brushed her teeth, grabbed her bag and then flew outside.

He flipped open the car door while she was still locking up, and seconds later she jumped in.

"Phew, you smell better," he said as they pulled away. "Oh, and just so you know, your car's been moved."

"Oh, that was quick. Thank you. Where is it?"

He took a card out of his jacket pocket. "There you go. Small garage. Ash said it's an easy enough job to bash out the side again. And no major damage but he'll check it over."

"Ah, that's brilliant. Thank you."

"Not a problem. Now then, fill me in quickly. What do you think's happened with your friend and why is she in danger?"

"Okay, long story short: Jeannie suffered abuse growing up in Curbeck and was having nightmares. She did need help and I was the one who found Estelle. But I got it wrong." She sighed, suddenly on the verge of tears. "I had an uneasy feeling almost as soon as Jeannie started seeing her. One reason was because she skipped normal protocol and saw Jeannie every single day, spent hours with her, sometimes three. Another was the appointments were at Estelle's own home. And another was she didn't charge her."

Joe pulled off the dual carriageway and headed out of town. "Bit too kind?"

"Yeah. Jeannie had an explanation for all of it, though. She was elated with how things were progressing, and on the day I crashed the car they'd finished recording everything and were going to discuss a treatment programme. I assumed that meant counselling, cognitive behavioural therapy, or past life regressions. I don't know. But that morning she suddenly dropped a bomb and said not to worry if she was admitted to the psychiatric unit. And like I said, you have to know how terrified of psychiatric units, Jeannie was! That's where her sister ended up and she never came out again. Not only that but she didn't trust Crispin Freeman one bit, yet she'd be in his care."

"But he's the psychiatrist, right? And presumably your friend wouldn't have known at that point?"

She looked out of the passenger window, aware that nothing sounded too wrong. The psychologist deemed admission appropriate, and the psychiatrist was who she'd make the referral to.

"You have no idea what's under that old hospital, have you?"

"Eh? Come again?"

"Sorry, I jump about a bit. You told me one of the girls who killed Molly was on that psychiatric unit for three years. Well, I've just spent three days on that site and as a medium I can tell you it's no wonder she ended up as mad as a box of frogs. And the boy who was haunting Molly's house, the one who told his mother to murder her husband and cut out his heart? Gareth told me he'd been on that unit, too. He was adopted. Mailing Street was built on an abattoir, which when verified, and if you dug up the old hospital you'd find it was built over a plague pit. They loaded up bodies on carts and just threw them in. Many weren't dead. The rats and foxes ate them live. That's what I've been seeing these past few days and why I couldn't stay another night. Do you understand now?"

"Oh, for fuck's sake."

"Yup. And they were operating on people. I don't mean like today. These wounds were horrific, like the patients had been experimented on. Parts of their brains were missing."

"You got all this in visions? Not side effects from the drugs?"

She regarded him steadily. "When I was under the drugs I can't remember anything. This was after I refused any more and started to wake up. But I take your point. I suppose the only way to prove it would be to excavate the area. You'll find a whole lot of evidence."

"That ain't gonna happen." He turned the car onto Moorlands Road. "Silverdown is apparently next door to the nursing home." Beth's eyebrows shot up. "Eh?"

"Not The Gatehouse. Other side. Ah, here it is," he said, slowing down. "Okay, well I'm quite prepared to accept the town's got a sordid history, but how does this relate to Jeannie?"

"I know I sound bonkers to ninety-nine percent of the population and I'm used to that. But once you come across the demonic you definitely know about it, so I'll go with this. I think you have a satanic cult in this town and they used the children's home and the psychiatric unit to recruit. The whole place is a simmering hotbed of resentment, fear and secrecy that people are barely managing to mask. It's built on the vile desecration of sacred land and the ley lines have been corrupted. Now the people don't even notice the lack of harmony because they're too busy paying for new houses, cars and gadgets. This is hypnotised Curbeck all over again and my friend is possibly in that unit. Thanks to ..." She motioned towards the large house they were now sitting outside. "Her."

"And who is in the cult?"

Beth shook her head. "Jeannie wasn't supposed to have ever left Scarsdale Estate. They overlooked her, you see? No one leaves it."

"How is it connected?"

She indicated Estelle's house. "Estelle put Jeannie under hypnosis and recorded it. Jeannie told her everything about Scarsdale Estate and Allegra Mantel, plus what happened to her mother and sister, to the kids in the school, and everything she could remember about past lives, which believe me is on a replaying loop – no lessons learned so round and round the ancestry goes. That's another place you'd find a lot of skeletons if it was ever investigated. Jeannie was having the same nightmares I'd already seen play out in graphic detail from her past, and those scenes were centuries old. Estelle went out of her way to get that information as quickly as possible, and then persuaded Jeannie it was necessary to run tests in a hospital. She basically told her, and got her to accept, that she was ill, not abused or traumatised but ill. And needed to be admitted."

"And someone wants that laptop? Or the memory sticks?"

"I wish now we'd spent more time together instead of working like crazy to save money. I could have helped her release the trauma. I should have done that…" *There's a reason…*

"You did what you thought best," said Joe.

"Why would Estelle convince a healthy woman who had actually escaped a horrific ordeal, that she had schizophrenia? That isn't helping someone come to their own conclusion or gain independence and a full life. And you can bet the authorities will say she's delusional and was given appropriate treatment. All as it should be, you know? To keep society safe from people like Jeannie."

"Yeah, it would run like that. But my honest opinion is you've got nothing in the real world to back this up and you've both used fake names."

"I know. We're in this weird parallel universe now. You shouldn't be seen with me, really. I worry about that. All I know is I can't leave my friend in that place, so I'm just going to ask Estelle when she last saw her client and where she's gone. I'll have to think on my feet. I'm expecting her to be coldly dismissive."

Joe nodded. "Yes, distant. That's the word for Estelle. Or vague…dreamy…Anyway, I'll park a bit further up and wait for you. Rita's been out for a pee so no rush."

Beth smiled. "Rita knows exactly where you are. Animals do. Okay, well wish me luck. I'm expecting this to be brief, as in door shut in face."

Silverdown stood in darkness at the end of a long drive whispering with laurels and rhododendrons. Rain glistened on the tarmac as she walked towards it, the hum of traffic and the hypnotic roll of the tide below becoming muffled, sea mist floating over the lawns.

I've been here before!

The porch was unlit, and she was almost at the door before full recognition kicked in. Exactly as viewed on the astral realm, the paint was ruby red, the nameplate read, 'Silverdown,' and on the arch above it was a caduceus. Having seen the same carving not an hour before, on Lord Freeman's vault, the sight jarred like a discordant note. That was Joe's connection. The symbol bound them. Tenuous, innocuous even, that was the only visible link.

She lifted her hand to pull the bell cord, a clang which echoed inside the silence of a vacuous hallway. No answer. About to ring again, hand half-mast, she hesitated. A door had shut somewhere inside, followed by the sound of footsteps, small and quick.

Too quick. Crossly quick.

Beth stepped back, expecting a torrent of rage to burst out from a woman disturbed at home in the evening. The door swung open and she stepped back further.

Immediately a scent of pear drops wafted on the air.

"Hello yes, can I help you?"

"Um…"

Wow, this was a surprise. Although Estelle Vickers looked exactly as expected, with a chlorosis complexion and two pink indents either side the bridge of her nose, her stance was not that of a middle-aged woman at all, but a frankly, cocky teenager. Folding her arms she looked Beth up and down.

"What do you want?"

"Um, sorry to bother you. Are you Estelle Vickers? Only I'm worried about a friend who–"

"Estelle can't speak. You've got me."

"Oh?"

"You'll have to deal with me."

This woman looked like Estelle and surely was Estelle.

Beth glanced into the hallway, noting a door left ajar. A pair of glasses had been left on the arm of a sofa. This was most definitely Estelle. Odd aura, though…mixed…

Puzzled, she stared back, and then it hit her. Jeannie said Estelle had been abused, and this is what had happened in Curbeck: the abused children had fragmented personalities. Maybe Estelle had alter egos when situations became uncomfortable? Oh bloody hell, how to handle this?

"As you would with spirit possessions," came Gran's voice. "Ask for her name."

"Pleased to meet you, er…?"

"Corinna."

"Corinna. Hi. Do you know where Estelle is? Could you ask her to talk to me, please?"

"She can't. She's pathetic and hiding as always." Corinna raised her eyes to the ceiling and sighed. "I have to do everything. So like I said, seeing as you're deaf, you've got me."

In the dimly lit hallway, several spectres had appeared. One bug-eyed child sat on the stairs sucking her thumb. Another leaned against the wall chewing gum, eyeing Beth through a curtain of long hair. And trailing through the corridors of yesteryear came screams and shouts from up the stairs, the slamming of doors and cranking of pipes.

"Oh, that's annoying for you. That she hides."

"Very. But she's younger than me so that's why I step in. I take care of everything."

"In that case I wonder if you know what happened to Maria? She's been coming here to see Estelle."

Corinna pursed her lips and shook her head. "Nope."

"I think Estelle made some recordings and–"

"Oh, yes! Are you the courier who's come to collect the laptop? Oh, that's all right then." She made a move towards a table in the hall, then stopped and cocked her head to one side like a parakeet. "What? No, you can't. No, I'm dealing with it." She looked back at Beth. "You're going to have to speak to Graham now. He says you're not the courier."

"Who's Graham?"

"He takes away people who cause trouble for us."

"We don't need Graham. All you need to do is what you were told to do, which is give the package to the courier. It's very important. Estelle's not brave enough to do it but you are."

Beth peered beyond Corinna to where a brown jiffy bag lay on the hall table. "You were told to give it to the courier, remember?"

Forced to play along she cringed inside, but there was too much at stake: Allegra would end up with every detail of their lives. Get hold of those recordings though, and they could end up with a lot of detail on hers! The electric charge of that realisation fired up every cell in her body as she stood there, willing this woman to give her the laptop. Who knew what Jeannie had revealed under hypnosis?

Corinna stared at her while arguing with herself. "Shut up, no. I'll tell her."

"Corinna, the package must be given to the courier. I'm here to collect it and I have to get going or we'll both be in trouble."

"I'm giving it to her so you can sod off. You're the one who'll get punished not me."

Corinna grabbed the package and handed it over.

But just as Beth's hand closed around it, she tried to snatch it back again. "Wait, no—"

Beth yanked it firmly off her. "Thank you."

Every sinew in Corinna's face tightened into a contortion of rage. Her eyes shot to black and a man's voice now boomed out of the fragile form. "No, I told you not to!"

Corinna lunged forwards with her teeth bared. "You fucking bitch, whore. You know what I do to women like you?" The slight body drew itself up into a cobra arch and one fist drew back for a punch. "You know what I do to little girls who snitch?"

She didn't think twice. Beth turned and fled, even as Estelle's quick, light steps chased her down the drive into the street, her breath hot on her neck.

***

CHAPTER THIRTY-THREE

"Well," said Beth, as Joe accelerated up Moorlands Road. "I didn't bloody expect that. Did you see?"

"I heard a bloke's voice. Then I saw you fly out of the drive like you'd caught fire."

"I've got Estelle's laptop! Don't ask me how because it was bizarre. Anyway, as soon as the real courier turns up, they'll know."

He shot her a quick sideways glance.

"She gave it to me. Well, kind of."

"I'll turn down Millers Lane and drive back that way."

She stared out of the passenger window at her ashen reflection. "Estelle's got a fragmented personality, Joe. What's the proper name for it? Not multiple personality but–?"

"Dissociative Identity Disorder. There's a lot of it in Crewby."

"Really? I thought it was rare. And that woman's a flipping psychologist so you know…" She shook her head. "I'm still stunned."

"What happened?"

"I managed to talk to the alter personality, or one of them, a teenage girl called Corinna. She assumed I was a courier and handed over the laptop, but that seemed to trigger something because then a bullyboy surfaced and tried to get it back. He was her and she was him. It was really bloody scary. I'm shaking all over."

The car sped along the moor top road, Crewby a maze of lights below.

"Jeannie's information must be very valuable."

"Put it this way, they'll definitely want to shut us up when they know we've got this. Guess they didn't bank on losing."

"Are we going straight to the psyche unit?"

She looked at the clock on the dash. "Please. The thing is, I cannot and will not believe Jeannie attacked anyone. That girl hasn't got a violent bone in her body and she's tiny. All she needed was a professional to talk to, not this. I have to get her out."

"I'll drop you down there."

A couple of minutes later the lights of the hospital complex came into view.

"Can I leave the laptop with you, would you mind? Just until–"

He nodded. "I'm going to park at the back of the labs and wait for you there."

"Thanks, I'll be as quick as I can. I really can't predict how this is going to go."

He drew alongside the gate leading to the back of the hospital. "Ring if you need help. I'll show up as an anonymous friend. Got your phone?"

"Yup. Thank you."

After the tailights disappeared she stood alone on the pavement for a moment. The evening was cold and damp, the hills dark beneath a glaze of silvery stars. Shivering, she took a deep breath and then headed in the direction of Lord Freeman's Mental Health Unit.

Here goes, then!

A couple of lights glowed from within and she hurried towards it. This had to be done. It had to. Failure was not an option. Steeling herself for what lay ahead, she walked up to the entrance. Tiredness washed over her and she put a hand to her stomach. What she wouldn't give for a lie down! But Jeannie could not be left here. And if that laptop was supposed to go to Crispin Freeman or Allegra Mantel, then soon one or the other would know she was out of hospital and had collected it. Who else would it be?

She pressed the buzzer.

A bored robotic voice droned, "Psychiatrics!"

"Hi! I was asked to come and see my sister, Maria Kitlowski. She's expecting me."

"Visiting's over."

"Yes, I know. I'm late. She was supposed to come home this afternoon but I was held up…at…"

Words were failing her, dizziness casting its fog. She was too tired, still drugged.

Gran Grace took over. "Tell her you're here after talking with her therapist. That's why you're late."

Aware of chattering and someone giggling in whatever office the robotic voice emanated from, Beth realised the listener wasn't paying much attention.

She spoke louder and with more authority. "I was held up and then went to see Maria's therapist to check what happened. Anyway, I'm here now. Better late than never. Can I see the nurse in charge?"

"Level Two."

To her amazement the door clicked open and she

walked straight through.

Once inside though, she hesitated. Which way? On the facing wall an arrow pointed to various wards, and at the far end of the corridor a neon light glowed from an un-manned reception desk. Someone had left a computer screen on. No one there!

The cloying smell of stale flesh, cigarettes and urine hung in the air. And within seconds the corridor began to fill with all the hideous thought forms of those who had gone insane. The walls wavered and the air crackled. At the foot of the stairs a woman stood cradling a baby, except the baby was withered to hide and had the face of an old man. Something the size and weight of a rat ran up the wall behind her, and maniacal shouting reverberated inside her head.

She pushed the energies away and tuned in. Jeannie's image came clearly…asleep, the room quiet, one bed…and Billy was with her. Following the magnetic pull, Beth headed for the staircase.

"Lavender Ward," said Gran Grace.

Silently thanking her, Beth now noticed the sign and hurried up to the first floor. At least there would be fewer staff on at night. But what would she say? Would the ward be locked? Doubt crept in. Of course it would.

At the top, she pulled open the double doors and peered down another corridor. Night lights lifted the gloom but it looked deserted. Good. Lavender Ward was indicated to the left and she began to walk in that direction. What if Crispin Freeman had Jeannie sectioned or restrained, though? And what if someone asked her who she was?

He knows I'm out!

"Trust," came Gran's voice. "You will succeed. Consider it done. My uncle is with Jeannie, waking her up."

On nearing the ward, she was just wondering what to do if the doors to Lavender Ward were locked with a pin number, when an orderly appeared with a trolley piled with teacups.

Beth hurried to hold it open. "Ooh, that was lucky for us both. Let me help. I'm just here to see my sister. She's been ever so poorly."

"Oh, what a shame," said the woman. "Thanks, love."

"No worries."

She left the orderly at the top of the ward and tentatively walked in, looking from left to right into bays of six. All was quiet, the nurses' station empty and the office behind it softly aglow. But there was an argument coming from further down. It seemed to be coming from one of the bays near the far end and was escalating. A scream suddenly ripped through the air.

Please God, don't let this be Jeannie!

She drew level. A man in a black t-shirt and jeans had an elderly woman in a half nelson as a nurse tried to inject her with something. The old woman, wild of hair and puce in the face, was shouting, "You fucking bastard demons. You fucking demons."

Easing into the shadows, Beth glanced over her shoulder at the office. There was someone in there! By the light of a reading lamp, a woman was reclining with her feet on the desk, flicking through the screen of a mobile phone.

Were these nurses? The old woman's face was now

275

the colour of an over-ripe raspberry, the purple veins on her cheeks dilating into a map as her eyeballs bulged. The more she swore, spat and kicked, the tighter the grip. The man now had both her arms up her back. It wasn't comfortable to watch, and even less so when the woman's body finally slumped, the fight left her, and the Brillo-pad head lolled onto her chest.

The smell in here was chemical, reminiscent of many years ago, and for a moment Beth stood transfixed, transported to another time and place.

"Beth! Concentrate!"

Gran's voice brought her up short. Snapping out of the trance, she continued down the corridor towards the blue light of the television lounge and a row of doors off to one side. Instinct told her Jeannie was in one of those. The picture of her lying on her own was clearer than ever…And good she was at the far end because the fire escape was there.

Footsteps suddenly clattered into the corridor behind and she darted into the communal lounge.

It was a grim place, and a quick scan was all it took to confirm the grey figures sitting in high-backed plastic chairs watching an action movie, were no longer living. She peeped around the corner as the nurses walked smartly into another bay, and was about to dart out when the creeping feeling of having been observed caused her to look back. A girl on the front row, most definitely still living, had swivelled around to stare. A girl with long dark hair and yellow eyes.

For a moment it seemed they were both equally surprised.

The last time Beth had encountered this girl was

during the exorcism of Mailing street, when Molly's final moments on earth had been revealed. This would be Toyah, then?

Toyah, it seemed, was also realising they had met before. Her blood-red mouth split into a malicious grin, and too late Beth saw what she'd unleashed. A battalion of spiders raced across the floor towards her. In every imaginable colour, the tarantula sized arachnoids scurried up the walls, clambered across the blinds, scooted behind the television set and ran into the shadows.

Toyah's grin broadened.

"I can see them," Beth hissed. "Now get rid of them or we'll do it for you and you won't like that."

Her smile vanished. "I can't."

Billy and Gran now appeared and she knew Toyah could see them, that this girl had the sight. "You can. Make them go away. Un-create them."

A yellow critter ran up the partition wall and even though she detested them, Beth picked it up by one leg and dropped it into the girl's lap.

Toyah recoiled. "Get it off me."

"You're projecting these but I can't be scared by you, do you understand? This does not work on me. It's an illusion and you know it."

Toyah glanced behind at the gloomy auditorium. The spectres in the high-backed chairs had started to shift and darken. Her aura was smoky brown, her soul engulfed. She began to bite her nails, to rock back and forth, muttering some unintelligible song. What on earth had been done to this child?

Gran's voice called, "Beth! Focus!"

Toyah heard and her head cranked up. "Hello, Beth!"

She looked over to the side wards, then back to the lounge, which was now crawling with multi-coloured spiders. The spectres in the chairs were moaning and swaying as collectively they began to rise. No one who came here stood a chance. She could help Toyah, but…

Gran's voice again, "Beth!"

It was getting late and those two nurses could reappear at any moment.

No, no time…

She flew down to the room where Billy was waiting, and yanked open the door to find Jeannie lying in bed exactly as imagined.

The door hushed into place behind.

"Jeannie, it's me."

Jeannie's eyes opened then closed again. Red marks had risen in wheals around her wrists. "Wha…?"

Beth shook her. "Come on, wake up. It's me, Beth. Listen, we have to go. Now."

Opening the bedside cabinet she pulled out a pile of clothes - at least in a psychiatric unit they didn't have to wear surgical gowns - and threw a t-shirt at her. "Hurry. Keep quiet. Get dressed fast as you can. This is a bad place. Leggings! Boots! Come on, hurry. We have to go."

Jeannie struggled to sit up. "Okaaaay."

Footsteps clicked down the corridor and they both froze.

Beth put her fingers to her lips.

The footsteps stopped.

"Toyah! What on earth are you doing? Get off the

floor this minute."

A guttural roar and what sounded like a chair being thrown at a wall followed, and Beth sighed with relief. Toyah was going to give the staff a hard time. At least they'd be occupied for a while.

Jeannie was trembling from head to foot. "I'm so cold, I'm freezing."

"Here, put your clothes on. Come on, help me!"

"I could hear a man telling me to wake up."

Beth nodded. "That was Billy."

"He said you were coming."

As soon as Jeannie was dressed, Beth took hold of her hand and pulled her towards the fire escape, praying the doors would open at ground level.

No officials, please! Please let no one be there. Please, please!

"Picture it done," came Gran's voice.

"And so it is. And so it is."

The door would open.

With Jeannie half falling down the stairs, they lumbered towards the double doors. Beth pushed down the release bar. Nope. She looked to one side, spotted a green square of plastic, pressed it, and the door opened into an unlit car park awash with fresh rain.

"Beth? Where are we? My legs are buckling."

"Shh! We've got to get to Joe's car. I just hope they don't ring the police."

"Police? Why?"

"Come on, walk faster, talk later. We might have to leave Crewby tonight, although I don't know how yet."

Inside the labs a single lamp was on, and several vans were parked outside.

"Little red jesters on the vans," said Jeannie.

She did a double-take. Sure enough, every single one had the Mantel's company logo stamped on the side. Maybe a coincidence? Laboratory supplies?

"Hmmm. Anyway, come on, keep moving. Joe's taking us home."

"Won't they come after me?"

Beth cranked open the gate and scanned the street. A car was parked in the cul-de-sac at the end and its lights flicked on as they emerged.

Oh, thank you, God, for Joe.

"I don't think so but they might call the police."

"They won't," said Billy.

Hobbling along with Jeannie a dead weight, Beth barely heard the words above the pounding of her heart. It banged in her ears and thudded in her chest, adrenalin consuming her with panic. Joe's car was now level and he leapt out to help Jeannie into the back. It was therefore only as they sped away, that she fully tuned into what Billy was saying.

"He's got no qualifications and nor has she."

She put her fingers to her temples and silently had the conversation. *What?*

Crispin. No qualifications. He flunked medical school. The rest is made up. Nor has Daphne. Nor has Estelle. They can't send officials for you.

What about Gareth, the town gossip?

A host of possibilities streamed in. Any number of things could happen.

She heard Gran sigh so loudly it was as if she was sitting next to her. *Beth! Child! They paid you both below the minimum wage and neither put you on the books or paid tax. They can't! The only way would be a trick.*

A trick?

Aware Joe was waiting for her to speak, Beth shrugged.

"You okay? Dare I ask what happened?"

"We're not safe here anymore. I just went and got her. She didn't assault anyone. I think they made it up to keep her incarcerated - to maybe use it later, I don't know. It doesn't look like they're following any rules in there."

Were those nurses even nurses?

Joe turned off the dual carriageway. "You should be safe. If she wasn't sectioned then Jeannie had a right to discharge herself, so apart from the fake names–"

"Gareth and Freeman weren't paying tax. They paid us cash below the minimum wage, so they can't get too official, can they?"

"Don't tell me anymore."

She disappeared into a warren of her own thoughts.

The people I'm worried about are the ones who work in the shadows.

"They're meeting at three, so they're busy," Billy chipped in. "Very. So rest up for a few hours."

Joe parked outside the house and looked into the rear view mirror as if he'd heard.

"Who's meeting at three?" Beth said out loud. "Why?"

"All of them. There's a lunar eclipse."

"Where?"

"The Gatehouse."

"Three tomorrow?"

"No, six hours' time."

"I can see an outline, Beth. On the backseat next to Jeannie."

"Oh wow! You've done it!"

"What am I looking at here in Crewby? I mean I get the old friends from the children's home and I get something sinister is at the root of this, but have there been any actual crimes? Recent ones?"

"You could check out the qualifications of Crispin Freeman, Estelle Vickers and Daphne French for a start, because they don't have any. They're charging a lot of money for that nursing home, and not only taking information from people seeking psychological help but admitting them to a place they will not emerge from as the same person. If at all. Oh, and you might want to check May Morris's toxicology."

"I can't do anything unless Carrie sanctions it."

She nodded. "What does she wear on her lapel?"

He looked into her eyes.

"What does she wear on her lapel that Crispin Freeman, Daphne French, Estelle Vickers and Lord Freeman also wear? What's on Estelle's doorway, which we now know was once the children's home? And what's on the door of The Gatehouse?"

He nodded.

"And I'll put money on Judge Gordon wearing one, too?"

"Isn't it a medical symbol? I mean, harmless enough?"

"I think that's the Rod of Asclepius. One snake. The caduceus is different. The meaning would be in the interpretation of course, but if it's purely medical then why put it on a children's home? And why would a police chief wear it?"

And why carve it into an underground vault?

He frowned.

"You've got to look it up," said Billy.

She nodded. "Think of the owl. Yet it's also used to depict Moloch! Everything depends on the watcher, on the intent, on the energies or emotions. I love owls. Innocent people wear a caduceus. So do the not-so-innocent."

"So the symbol binds them together and no outsider would guess the nature of their particular club."

"Exactly. Anyway, you've got the laptop, and I think you have more chance of keeping it safe than me. No one knows you've got it and I have a feeling that one day, don't ask me how, it will be needed. We're not just talking about a rogue cult in one small town, by the way. What's happening here is linked to Scarsdale, and the tunnels are connected to global ports. It's all underground, Joe."

"There's just nothing to physically go on apart from this lot with no qualifications."

"Devil's in the detail."

"Satanists," said Jeannie, from the back seat.

Joe turned to look at her.

Her voice was syrupy and slow. "It's all been coming back to me. They get you to do things…with the camera running…" She put her head in her hands. "So you can't say."

"Say?"

"So you can't ever say who they are."

***

CHAPTER THIRTY-FOUR

Jeannie fell deeply asleep as soon as her head hit the pillow, and Beth sat downstairs in the dark rolling a smoke. Every couple of minutes she glanced at the clock. With no car parked outside and no lights on the house would look empty, but it was a risk being here. Without transport though, what choice was there?

Nightmare scenarios played out in her head: men in uniform banging on the door...being bundled into a van...locked in a cell...forcibly injected... Her thoughts flailed into terror, and it was only at the point where she'd imagined a baying mob outside – previously pleasant market stall holders and fishermen – throwing bricks through the glass, calling them liars and witches, that she took a hold of herself.

"I'm too far away. I'm drifting... I can't see what to do."

She bent her head in prayer, and then focused on one central object - a clear, glinting crystal pyramid - until her mind slowly cleared of turmoil. Sensing the healing presence of the soul tribe around her, she leaned back against the sofa, falling quickly into the white room and her sanctuary of inner calm. A flipchart on a board had been set up by a long sash window and next to it was a pot of gold paint. The paint shimmered warmly. She picked up the brush and wrote the word, 'Peace.' The word resonated, inspiring feelings of love and hope, reassurance and faith. Her heart chakra opened and her body was filled with bliss. Light streamed in, and it was as if she became lit from within. Unlike previous meditations though, the feeling didn't level off but carried on, gaining momentum. Euphoria charged up every cell and her heart seemed to expand until she felt it would burst. Tears streamed steadily down her face. There was so much light now…white…dazzling… And still the glorious sensation continued. Until finally, at the point it became physically impossible to infuse any more light and love, The Silence spoke.

It was in a vision. The day was so bright it hurt the eyes. She was sitting on a beach of fine, white sand. Water lapped onto the shore - a pure turquoise lagoon - the horizon a shimmering haze.

"Turn around," said a deep voice so gentle it caressed the soul.

In the dream state, she observed crystal grains sparkling on her toes, intensely aware of being in the 'now,' of the rhythmic hiss of the waves, one part of her afraid, another not wanting to break the trance.

"Turn around, Beth."

Time stood still, the summer breeze dancing with flecks of gold.

Who are you?

"You know who I am."

The beating of her heart paused. Had she died?

"Have courage. Turn around."

Slowly, oh so slowly, she began to turn. The glare was blinding. She brought her hands up to her eyes to shield them. But just at the moment she moved her hands away, to see who had called her name, she woke with a bang like a horse-kick in the chest. And the memory of a voice so soft as to be a murmur, yet with more power than a cathedral echoing a thousand chants.

He had said, "I am with you."

For a long while afterwards she sat staring at the mantelpiece, at the tiled hearth and the grey bars of an unlit fire. There were no words, and there was no living soul she could tell. Yet the experience had left her with the conviction that she could and would do anything, absolutely anything, to expose the hidden evil that kept people from the love they had lost.

We're all adrift…everyone…all of us…

"What's coming has taken over two thousand years," said Gran.

"Gran! What is this? What am I to do?"

Gran Grace was wearing her favourite turquoise shawl with the topaz brooch. "You have to find out in bits, Beth. Or it will send you insane. And each revelation will widen the gap between you and the rest, remember? They will think you insane and that in itself will be difficult to bear."

She nodded. They would not give more than she could cope with, but she was being given the maximum. She glanced at the clock. "And what are we doing at three?"

"We're going to The Gatehouse."

"Yes, but what's happening there?"

"We've been preparing for a while, and those who can do what you do, have been woken in their sleep. We're almost ready. What they have under The Gatehouse is ancient, and the black mass is on a lunar eclipse. We need to disrupt it and you are the channel. We will all be there this time."

All?

Beth rolled another smoke and thought about the building.

I don't mean the town. I mean the earth. We have orders to escort you off.

"Okay. How do I get in? It's barred."

"Max," came Billy's voice.

She shook her head. "How?"

"Trust us."

Remembering the vision she'd just had, she stood up. Whatever it took, however far down the path of potential madness, no matter the dangers or the fatigue, she would carry out God's work. To those who called it nonsense, she could not explain. However, for those who had encountered the dark ones, and for the poor tortured souls trapped underground, she would be there.

"I'd best grab a few hours' kip, then."

She was permitted to sleep for a while, to drop through the layers of consciousness into deep delta waves. Here she rode the tide of oblivion, in full rest mode. At some point, Yukon settled on the bed, and later, much later, a cool breeze wafted across her face and she began to lift away.

Soon it would begin.

The Gatehouse stood in the cold blackness of a night drizzling with fine rain, and from the direction of the hills a vixen's cry pierced the air. Half expecting to see the man in black again, she focused on the wall of the house itself. And as she concentrated it became evident a once large archway had been concealed with identical stonework. Only a barely discernible outline now remained, but a monumental doorway had originally been there. Propelled closer, she quickly disguised her appearance.

Something was coming…

That the cult was inside was not in doubt, yet there was no visible entry point a human being could have used. As before, she attempted to push through the energies, only to be rebuffed by an invisible wall as impenetrable as stone. It jarred like a flat note and sickly concussion reverberated through her. No way could a remote viewer get past that!

Something…no, someone…was coming…

"Prepare for what you will see," came Billy's voice. "We're going ahead."

Without any further time to think, the glittering form of Max folded her into his cloak. And when she became conscious again it was from within the house.

Immediately the atmosphere hit her. Heavy and thick as treacle, it was clogged with burning incense and the stench of sulphur, the preparations for a black mass already underway. Was this really inside a house? The place was cavernous with no separating floors, but it looked like… a church… except it wasn't…because everything was upside down.

The Satanists of old had transferred the entire

contents of a church and suspended them from the ceiling - from the pews and the altar to the organ pipes. On great iron chains like those from the abattoir, they hung over the ceremony in a diabolical inversion. And far below, in the fiery darkness, was a ring of stone boulders. Some of the hooded figures humming and swaying were within the circle, others outside it.

The stone walls, which flickered in smoky shadows, had been elaborately adorned with grotesque images similar to gargoyles, but were largely sexual, bestial, defilements of sacred images. Coiling serpents wrapped around cherubs in lascivious paintings that mocked the holy trinity. Viewing it from the astral was difficult, and Beth had to concentrate on keeping the vibrations steady amid the jarring, mechanical scraping noises of the low energies conjured. The stage set was like nothing she had ever seen, could have imagined, or been prepared for.

The robed figures were in a hypnotic trance, the monotone a prolonged, discordant key, the air sour, reeking of animal fear and the tang of blood.

She hung back, waiting for instruction, aware now of sparks beginning to disrupt the dark energies. The anticipation was building, but as yet the participants were unaware of what was going to happen.

In the centre of the circle, she saw now, was a table. Seven sided, it had a black marble fascia over ebony, the design on top one no human eye should see. No artisan could have created the face of the enemy in such intricate detail. Beautiful and horrifying, the eyes followed anyone and everyone at any angle and from any aspect in whichever room it was placed. Two items had been placed on the table, one at each end – a sword and a black obsidian chalice. And on the floor, at the foot of the altar a disembowelled human body adorned with flowers as Molly's had been, lay as a sacrifice.

Someone coming…

The person who would conduct the mass was not yet in the room but they were much closer now, the quickening of their breath a barely suppressed excitement, a hunger…

But from within the haze of smoke and static there were ever increasing flashes of gold and silver, and what had been a faint tribal drumming was now amplifying.

The clash of energies was rapidly becoming disruptive, the hooded ones below glancing at each other uneasily. The humming faltered, the madness in their auric fields ugly thought forms, as each began to feel the rebound of what they had summoned. And with a surge to her heart, Beth realised what was about to play out. The powerful presence of the heyoka was here. Each participant would be getting a mirror!

Their insanity grew along with the visions of what they had done. Rows of hooks hung around the walls. Huge meat hooks from the abattoir had been nailed into stone. Hooks that dripped with the ghostly cadavers of the long-since sacrificed, some slashed open from throat to pelvis, others missing part of their heads, gouged through the face, through the eyes. With a shock, Beth noticed a boy. A boy with sandy hair…

And the souls of the murdered were still here, trapped in fear, re-living the pain and horror of what they knew was coming…again…the kind of evil they never knew existed. Until it was too late.

Jeannie's voice echoed in the bowl of her head, 'I know if I ever saw what was on the other side of that door…'

A cold draught drifted from the far side wall, and now it was easy to see how the cult had entered the building. A set of stone steps led deep into the earth, the tunnels still howling with lost screams. The fear of the victims tasted like blood on the tongue, the slip into madness their only door of escape.

Beth!

Satan would gleefully take them all to the halls of insanity, she knew, and that would include herself for even looking. Yet all this had happened. It was here. All real. The horror of it - of what human beings had done, and were still doing.

Beth!

She forced herself to pull back.

Gold, silver, violet and magenta beings flashed and flickered in the darkest of corners, closing in on a summer storm. And Billy was clamping off connections, a long and painful task due to the ancient and long held dense energies. They must turn dark to light, and lingering on base horrors wouldn't help. She began now to pray, calling on the Children of the Light. She must find the soul of the one sacrificed so it could not be used.

Tuning in, she followed the energies around him but found nothing. There wasn't a man lingering around the body.

She sensed the heyoka. "Not a man! Stop looking for a man."

Not a man? Then…?

Beth allowed her mind to go blank and in an instant a fruit box appeared. A fruit box hidden in the far corner of the room. And in the box was a baby. The man's soul was still a baby. Immediately she went to pick the baby up, and sent the soul into the light with prayer. Love flowed through her for what she now knew had been an abandoned child, and then a homeless man. At least now he could go home. And be loved.

The tribal ritual was building rapidly. With every beat of the drum the energy lifted another notch, all light beings channelling the highest vibrations, the love of God. Recalling the euphoria from just hours ago, Beth tapped into that immense power and with repeated prayer, radiated the higher energies. The effect was like switching on a light bulb in the basement. It lit a few square feet but the rodents still scuttled around the edges, skeletons unseen. Then another was lit, then another….No one must tire. The work continued, the quota of light increasing steadily along with the drumming…on and on and on…building it up until finally the darkness began to fracture and its canvas frayed.

Down below, the humming had resumed but not as strongly. Having faltered it had lost its momentum and failed to recover. Panic was gripping the players, fear weighting them in their own chains. Whoever was coming to lead the ritual was on the approach, and he or she absolutely terrified them.

The air in the stone circle was thick, dirty and greasy.

They've lost!

A breeze blew up. Their worst nightmares were

looming, the ones that plagued and threatened to devour them should they ever stop providing what was needed. Again the humming stalled. Several of the candles snuffed out.

The heyoka was about to pierce their veil.

A lull. And then the breeze became a shrieking banshee and suddenly the heyoka broke through the cleared channels and roared into the face of the masked figure at the helm of the ceremony. Every diabolical act he had ever committed was flashed before him in one hit. The staff he was carrying fell to the ground and urine gushed down his leg.

All of the candles went out.

The drumming now over-rode the humming with ease. Light filtered in as if through a forest canopy, widening, cracking open the blackness. From the other side of the world, Father Greg had joined in prayer, called in sleep like Christine and many others united in the fight against the archon darkness. Divine beings were everywhere, and love, faith and joy burst through. The air began to flash like sheet lightning illuminates a night sky and the drumming reached its height. At which point, as a glass is shattered by a soprano, so did the black obsidian chalice. Exploding on the altar at the same time as a rumble of stones shifted underground.

The effect was as if a bomb had dropped.

For a moment the Satanists continued to sway drunkenly, muzzy and confused. Drugged, their minds hinged between fear and insanity as the heyoka now seized the perfect line of shot and lunged directly into their minds. Mirrored a thousand fold, everything they and their predecessors had ever inflicted on their helpless victims was projected. Every terrorising, cruel, excruciatingly painful act now became their own. The hunter became the hunted, their night terrors demonically real.

They stood, mouths agape, some soiling themselves as once their innocent victims had done. Their personal private terrors would replay every time they tried to sleep for the rest of their lives. What they had raised into this world would visit them every single night. Beth saw what they saw: the demonic cloak of terror standing over their beds, the curl of cruelty on the lips of the one with liquid black eyes, the cold demand for the ultimate sacrifice of the eternal soul.

Now it was their turn.

The master they had chosen did not do mercy.

In a panicked herd they bolted for the far side of the hall and clattered down the steps.

Only to find the exit blocked by fallen stones. No way out. While above them hundreds of pained, tortured souls rose as one into love and freedom, at long last released.

Then in less time than a blink, Beth found herself outside The Gateouse once more, standing in the fine rain of early dawn. Streaks of pale aqua painted the sky above the crags on the moors. And she knew then, saw in her mind's eye, that the person who was to lead the mass had never made it into the room at all.

Because she knew before she got here.

The countess's chauffeur had stopped the car and was poised on the precipice overlooking Moorlands Road. It was the last thing Beth recalled before she dipped back into sleep: the back end of a Bentley with no number plate, turning around before merging smoothly with the fog of dawn.

***

CHAPTER THIRTY-FIVE

Beth's sleep was deep, her body aching as badly as if she'd been kicked all over. It therefore took a while for the insistent knocking on the front door to permeate. When it did, however, she catapulted out of bed in one move. Police. Had to be. Instinctively she darted into Jeannie's room and shook her arm.

"Wake up! Jeannie, wake up!"

Jeannie squinted through red-rimmed eyes. "Who?"

"You. No time. We're going to have to leave Crewby today. This morning."

"Where am I?"

"You're at home. We came back here last night, remember? Here, have some of your water."

The rap on the door started up again. Whoever it was, clearly wasn't giving up.

"Crap." She kept her voice to a whisper, contemplating an escape through the back door. Surely they wouldn't break in? She pictured armed officers in riot gear. "Do you remember being on the psyche unit?"

"Yes."

"And you definitely didn't attack anyone, did you?"

"No, of course not. Why?"

"Did any police officers come to see you?"

"No."

They can't send officials… the only way would be a trick…

"Okay, look I have to go get the car no matter what state it's in. Can you pack the bags? Without being seen? And don't make any noise. Not a squeak. I don't think they can barge in here without a warrant, so just be really quiet. We'll talk later."

Jeannie sat up. "I'm parched. Ugh!"

This time the rapping on the door was a continuous banging and they looked at each other askance.

A man shouted, "Beth!"

"That's Joe's voice."

"Your fancy copper?"

Beth nodded. "Not mine and not fancy but–"

"He's double-crossed you?"

She looked over at Billy, who was holding Spot and peering through the curtains. He was going to miss that little cat.

"Is it Joe? Is he alone?"

"Yes. He needs to speak to you."

"Okay." She turned back to Jeannie. "We still have to leave. Can you sort out coffee and whatever there is to eat and get packing?"

"I feel really sick."

"I know, sorry. This is rough for both of us." She stood up. "Okay, I'll speak to Joe and then get the car. Eat something, you'll feel better."

"No shit, Sherlock," said Jeannie, clambering out of bed. Decidedly green about the gills, her hair was pancake flat at the back and Beth's heart went out to her. What bizarre trip had she been on over the last few days?

And Joe, when she let him in, also looked as if he hadn't slept.

Soaked to the skin, he wiped his feet. "Thank God. I thought you'd already scarpered. It's pissing down out here."

"What's going on?"

He was rubbing his hands together, wiping his feet on the map and shivering. "Can we have a quick chat?"

She glanced down at her dressing gown and grimaced. "Yes, come in. But would you mind waiting five minutes while I wash and put on some clothes?" She nodded towards the kitchen. "Feel free to make coffee. Jeannie will be down in a bit and she's in dire need of some, too. Sorry, it ended up being a late night."

He narrowed his eyes.

"Astral."

She dashed upstairs to the bathroom. The last few hours had been a roller coaster of euphoria and shock: the light too brilliant and blissful to comprehend, the dark too evil to come to terms with. What was this world they lived in? Was any of it, she wondered, as we had been led to believe? Images of tunnels and crates, ports and containers, whipped through her mind in quick succession as she washed and brushed her teeth. Why was the countess involved with a place like Crewby? Who had been at the ritual and, oh…She stopped and stared at her face in the mirror, toothbrush mid-air…

Downstairs, plates and cups clattered, the sound of voices muffled.

They, whoever they were last night, would still be trapped in the rubble!

So…?

Whirling around in the hope of talking to Billy or Gran, she found only an empty space. Thus, returning to the mirror she continued to regard her ghostly complexion and bleary eyes. Then all at once it clicked. The lock of confusion sprang open. And a huge grin spread across her face.

Genius! Oh my God!

God was amazing. Of course! No one would be coming for her and Jeannie because the powers that be were all trapped underground. The whole lot!

Tearing downstairs she burst into the kitchen. "Oh, what a beautiful morning, oh what a beautiful day–"

"It's raining," said Jeannie, grimacing at the taste of black, instant coffee.

"I haven't slept," said Joe. "I can't stop thinking about what you've been saying about this town. I thought it was all right here. But now–"

She took the cup Jeannie handed her. "Thanks. Ugh! Ooh, yes that's bad. Anyway, listen, I'm going to dash out and get the car."

"I'll give you a lift," said Joe.

"Oh, thank you. Brilliant." She giggled at the looks on their faces. "And Jeannie, please will you start packing? Although, maybe it's not so much of a rush as I thought."

Joe was looking at her as if she was speaking in Russian.

"Sorry, it's just that everything's fallen into place." She smiled. "Well, sort of tumbled into place, ha ha!"

"I have no idea what you're talking about, woman," said Joe. "But what I came over to tell you was that I spoke to my mate, Colin, about the incident at the psyche unit with Jeannie. I said I was asking for a worried friend. Anyway, he told me there was nothing to worry about and as far as he knew it wouldn't be going any further. But here's the thing – there was absolutely no mention of Jeannie absconding. So clearly it hadn't been reported. If she'd posed a violent risk to society it would have been, would it not? Also, Gareth! I dropped in for a word but he wasn't there. First time ever I've been to that pub and he wasn't around. The barrels had just arrived and the delivery guy couldn't even get him on the phone. So I don't think anyone's coming after you."

"Told you!"

Smiling inwardly at Billy's words, she said. "Not today, anyway."

"I thought you might be worried and I wanted to put your mind at rest. Actually, it's a bit of an odd morning altogether. Word's out that Carrie hasn't turned up for work this morning, either."

"A few haven't," said Beth. "I imagine there'll be a search party out soon."

"Tell me on the way," said Joe. "I've got to go and pick up some documents in Fleet soon, so let's get going."

She took a little time getting ready, giving Jeannie and Joe their first proper opportunity to talk. Both had a lot to take on board.

"I still don't get why I was guided to send Jeannie to Estelle," she murmured to herself. "That was bloody close to the knuckle. It was nearly the end of her."

"That's what it took to wake her up," said Gran Grace. "She trusted someone she didn't know. Big house, posh accent, letters after her name. Tch!"

"She trusted her more than me."

"Yes. Over the one person who had nothing to gain and who'd looked after her. She's going to feel bad for a while but she must see it as a lesson, and you will see it as an opportunity to forgive."

Beth nodded. "It brought the deeper fish up to the surface too, I suppose? They…"

She looked round, but Gran had gone. Beth nodded. Everyone needed a break whether in flesh or spirit, and the amount of energy needed for spirits to materialise was huge. What had been expended on Crewby during the last few days had taken it out of all of them.

Grabbing her coat two minutes later, she shouted, "Ready, Joe?"

They drove in silence, the morning drizzle typical for early March. On the grass verges and roundabouts, daffodils shivered brightly, vivid against the green.

An old song came into her head. 'Nothing ever happens…nothing happens at all…'

It wasn't until Joe drove into the garage forecourt, this one a small yard behind the harbour, that he finally spoke. "So where's Carrie then, Beth?"

"I'm going to take a punt she's under The Gatehouse, but since it's all stoned up I don't know how she got in there, do you?"

He looked at her. "You do my head in."

"Thanks. I see tunnels all the time now, Joe.

They've been cut into ley lines that were meant to be used for the good. The whole thing is made to look as if they're being used for drains, cables and pipes. But like bindweed twisting through flowers, you don't notice if you don't look. I'm being shown rail tracks as well - like inside mines – and shelves stacked with cages, although I don't know where they are yet. Anyway, your search parties might find an entrance beneath the labs or the old hospital. I'm going to suggest they take rescue equipment and sick bags with them."

"How–?"

She shook her head. "When I've gone you could maybe tell one or two of the more open minded that you had some help from a spiritual medium? They won't like it and they won't accept it, but that's up to them. They won't find a comfortable explanation, that's all I can say."

"What happened? I mean how do you know?"

She took a deep breath and told him. "And this is what they do, Joe. This is how they get and hold onto power because once people sign into that, they're done. If they speak out they will be killed or humiliated into killing themselves. It's over. And worst of all, many are recruited as children. Crewby is a quiet port and I'm guessing it's been used for international trafficking for a long time now."

He was staring out of the window at a guy in overalls holding a spanner. "And yet everything looks so normal."

"Bizarre, isn't it? When you find out there's this whole parallel world going on, and it's about as sinister and hellish as you could possibly imagine. Worse, you're the only one who knows and no one you tell believes you."

He gave the thumbs up to the man with the spanner.

"I've left you with a rabbit warren," said Beth. "Fall guys will be chosen once you locate your boss, I guess."

"We call them patsies."

"Yes, those pesky loners with mental health issues, eh?"

He smiled. "Can I just ask - Lord Freeman?"

She shook her head. "No, I don't know where he is, although I suspect he will be choosing the patsies. The last time I saw him he was opening a vault. It looked as if it was in the London Underground. There was a rumbling noise above him...I don't know."

He shook his head. "You're like, I don't know what. I'm just wondering how the hell I'm going to suggest to the team that our chief of police is under a building with no entrance, stuck in a pile of rubble."

"Naked," she added.

"What?"

She opened the door. "None of this is me, you know? I don't do religion and I don't do preaching, but I'm just saying straight up that all the glory is God's. We channel his love. That's it. It really is that simple. Forget black, white, male, female, status, wealth or beliefs - everything is about love. That's the only thing we came here to learn and the only thing we take with us when it's over."

She did not wait for a reply. Joe would find it impossible to understand how she knew where Carrie and Crispin Freemen were. There was no way into that house and the tunnels were barred by locked, wrought iron gates they would have to cut through. Ultimately, there would be no other explanation other than the one she had given.

As he reversed and exited the yard she watched him go, and raised her hand until he was out of sight. In another world and another life, she could have fallen for him.

***

EPILOGUE

It was evening by the time Beth parked the Peugeot at a beauty spot an hour's drive south of Crewby. She and Jeannie sat for a while watching the waves break onto a deserted shore. Tufts of grass quivered on wind-blasted dunes, a double-halo of sun dropping behind the horizon.

Beth zapped down the window and rolled up a cigarette.

"Want one?"

Jeannie shook her head. She'd barely said a word since this morning, the journey so far in silence. "There's a lot I don't get."

"I know."

"It's just, well, both you and Joe seemed to think I'd been in some kind of incident at that hospital, but I hadn't."

"To be honest, I was expecting the mother of all rows when I got there last night. I thought, from what I'd heard, that you'd been sectioned; but there you were, all alone in a side room."

"I've been out of it for days, Beth." She rubbed her wrists. "I do vaguely remember being restrained, but not roughly, and it wasn't anything to do with violence. I was at Estelle's and felt drowsy. I walked into that hospital like I was in a dream and just got into bed. I remember faces all woozy above me and then this girl with yellow eyes…stroking my face and singing… "

Beth shuddered.

"So we were both drugged to the eyeballs for three days?"

"Why, though?"

Beth shook her head. "I can only think we weren't supposed to have come out again. And meanwhile a ritual was being planned to put a strong seal in place." She blew smoke out of the open window. "Everyone can feel a bad atmosphere, right? Well, times that by a thousand and you've got such a dark energy trap that people remain in a low state of fear and anger, petty jealousy and ego. They can't pursue dreams or expand their minds when they're in that low vibration. They don't love and respect each other, or themselves. It becomes about survival and they drain each other. So you have an entire community that's absolutely controllable. Unseeing. Everything is energy. Everything. Anyway, there was a lunar eclipse last night. The powers that be know about gematria and merkaba, physics and alchemy—"

"And you stopped it?"

"Not me. God. Pure love." She smiled. "Suffice to say the energies were so disrupted they couldn't summon as much as a cup of çoffee. Mantel never even made it into the building. And on top of that the vibrations we caused were powerful enough to cave in their tunnel. And that, my friend, is where they remain."

"Who? Crispin Freeman and Daphne French? Carrie Gordon?"

Beth nodded. "I definitely picked up Crispin Freeman's energy signature. I think he was leading the preparations. I can't be sure about the others except Carrie Gordon didn't turn up for work today. All I know for sure is they're trapped."

"Oh my God!"

"They can breathe. Call it a tragic accident. And frankly I think all of them will want it hushing up when they're rescued. A lot of minds imploded, Jeannie - nightmares they won't recover from. The inside of The Gatehouse is horrific, by the way. And they won't be able to keep that a secret anymore."

"How so?"

"For a start they had a human sacrifice laid out."

Jeannie stared straight ahead.

Dusk was descending. A sharp gust rocked the car, blasting the sand dunes, flattening the tufts of grass.

"I wish I could have gone back to say good-bye to May."

"May passed yesterday, Jeannie."

"Ah!"

"In her sleep."

Jeannie nodded.

"I felt her soul depart as I was getting ready to come and find you last night. She wanted to pass on a message but all I got was your name. There is a reason you worked at that home and I think it was to meet her."

Jeannie turned to face her, her thoughts not quite forming on her lips.

"What puzzles me is why they separated you and sedated her so heavily. Because what she'd written was already out there and they had her captive. She was no threat to anyone."

"I know why." Jeannie yanked the travel bag from the back seat and pulled out a wad of papers. "She gave me this."

On the front page was the word, 'Caduceus.'

"Ooh!"

"I've not had time to look at it properly yet, but May was born in Crewby. She retired here, a place to end her days. Only she became interested in the town's history and began to research Silverdown and the ancient forest. She knew the stones had been moved and that there'd once been a church on the site. To be honest, I didn't see the relevance when she started to tell me all this stuff. But then she told me about the man in black at the house next door, and also about the children's home. Said it was all in here. She kept it in a secret compartment in her suitcase, one she'd had in the secret service."

"I wonder how Daphne and Crispin knew what she'd   found?"

"She said everyone knew about Silverdown and they didn't want to talk about it, either. Most said it was ancient history now. But she did a lot of research and asked a lot of questions, and she said absolutely no one knew what was in The Gatehouse. The only reason she'd become suspicious was because she'd seen the man in black and knew he was demonic."

"She was a sensitive."

Jeannie nodded. "She also pieced together who'd

grown up together in Silverdown Children's Home."

"The symbol. The caduceus. The link."

"I think Daphne and Crispin Freeman just kind of knew she'd told me things…"

In the rear view mirror, Elise Lockwood was nodding.

"Yup."

"You've left Joe quite the hot mess to sort out."

She nodded. "It was bubbling up anyway. So, I know what I wanted to ask - do you remember a photo on Estelle's bookcase, of a couple in a white Morgan?"

"Yes, I used to drift off to sleep looking at it. Apparently it's the founder of the children's home, Lord Freeman. She grew up there and was adopted by the man who ran it, Eric Vickers."

"Lord Freeman was the founder?"

"Yes."

"But that photo was what, 1930s, 1940s? And he looks middle-aged." She frowned. "So that would make him, what?" She did a quick calculation. "A hundred and twenty? Or …no…."

They looked at each other.

"Not possible," they both agreed.

Beth got out of the car with her tin of obsidian ashes and set off towards the ebbing tide. The man deep underground who'd gone into that vault had indeed been ancient. But a hundred and twenty or more? At the water's edge she pulled off her boots and paddled into the icy ocean before tipping out the contents of Mailing Street's demons, closing her eyes and praying for the conversion to light and love. And when she turned around again to face the starlit shore, Gran Grace was standing there with Yukon.

"This isn't over, is it? Where are we going next, Gran?"

"A river. We're looking across a delta at a headland and the skyline at the other side is totally different from the one we're on."

"The place you came to after you left Canada?"

"Escaped, child. We were hunted down. And this is one reason why you have to find them. They're still free. All of them."

Beth looked up at the car on the headland, and the diminutive figure of Jeannie leaning against the bonnet. "Who? Allegra? Freeman?"

Gran shook her head. "Same ones through the ages. This has been coming two thousand years and now it's time. Now it ends. You're the one, Beth."

"How?"

"Trust us. You will be guided."

She picked up her boots, noting the paw prints in the smoothly washed sand, before walking back to the car. Jeannie had saved up more than enough for a hotel stay and after that they would head south.

"It's some mountain to climb." Her words trailed into the breeze of a dying day. The air stilled then, and so did her heart, the moment silent and crystallised. She stood paralysed as her body was filled once more with overwhelming bliss.

The light became blinding.

I am with you…

The moment passed in an instant. And when the sea rushed back into her ears she almost stumbled. Turning around again, not wanting Jeannie to see her crying, it was just in time to catch a shining ripple of rose-gold spreading across the surface of the ocean. Who knew the secrets of this earth? Who could honestly say?

"One day I will wake up from this," she murmured.

In a heartbeat the golden glow faded, and by the time she reached the car, late afternoon had become dusk.

"I've been shouting you," said Jeannie as they both jumped in.

"Sorry."

She began to reverse off the headland.

"Anyway, I found something out."

"What?"

"It's immortality," said Jeannie as they headed towards the main road. "I was just looking it up on the internet. That's what some believe the caduceus represents - immortality."

I don't mean the town. I mean the earth. We have orders to escort you off.

The dual carriageway leading to the motorway south was dark and empty, headlights reflecting on a wet road.

Orders from whom?

The words just popped out of her mouth unbidden. "He lives that long in the flesh because he's a vessel."

"For what? A demon?"

The cold shard of fear tried to rip into her heart but did not succeed.

"Only for so long, though," said Beth. "Used vessels die. The soul, however, is eternal. Don't ever give it away, will you?"

***

REFERENCES

1. The Nag Hammadi Gnostic Gospels.
2. 'On the Mechanics of Consciousness' by Ishtar Bentov
3. 'The Committee of 300' by Dr John Coleman

GLOSSARY

Rod of Asclepius

A symbol of medicine and healing.

Caduceus
There are many diverse interpretations and legends associated with this symbol. For the purposes of this book, however, the following was the inspiration:

(Source: Mackey's Encyclopaedia of Freemasonry)

'The Caduceus then-the original meaning of which word is a herald's staff-as the attribute of a life-restoring God, is in its primary. meaning the symbol of immortality; so in Freemasonry the rod of the Senior Deacon, or the Master of Ceremonies, is but an analogue or representation of the Hermean Caduceus. This officer, as leading the aspirant through the forms of initiation into his new birth or Masonic regeneration, and teaching him in the solemn ceremonies of the Third Degree the lesson of eternal life, may well use the magic wand as a representation of it, which was the attribute of that ancient deity who brought the dead into life.'

***

MORE BOOKS BY SARAH ENGLAND:

FATHER OF LIES
A Darkly Disturbing Occult Horror Trilogy: Book 1

'Boy did this pack a punch and scare me witless...'

'Scary as hell...What I thought would be mainstream horror was anything but...'

'Not for the faint-hearted. Be warned – this is very, very dark subject matter.'

'A truly wonderful and scary start to a horror trilogy. One of the best and most well written books I've read in a long time.'

'A dark and compelling read. I devoured it in one afternoon. Even as the horrors unfolded I couldn't race through the pages quickly enough for more...'

'Delivers the spooky in spades!'

'Will go so far as to say Sarah is now my favourite author – sorry Mr King!'

***

Ruby is the most violently disturbed patient ever admitted to Drummersgate Asylum, high on the bleak moors of northern England. With no improvement after two years, Dr. Jack McGowan finally decides to take a risk and hypnotises her. With terrifying consequences.

A horrific dark force is now unleashed on the entire medical team, as each in turn attempts to unlock Ruby's shocking and sinister past. Who is this girl? And how did she manage to survive such unimaginable evil? Set in a desolate ex-mining village, where secrets are tightly kept and intruders hounded out, their questions soon lead to a haunted mill, the heart of darkness…and the Father of Lies.

***

TANNERS DELL – BOOK 2

Now only one of the original team remains – Ward Sister Becky. However, despite her fiancé, Callum, being unconscious and many of her colleagues either dead or critically ill, she is determined to rescue Ruby's twelve-year-old daughter from a similar fate to her mother.

But no one asking questions in the desolate ex-mining village Ruby hails from ever comes to a good end. And as the diabolical history of the area is gradually revealed, it seems the evil invoked is both real and contagious.

Don't turn the lights out yet!

***

MAGDA – BOOK 3

The dark and twisted community of Woodsend harbours a terrible secret – one tracing back to the age of the Elizabethan witch hunts, when many innocent women were persecuted and hanged.

But there is a far deeper vein of horror running through this village, an evil that once invoked has no intention of relinquishing its grip on the modern world. Rather, it watches and waits with focused intelligence, leaving Ward Sister Becky and CID Officer Toby constantly checking over their shoulders and jumping at shadows.

Just who invited in this malevolent presence? And is the demonic woman who possessed Magda back in the sixteenth century the same one now gazing at Becky whenever she looks in the mirror?

Are you ready to meet Magda in this final instalment of the trilogy? Are you sure?

***

THE OWLMEN

IF THEY SEE YOU, THEY WILL COME FOR YOU

Ellie Blake is recovering from a nervous breakdown. Deciding to move back to her northern roots, she and her psychiatrist husband buy Tanners Dell at auction – an old water mill in the moorland village of Bridesmoor.

However, there is disquiet in the village. Tanners Dell has a terrible secret, one so well guarded no one speaks its name. But in her search for meaning and very much alone, Ellie is drawn to traditional witchcraft and determined to pursue it. All her life she has been cowed. All her life she has apologised for her very existence. And witchcraft has opened a door she could never have imagined. Imbued with power and overawed with its magic, for the first time she feels she has come home, truly knows who she is.

Tanners Dell, though, with its centuries-old demonic history…well, it's a dangerous place for a novice…

***

The Soprano

A Haunting Supernatural Thriller

It is 1951 and a remote mining village on the North Staffordshire Moors is hit by one of the worst snowstorms in living memory. Cut off for over three weeks, the old and the sick will die, the strongest bunker down, and those with evil intent will bring to its conclusion a family vendetta spanning three generations.

Inspired by a true event, *The Soprano* tells the story of Grace Holland – a strikingly beautiful, much admired local celebrity who brings glamour and inspiration to the grimy moorland community. But why is Grace still here? Why doesn't she leave this staunchly Methodist, rain-sodden place and the isolated farmhouse she shares with her mother?

Riddled with witchcraft and tales of superstition, the story is mostly narrated by the Whistler family, who own the local funeral parlour, in particular six-year-old Louise – now an elderly lady – who recalls one of the most shocking crimes imaginable.

***

Hidden Company

A dark psychological thriller set in a Victorian asylum in the heart of Wales.

1893, and nineteen-year-old Flora George is admitted to a remote asylum with no idea why she is there, what happened to her child, or how her wealthy family could have abandoned her to such a fate. However, within a short space of time, it becomes apparent she must save herself from something far worse than that of a harsh regime.

2018, and forty-one-year-old Isobel Lee moves into the gatehouse of what was once the old asylum. A reluctant medium, it is with dismay she realises there is a terrible secret here – one desperate to be heard. Angry and upset, Isobel baulks at what she must now face. But with the help of local dark arts practitioner Branwen, face it she must.

This is a dark story of human cruelty, folklore and superstition. But the human spirit can and will prevail...unless of course, the wrath of the fae is incited...

***

MONKSPIKE

You are not forgiven

1149 was a violent year in the Forest of Dean.

Today, nearly 900 years later, the forest village of Monkspike sits brooding. There is a sickness here passed down through ancient lines, one noted and deeply felt by Sylvia Massey, the new psychologist. What is wrong with Nurse Belinda Sully's son? Why did her husband take his own life? Why are the old people in Temple Lake Nursing Home so terrified? And what are the lawless inhabitants of nearby Wolfs Cross hiding?

It is a dark village indeed, but one which has kept its secrets well. That is, until local girl Kezia Elwyn returns home as a practising Satanist, and resurrects a hellish wrath no longer containable. Burdo, the white monk, will infest your dreams… This is pure occult horror and definitely not for the faint of heart…

***

BABA LENKA

Pure Occult Horror

1970, and Baba Lenka begins in an icy Bavarian village with a highly unorthodox funeral. The deceased is Baba Lenka, great-grandmother to Eva Hart. But a terrible thing happens at the funeral, and from that moment on everything changes for seven year old Eva. The family flies back to Yorkshire but it seems the cold Alpine winds have followed them home...and the ghost of Baba Lenka has followed Eva. This is a story of demonic sorcery and occult practices during the World Wars, the horrors of which are drip-fed into young Eva's mind to devastating effect. Once again, this is absolutely not for the faint of heart. Nightmares pretty much guaranteed...

***

MASQUERADE

A Beth Harper Supernatural Thriller

Book 1

The first in a series of Beth Harper books, Masquerade is a supernatural thriller set in a remote North Yorkshire village. Following a whirlwind re-location for a live-in job at the local inn, Beth quickly realises the whole village is thoroughly haunted, the people here fearful and cowed. As a spiritual medium, her attention is drawn to Scarsdale Hall nearby, the enormous stately home dominating what is undoubtedly a wild and beautiful landscape. Built of black stone with majestic turrets, it seems to drain the energy from the land. There is, she feels, something malevolent about it, as if time has stopped…

Newsletter and more info on:
WWW.SARAHENGLANDAUTHOR.CO.UK

Printed in Great Britain
by Amazon

65974982R00188